BY MONICA MURPHY

THREE
BROKEN
PROMISES

THREE
BROKEN
PROMISES

A NOVEL

Monica Murphy

BANTAM BOOKS TRADE PAPERBACKS | NEW YORK

A Bantam Books Trade Paperback Original

Copyright © 2013 by Monica Murphy
Excerpt from *Four Years Later* by Monica Murphy copyright © 2014 by Monica Murphy

Published in the United States by Bantam Books, an imprint of The Random House Publishing Group, a division of Random House LLC, a Penguin Random House Company, New York.

BANTAM BOOKS and the HOUSE colophon are registered trademarks of Random House LLC.

This book contains an excerpt from the forthcoming book *Four Years Later* by Monica Murphy. This excerpt has been set for this edition only and may not reflect the final content of the forthcoming edition.

ISBN 978-0-8041-7680-4
eBook ISBN 978-0-8041-7681-1

Printed in the United States of America on acid-free paper

www.bantamdell.com

9 8 7 6 5 4 3 2 1

To the readers. This series would be nothing without you. Thank you for your endless support.

THREE
BROKEN
PROMISES

PROLOGUE

I don't want to let her go.

She's going to leave me and I can't stand the thought. I've been coasting through life, confident with the fact that she's always there. Working with me, living with me, talking with me, laughing with me, and, sometimes, in those rare moments we never discuss, late, late at night when we're all alone, crying with me.

Lying in my bed, wrapped around me like a vine wrapping around a trellis. Her hands in my hair and her breath on my neck, making me feel so alive I want to tell her how I feel. Tell her what she makes me feel.

But I've never had the courage to confess.

Now, she's leaving. Wants her freedom, she claims. As if I've been holding her down, holding her back. I'm offended, when I know I shouldn't be. She's not ungrateful. She appreciates everything I've done for her. And I've done a lot—probably too much.

Guilt eats away at my insides. I started doing everything for her out of that sense of guilt. Truthfully, it's my fault she left her family. My fault she ended up all alone, on her own, struggling to make it, subjecting herself to things no woman should ever have to do. Until I swept back into her life like some sort of Prince Charming on my mighty steed, saving her from a world of shit.

As time went on, the guilt I felt slowly but surely morphed into something else.

Something real.

I have to be honest and tell her how I feel. I need her. Desperately. Losing her would be like losing a part of myself. I can't risk it. I think . . . holy shit, I'm pretty sure I'm in love with her.

But I'm the last guy she should be with. I have this way of ruining those I'm closest to. No way could I do that to her.

No way can I let her leave me, either.

CHAPTER 1

Jen

"So why a butterfly?"

I lean forward, my boobs smashed against the back of the chair. I've been sitting here for what feels like hours, a needle pressing relentlessly into the sensitive skin on the back of my neck. The needle's buzz fills my head, drowning out all the chaotic noise that usually occupies it.

I much prefer that incessant buzz. Easier to deal with compared to the endless stream of questions and worries that run through my brain.

"Yo, earth to Jen." Fable waves her hand in front of my face, then snaps her fingers twice. Brat. I wish I could smack her but I'm too busy gripping my knees, bare-knuckling them like a little wimp.

"What?" I grit out from between clenched teeth, wincing when the needle sketches over a particularly sensitive part.

Oh, who am I kidding? *All* the parts are sensitive. Time to face facts. I'm a complete weenie. I thought getting a tattoo would be a cinch. I've dealt with a lot of emotional pain in my life, but not too much physical. What's an hour or so sitting in a chair under a needle?

Apparently it's pretty shitastic, considering how much it hurts, and how much I have to gird my loins to get through it all.

Gird my loins—something silly my mom used to say. Back when she was happy and carefree and our family was whole.

Now we're broken and distant. I don't talk to my father. Mom calls only when she's crying and drunk.

It sucks. That's why I had to get away from my family. I have other reasons for wanting to escape *this* place now.

"I want to know why you chose a butterfly for your tattoo. What's the meaning behind it?" Fable asks, sounding beyond irritated with me though she's smiling, so I know she's not. She came with me downtown to Tattoo Voodoo, the little shop she recommended for us to get our tattoos.

She got one, too, but she's already finished, considering it was only a line written in elegant, simple script. A surprise tattoo for her boyfriend, fiancé, or whatever you want to call him, though considering they can't keep their hands off each other for too long, I'm guessing he'll discover his "surprise" sooner rather than later. Drew Callahan is so madly in love with her, it's sort of disgusting.

But it's also cute. Super, super cute, especially since it's a line from one of the poems he wrote for her. How they make Fable swoon, and nothing makes that girl swoon. She's pretty hardcore. She's had to be, what with the things life has dealt her.

I could take a lesson or two from her. I'm too soft. I let people in.

And then they stomp all over me. Or worse, ignore me completely.

"Freedom," I finally tell her, exhaling loudly when the buzzing stops and I feel the washcloth brush across my freshly tattooed skin. "I'm ready to break free of this stifling cocoon called my life and find my own way, instead of relying on someone else. A butterfly's a perfect representative of that, don't you think?"

I can practically taste it. Freedom. I've always relied too heavily on others. My friends. My family. My brother especially, not that I can anymore considering he's been gone for a while now. I might have run away that one time and tried to make it on my own, but I failed.

Spectacularly.

Not this time around, though. I've thought things through. I've saved money. This time, I have a plan.

Sort of.

"You really believe leaving is the best thing for you?" Fable asks, her voice incredulous, her expression . . . sad. She's my closest friend, the first real friend I've made since I fled my old life. But even she doesn't know everything. She'd never look at me the same if she knew. "Do you want to leave because of what happened to you before?"

Nodding, I wince when the tattoo artist—Dave—wipes the washrag across my skin yet again. "Finished," he says matter-of-factly.

"Yeah, I can't deny that my past comes into play." I'd told Fable what happened for the most part when I worked at Gold Diggers, that sleazy strip club on the outskirts of town. My family doesn't know, and I swore Colin to secrecy. The public story is that I was a cocktail waitress. The private story is that I stripped.

The secret, no-one-else-can-know story is one I can hardly think about, let alone admit.

"We all have a past," Fable points out. She has a pretty bad one, not that anyone calls her on it. Drew won't allow it.

"I know. I just . . . I can't stay here forever. Even though you want me to," I murmur, sending a pleading look in Fable's direction. I don't want the lecture again, especially in front of our new friend Dave. I don't think I can stand it. I know she means well, but the words she says halfway convince me I need to stay every single time I hear them.

"I'm not the only one who wants you here," Fable points out, brows raised, a knowing look on her face.

Her statement doesn't need an answer. I know who she's referring to. He'd want me to stay indefinitely, but I haven't even told him I'm leaving yet. I'll let him know tonight.

Hopefully.

He provides the place I live, my job. He does it all with no strings attached, or so he claims. Really, I believe him. A deep, dark secret part of me wishes there *were* strings. Plenty of strings that tie me to him, bind us together until we're so connected that we'd become one long word. Not just Jen. Not just Colin.

JenandColin.

No way is that gonna happen.

So if I can't have him—and really, I shouldn't want him, or have allowed myself to become completely dependent on him for far too long—then I'm going to claim my freedom completely.

Stupid and risky and totally freakin' scary, but . . . I need to do it. Recent events have pushed me into doing it. My past has come calling in the form of a customer at The District just a few nights ago. He came into the bar and ordered a drink. Thankfully, I was able to avoid him and he left without incident.

This could happen again, though. Having the man there was a reminder that I can never escape my past. I don't want Colin to know what I've done. He won't like me anymore. He'll look differently at me.

I don't think I could stand that.

Desperately needing to change the subject, I ask, "How does it look?"

Fable tilts her head, examining the tattoo on the back of my neck. "It's beautiful. But you'll never really see it."

"There's such a thing as mirrors, you know." I take the very one Dave is handing to me and I look into it, see my reflection bouncing off the mirror that lines the entire wall. My long hair is piled on top of my head in a sloppy bun, revealing my neck, the reddened skin, and the butterfly.

It's a delicate sketch in gentle shades of blue and black, looking as if it could somehow flutter its wings and fly right off my skin. If I like it this much now, imagine how awesome it'll look when the skin is healed.

"I love it," I breathe as I hand the mirror back to Dave, who sets it on the counter beside him.

"It's pretty," Fable agrees with a smile on her face. "I'm proud of you, Jen. I know you were scared to come here."

More like petrified, but now I'm proud, too. I did it. I got a tattoo and I didn't cry or run out of the shop before big, burly Dave got his needle on me, which I was afraid I might do. Kind of stupid, to be proud of something as simple as this. If my mom ever sees it, she'll flip out. My dad will think I'm a common gutter tramp—his words, not mine. Not that I plan on seeing them anytime soon. I don't want to go back, and they're not exactly welcoming me. I think they're almost glad to be rid of me. I was a burden.

I have a feeling Colin won't really like my tattoo either. But I didn't get it for anyone else. Just me.

Dave's now placing a bandage on my fresh tattoo, rattling off the care instructions in a monotone, as if he's said this a million times before, which he probably has. He hands me a sheet of paper with the instructions listed on it and I glance it over, not really seeing the words. My brain is too occupied with these people in my life who I wish I could please but rarely do.

They haunt me, hang out in my head like ghosts I can't get rid of. Even Colin makes an appearance there, which is dumb considering I live with the man.

Fable's cell rings, and from the smile that pops onto her face when she glances at her phone, I know it's Drew. I watch her step away to talk to him privately and jealousy clutches at my heart, making it hurt.

I want that, though I'd never admit it out loud, and certainly not to Fable. Unconditional love, a man who would do anything—and I mean anything—to ensure I'm happy. Safe. Secure. Loved.

If I'm being honest with myself, I'd like to have that with Colin.

He acts like he wants more, but then he always pulls back. I've shared more intimate moments with him than with anyone else in my entire life. I've slept in his bed. He's held me close. He's kissed me . . . but nothing beyond the sort of kiss a brother bestows on his sister's cheek or forehead.

Confirmation that's the only way he'll ever think of me. We grew up together, Colin and I. Well, Danny, Colin, and I. My brother and Colin were best friends. They were supposed to join the Marines together, but somehow Danny was the only one who ended up going into the service. Then he went to Iraq.

And never came back.

He's the ghost who hangs in my head the most, though he doesn't judge or make me feel bad. Not necessarily. It's more like my big brother reminds me that sometimes, the choices I make aren't always the best ones. If he knew everything, he never would have forgiven me.

Also, he makes me feel guilty for having certain . . . feelings for Colin. I always wonder if Danny would approve. Would he want me with Colin? Or would he have fought like hell to ensure Colin and I never happened?

It doesn't matter. Danny isn't around, and Colin and I are never going to happen. No matter how badly I want us to, he doesn't. Not really. He likes having me around. He likes counting on me being there as a sort of crutch for him when his emotions, his demons, get out of hand.

But he doesn't want me. Not in the way that matters most. Not in the way that I want him to.

So forget it. Forget us.

Tonight, I'm giving a month's notice to Colin. More than enough time for him to find a replacement waitress. That's also more than enough time for me to find a new apartment, a new job, and a new life in a new city. I know exactly where I'm going, so it's not like I'm flying by the seat of my pants and changing my life on a whim.

Well, sort of. I've always been an impulsive person. That's gotten me in trouble in the past. Hopefully it won't get me in trouble now.

Colin's going to be angry that I'm leaving, but maybe, just maybe, the tattoo will give me strength. Will remind me that what I'm doing is the right thing. I need to go. I need to really learn how to live my life on my own, not this childish running-away shit and living out of my car like I did last time. I'm older now. Smarter. Wiser.

I need to fly and be free.

Colin

The restaurant is hopping. It's late August and the students are back in earnest, which means The District is back in business. The bar is packed, my staff is hustling, and the kitchen is a steamy pit of never-ending appetizers, giant plates being taken out again and again, since it seems none of the customers want a full meal tonight.

They all want to get their drink on. Celebrating being back at school, or drowning their misery in alcohol because they're . . . back at school.

I don't care which it is. As long as they keep buying drinks and leaving hefty tips for the hardworking staff, I'm satisfied.

"Hey, you're the owner, right?"

Glancing up, I see a pretty girl standing in front of me, a hopeful smile on her face. She probably wants a job. I just hired a new hostess late last week, so at the moment I'm not looking, but I always give out applications. You never know when you're going to lose someone, and good help is hard to find. "I am," I answer, returning her smile, my gaze dropping to take her all in. Check her out.

She's attractive. Not makes-my-heart-feel-like-it's-seizing-in-my-chest gorgeous, but not put-a-paper-bag-over-her-face-while-I-bang-her, either. I like the way she looks at me.

So I look back at her.

"I thought so." She takes a step closer, leaning her forearms against the hostess station counter, plumping up her breasts, which threaten to spill out of her skimpy top. She's stacked. I have a thing for big breasts but I keep my gaze fixed on her face for as long as I can, tomorrow's printed-out schedule clutched in my hand forgotten. It's already near eleven and the kitchen's just closed, which means I can get the hell out of here if I want to.

But I don't. Jen's scheduled till midnight, so I'll wait for her and give her a ride home. Like I always do. Anything to spend as much time with her as possible.

"Are you looking for a job? We don't have any positions available at the moment." Finally, I give in and let my gaze drop, blatantly studying her cleavage. It's been a while. Hell, I seriously can't remember the last time I got laid. And with where I work, with the endless stream of women that come in on a daily basis, I'm not being an asshole when I say I could get laid anytime I want.

Not being an arrogant prick, just stating fact.

She still hasn't answered me. "Let me grab you an application." Leaning down, I'm reaching for the stack of blank applications on the shelf when the girl laughs and shakes her head.

"I'm not interested in a job. I'm interested in *you,*" she says point-blank.

Blinking, I stand up straight, studying her. The smile curving her glossy peach-colored lips is coy, the look in her eyes hot. As in, she's definitely interested in what she sees.

Women rarely leave me at a loss for words, but lately I haven't been myself. Despite my hangups, despite my not wanting to disappoint the one woman who means the world to me, I like what I see standing in front of me, too.

I've fucked plenty of women, and this one looks ripe for the picking. She smells good, looks good, and the gleam in her eye tempts. Invites.

I'm no saint. Some might even call me a man whore, though that's more in my past. What can I say? I like women and they usually like me. I'm not stupid. This pretty face of mine has gotten me into trouble. Both the good and the bad kind.

Only one woman is off limits. I might be an asshole, but I at least have a small amount of scruples left within me. Besides, there has to be something untouchable and holy in my world, right? She's it. The sweet little girl I knew when we were kids. The pretty teenager who I tried my best not to look at for fear she'd know I was lusting after her.

The woman I deny myself from ever having. We're friends, and that's all it can be. I'm scared I'll ruin our relationship if I take it further. I need her friendship more than I want her body.

Well. Just barely.

Thinking of her makes my heart and libido sink, and my interest in this woman in front of me withers up and blows away like a dead, dried-up leaf.

That's all it takes. Think of Jen and I'm done for.

"Uh, I'm flattered, but . . ." I run a hand through my hair, wondering how I'm going to let her down easy. I've never had to do this before. When a woman's interested, I usually let it happen. I let her in. Not all the way, but just enough so we both get what we want.

I let no one in all the way. Jen's the only one who's ever gotten close. I still keep her at arm's length, though, for the most part. Except for those quiet, intimate moments in the dark, when the despair threatens to overwhelm me and she sneaks into my room to offer me comfort.

Those moments I keep to myself. We've never talked about them. They're like our dirty little secret.

"So I guess you have a girlfriend?" The woman laughs, cocking her head. She has dark blond hair, with perfect curls that tumble past her shoulders. Her makeup is subtle, her out-fit tempting. A few months ago, she would have been my type. I would have had her naked and been buried deep inside her within an hour of this meeting, if not sooner.

But anonymous sex doesn't appeal to me anymore. And the woman I want, I can't really have. Correction: I don't let myself have her. So instead of having *her* naked and me bur-ied deep inside her like I desperately want, I suffer. Like a true martyr.

Or try more like a true asshole.

Clearing my throat, I decide to be honest. "I—"

"He does." Jen appears beside me as if I conjured her up like a magical spell, made of smoke and mirrors and so much beauty it hurts to look at her. She curls a slender arm around mine, her fingers settling on my biceps, and my skin burns where she touches me. Nestling in close, that sexy lean body of hers is plastered to mine, making me sweat, making my skin tighten. She's wearing a mysterious smile and a defiant glare in her dark brown eyes that would deter even the most aggressive female on the planet.

The look clearly says, *Back the fuck off, he's mine.*

Hell, I wish.

"Sorry." The girl doesn't sound sorry at all as she pushes away from the counter and walks off, shaking her head. "Didn't mean to step on any toes."

"Keep walking. Nothing to see here," Jen calls after her as the girl disappears back into the bar. Then she releases her hold on me immediately, stepping away, and I feel the loss keenly. "God. Don't you ever get sick of that?"

"Sick of what? Women hitting on me?" I once lived for that shit every single night. Flirting, drinking, being surrounded by beautiful women—they all helped me forget what I'd done. How I disappointed an entire family. How I abandoned my best friend and he ended up dead. How I let this girl in front of me down most of all.

My fault. All of it.

"Yes." She sounds irritated, but she looks hot. The simple black dress she wears accentuates her curves, stops about mid-thigh, and showcases those endless legs of hers. Legs I'd like to have naked. I imagine gripping her slender thighs and wrapping them around my hips. "She's been circling you for the last twenty minutes like she's a shark and you're blood in the water."

I hadn't noticed. Am I a dick for liking that Jen had? This hint of a jealous streak is new. I wish I knew what spurred it on. "I would've taken care of her."

"By what? Inviting her back to the house?"

Glancing around, I'm thankful no one's left in the restaurant. The remaining customers have moved on into the bar. I don't need anyone witnessing this exchange, especially my employees. The rumor mill at The District is bad enough. Jen and I don't need to add fuel to the fire. They already talk about us. Wondering what the heck we're doing, if we're together, if we're not. The constant speculation is exhausting.

"I don't do that. Not when you're there," I finally say, my gaze meeting hers once more. "Since when do you care, anyway?"

Wrong thing to say. She looks ready to blow up—all over me. "So you would've brought her back to the house if I wasn't there? Is that what you're saying? God, you're such an ass," she mutters as she stalks off.

I follow her, my gaze zeroing in on the back of her head. Her long brown hair is down tonight, but when she tosses her head I see the edge of a white bandage peeking out between the thick, silky strands. "What happened to you?"

She glances over her shoulder with a withering stare. "What are you talking about?"

"The bandage." I grab hold of her arm and stop her in her tracks. She almost stumbles, what with the high heels she's wearing, and I grip her tighter to keep her upright. "Did you hurt yourself?"

She reaches for her neck with her free hand, rubbing the back of it self-consciously, a little frown wrinkling her brows. "I, uh . . . it's nothing."

Crossing my arms in front of my chest, I block her from

ditching me. I know that look. She's ready to run. Something she's real good at. "You're hiding something from me."

"I really don't want to do this here." She blows out a harsh breath, and I wonder what the hell she's talking about. "Can't we talk about this when we get home?"

"Talk about what?" I'm confused. Where is she going with this?

Jen yanks out of my hold and throws her arms up in the air, frustration written all over her beautiful face. "Fine. Let's do this. I need to give my notice, Colin. I'm quitting."

CHAPTER 2

Colin

"Quitting? What the fuck are you talking about?" I'm yelling. I notice her wince and I clamp my lips shut, feeling like a jackass. But her words send me reeling, and I'm trying my best to rein myself in.

Jen can't quit. She's worked here almost a year. She's one of my best waitresses. This place, specifically the bar, runs more smoothly when she's here.

But that's not why I don't want her to leave.

"I can't stay here anymore." Jen glances around the empty restaurant, her fingers curling around the back of her neck, playing with the edge of the mysterious bandage. "Consider this my generous four-week notice. That should give you plenty of time to replace me."

Doesn't she know she's irreplaceable? "Did you find another job?" It's the only explanation. And if she hated working here that much, I wish she would have told me. I could have done something to make it better for her here.

But what? What more can I do?

Slowly she shakes her head. "I'm leaving."

What the hell? "Going back home, then?" I find it hard to believe, but maybe she's finally ready to see her mom and dad after everything that's happened, after she ran away. She's never gone back and I know they miss her. Her mom has called me more than once asking about her. I know they've talked but it's rare, and that's on Jen's part. Maybe she's had a change of heart.

There's really no other explanation for her leaving. At least in my mind.

"No." She spits the word out as if it were poison and drops her hand from her neck, straightening her shoulders. "I refuse to go back home. I'm moving to Sacramento."

"Sacramento? Are you kidding me? Why?" I'm at a loss. I can't figure out her motive, why she wants to leave, and what the hell Sacramento has to offer that's so much goddamn better than what I can give her.

"I need a change of pace, okay? I'm tired of the small-town thing. I run into the same people again and again. Most of them I don't want to see anyway." She starts to walk past me. "We so shouldn't be having this conversation here."

I grab her again, stopping her progress. Curling my fingers tight around her upper arm, I pull her in close, invading her space. Her scent fills my head, like an exotic bloom that permeates the air, fragrant and heavy. Intoxicating. My gaze drops to her mouth, and I'm momentarily transfixed as she sinks her teeth into her plump lower lip.

Fuck. This is pure torture. Having her close. Arguing with her where anyone could see us. Acting like lovers in the middle of a heated discussion . . .

We pretend we don't really matter to each other, but it's time for me to be honest with myself. She's so immersed in my world, I can't imagine her out of it.

I don't *want* to imagine her out of it.

"Where else do you suggest we have this conversation, then?" I ask, keeping my voice low and as even as possible. While deep inside, I want to rage and yell and throw shit.

Jen can't leave me. What she's saying, I can't even begin to comprehend.

"Your house?" She rolls her eyes and actually laughs. "Not that we ever really talk there, though, do we? We never really talk anywhere."

Letting her go, I step away from her, needing the distance. She's right. Our situation is . . . weird. I take care of her because of my own twisted sense of guilt, and she stays with me because where else is she going to go? I know she appreciates all I've done for her. We keep our linked past a secret from the other employees at the restaurant with the exception of Fable. Jen confessed our long connection months ago.

At first, I was mad that Jen told her about our shared history. Then I got over it. I like Fable. She's troubled—was extremely troubled when I first hired her, but she's come out of her shell, and she and Jen are now best friends. I've even become somewhat friends with her boyfriend. Hell, the four of us have gone out to dinner together once or twice, like we're on a double date or something.

Stupid that I can keep what's between Jen and me so casual, so . . . easy, but I can't turn it into something real. Something true. I'm just too damn afraid to make a move for fear I'll ruin it.

Considering I've ruined a few things in my personal life, it's a legitimate fear.

"You really want to talk when we get home? We'll talk," I finally suggest.

Her eyes widen. "Seriously?"

"Absolutely. Whatever you want, all you have to do is ask." I spread my arms wide, then let them drop to my sides. She's watching me with those dark, fathomless eyes, taking me in, making me want to squirm. She's tall in the heels, almost eye level with me, and I'm a solid six-one.

"Whatever I want, you'll give me." It's a statement, not a question, and I wonder at it.

"It's yours," I agree. "When have I ever denied you anything?"

She laughs, but there's no humor in it. "You deny me almost every day of your life."

I scratch the back of my head, puzzled. She means something else, I know it, but I can't figure out what. Plus, I'm tired as fuck and not in the mood for a bunch of games, not that Jen is a game player. But she's being evasive. Mysterious. Trying to pull a fast one on me, I'm sure.

"Make your request. I'll do my best to accommodate you." I grimace the moment the words come out. I sound like a boss, which I am.

A tiny smile curves her lips. "All right, then. Let me go. Let me do this, Colin. I can't be dependent on you forever."

Realization washes over me, making me feel like a fool. "Is that the problem? That you feel bad because I help you out? You're never a burden, Jen. You know this."

"No, I don't know, but that's not the point." Sighing, her smile turns sad. "I appreciate your help. More than anything, I appreciate how you pulled me out of a bad situation before it could've become . . . a lot worse. You saved me."

"It was the least I could do." A major understatement. If I couldn't save her brother, my best friend, then I could at least save his baby sister.

"And I'm forever grateful to you for it. Really. But I gotta admit, I'm tired of being saved by you. Of being the problem you're constantly trying to solve. I want to leave. I need my freedom to try something new and explore other options. Staying here in this stupid small town doing the same thing day in and day out won't solve my problems."

"You have problems?" Why hasn't she told me about them?

"Yes! Tons of them. All sorts of problems, but you don't notice because you're too wrapped up with your own."

Isn't that the truth. "I don't want to give you your freedom just so you'll leave me," I murmur, feeling like a selfish ass. The look on her face tells me she thinks I'm an ass for saying it, too. "Ask me for anything else, Jen. Anything. I . . . I don't want to let you go. Not yet."

Irritation flits across her face, making her lips thin, her eyes narrow. "Ask you for anything else?"

"Anything. I'll give it to you. No questions asked."

"All right." She takes a deep breath, as if she needs it for courage. "I want *you.*"

Jen

He's staring at me as if I've lost my mind, which I probably have. What possessed me to just say that? He's going to reject me. I feel it in my bones. Not that I blame him. We wouldn't work. I know this. So does he. I'm keeping a huge secret from him that I can never let him know. That alone will prevent us from having any sort of a relationship.

But I couldn't help myself. I had to say it. I think he secretly wants me, too.

"You don't want me," he finally says, dropping his head to stare down at the floor, a self-deprecating chuckle escaping him. "Trust me."

Every single day that passes, he breaks my heart. The way he just said that, those six words infused with so much sadness, threatens to shatter my already broken heart into a bazillion pieces.

"You said I could ask for anything," I remind him, my voice small. "No questions asked." I throw his words back at him because I can.

He tilts his head back and stares up at the ceiling, seeming at a loss for words, which I don't think I've ever seen happen before. The man is a talker. A charmer. He has to be, as successful as he's been at such a young age. Yeah, his extremely wealthy and negligent dad gave him money to start the first restaurant he owns, but everything else he's accomplished has been all him.

He's also gorgeous. And he knows it. The dark blond hair, the piercing, pale blue eyes, and his face . . . no words can describe it. It's too damn beautiful.

"You're blowing my mind tonight," he finally says, still staring at the ceiling.

"It's been an enlightening day for the both of us," I return, irritation making me snippy.

Dropping his head, he studies me. "I want to pretend you didn't say that."

Anger fills me. Of course he wants to pretend. It's the story of his life. The way he always operates. I'm so sick and tired of pretending. Avoiding. Doing one thing while saying another.

My life with Colin feels unreal. I hate it.

"Go ahead. Pretend like you usually do." I want to run but I stand my ground, glaring at him.

He ignores my comment. "We should go."

"I'm scheduled till midnight." And I'm not ready to leave. We need to finish this conversation. Besides, what if we go home and he helps me pack my suitcase and sends me on my merry way? That's the last thing I want to happen. I'm not ready yet. I should have gone on about telling him my plan more . . . delicately. I've handled this all wrong.

Wrong, wrong, wrong.

"They've survived without you for the last fifteen minutes we've been talking. I think you clocking out early isn't going to matter. Besides, I'm the one who made your schedule. You can leave when I say." He flicks his head, looking every inch the arrogant, controlling boss. "Let's go."

And like the silly, obedient girl that I am, I follow him.

We drove home in silence, the air between us thick with tension. I spent the entire time texting with Fable, telling her I manned up and gave my notice to Colin. I thought she would be happy for me. At the very least, proud that I finally found some courage and did it.

Instead, I received a string of whiny texts in reply, begging me not to leave. I mean, what the hell? Even my new best friend is trying to hold me down. This town is too small and everyone knows each other. After my last close call, I don't want to take that chance again. I'd rather go and forget this place ever existed.

I'll miss my friends. I'll miss Colin. But it's best that I go.

I don't even quite know how I ended up here. I grew up about two hours away, in a small, seemingly idyllic but really super boring town in the mountains. Where everyone knows each other and the air is crisp and clear, filled with the scent of pine. Where gossip prevails and the secrets that aren't so secret anymore go generations deep. Colin grew up there, too; his mom lived right next door.

His father has never been a part of his life. I've met Conrad Wilder a few times but always briefly, and I don't know much about the man. Only that he's very generous with his money—and he has a ton of it, a fortune he'd inherited from his father when he died—handing it over to Colin every chance he gets, in lieu of the two of them actually spending time together.

Not that Colin ever complained. He keeps most of his emotions to himself.

The moment we arrived at his house, I closed myself off in my room. Didn't bother saying good night, let's talk more, screw you, I hate you—nothing. Just ran away from him, heading down the hall like a coward. I turned the lock on my bedroom door, shed my clothes, and curled up under the covers. Squeezing my eyes shut tight in the hope that sleep would take me swiftly.

It didn't. Hours later I still lie in bed, frustrated, hot even though the ceiling fan turns lazily above me. I've kicked off the covers, clad in only a pair of panties and an old tank top, feeling like I might burst out of my skin, I'm so restless.

And then I hear it. Him. Colin's room is next to mine and the walls are remarkably thin. Thank God he's never brought a woman here—at least he hasn't when I've been around. Hearing him do . . . whatever he might do to another woman would send me straight over the edge.

I'm already teetering there, hanging on by a tenuous thread thanks to Colin.

It always starts out quietly. A whimper, or sometimes a growl, though it's never fierce. Rolling over on my side, I face the wall we share, waiting breathlessly for the next sound.

His voice is guttural and deep, though I can't quite make out what he's saying. I usually can't. When he starts talking, that's my signal to climb out of bed and go check on him.

So I do.

Chilly air smacks my face when I open his unlocked bedroom door. He's left the windows open and the night has cooled considerably, a sign that fall is on its way. Tiptoeing into his room, I stop at the foot of the bed, watching helplessly as he tosses and turns, overcome with whatever demons come to him in his dreams on an almost nightly basis.

It's dark, but I can make out his form in the light of the moon shining through the open windows. He's shirtless, of course. The sheets bunch around his hips and his broad shoulders and chest gleam in the moonlight. I've never seen him like this in the light of day—naked and mouthwateringly perfect—but I want to.

His voice rises, I can understand what he's saying now, and the words break my heart.

"Gotta save him. Gotta find him." He pants, as if he's running, searching for the one he's lost, and without thought I slip into bed with him, snuggling up behind him so I can wrap my arms around his waist.

I know who he's looking for in his dreams. I used to dream about him, too. Right after we lost my brother for good. This is our shared loss, the strong connection that has kept us together, that made him search me out when I ran.

Colin found *me*. Colin saved *me*. It's the least I can do, to try and save him back.

Holding him close, I rest my chin on top of his shoulder, my mouth close to his ear. "It's okay," I whisper as I run my hands over his flat, firm stomach, feeling extra daring tonight. I'm tired of holding back, holding everything in. I want to feel him, know him in every intimate way possible. "Everything's okay. You did what you could."

His nightmares haunt him. They're dark and desperate. Though he never talks about them, it doesn't take a genius to realize just how awful they are. How they torment him almost every single night. I don't know how he lives like this. He acts like everything is fine in the daylight. Happy and carefree, as if nothing ever bothers him. But in the dark, in his sleep, his other world reveals itself.

And it's not pretty.

"Jennifer." He whispers my name, turning his head so his mouth is in near perfect alignment with mine. He settles his hands over my wandering ones, intertwining our fingers, and I sigh at his touch.

It's as though he's not even aware of what he's doing. He touches me as if he wants to own me. As if we're really together. But we never take it any further than this. No kisses, nothing sexual. Though the tension and heat that radiates off his big body isn't only from his bad dreams.

It's because of me. He wants me. His body always, always responds to my touch. I wish that for once, he could admit it.

"I'm sorry." He sounds so distraught, so forlorn. I hate that. Tilting his head closer, his lips brush mine when he speaks. "Don't leave me."

And then he kisses me.

CHAPTER 3

Jen

His lips are warm and soft, the kiss simple. My emotions are anything but, colliding within me and dying to get out. Chaotic and out of control, as I realize this is the very first time our lips have actually touched. We've kissed each other's cheeks and foreheads, but never lips.

I've wanted this for far too long, but I think . . . no, I *know* he's half asleep. He probably doesn't even realize what he's doing . . . does he? He called me Jennifer and he never, ever calls me that. I'm simply Jen.

Good ol' I-can-always-count-on-her Jen.

Colin releases his hold on one of my hands and reaches for me, cupping my face, his thumb caressing my cheek as he turns more fully toward me. His chest brushes against mine, my nipples harden almost painfully, and I slide my hands up his chest, over his pecs, winding them around his neck so I can bury my fingers into his silky, soft hair.

I love touching him. Hate how secretive it always is, under the cover of darkness, the shroud of nightmares, the bleakness of night. I have my own secrets that I hide. Ugly, terrible things I'm desperate to keep locked inside. If he ever found out, I know he'd never look at me the same again.

This time between us is different, though. Our mouths

cling to each other, our lips slowly parting with every pass, but I refuse to be the first one to take this deeper.

Refuse? More like I'm too scared to take this deeper. What if he turns me away? I don't think I could deal with that.

"God, what you do to me." He murmurs the words against my lips, his breath hot as he exhales shakily. His other hand is at my hip, nestling me closer, and I can feel him. Every blessed, hot inch of his bare, firm skin, the boxer briefs he wears, the thrust of his erection beneath them.

A matching shuddery breath leaves me when I realize he's hard. His hand slips up my cheek, into my hair, until his fingers are at the back of my head, tightening around the long strands until I have no choice but to bend my head back, my new tattoo aching, the adhesive from the bandage tugging the few hairs that are captured beneath it.

It hurts, but I revel in the pain. Because it means I'm alive and Colin is touching me, kissing me. I want more.

So much more than what I'm willing to ask for.

He shifts his position, towering over me, dominating me, and a delicious shiver runs over my skin and through my veins, settling between my legs.

"I could take you like this." His hips thrust against mine, a slow, sensual roll that nearly makes my eyes cross. I try my best to withhold the whimper of pleasure that wants to escape, but it's no use. "Would you like that?" he asks, his perfect full lips tilting up at the corners. He's looking right at me, his lids lowered, his gaze smoldering and nearly setting me on fire.

I don't answer. I freaking can't find my voice, I'm so turned on, turned inside out. Trying to lift my head to connect our mouths again, he tightens his hold on my hair, sending a ripple of pain across my neck. My freshly tattooed skin hurts, the bandage isn't helping, but I ignore it. I focus instead on

Colin, how he's keeping me in place. Keeping me under his control.

He likes control. I've known this for years. I had no idea it carried over sexually, though I shouldn't be surprised.

"I won't fuck you, though. I can't have you," he says, disappointment ringing in his deep voice. He runs his lips along my neck, covering my sensitive skin with tiny, hot kisses, and I moan, wishing I were naked.

Wishing he were inside me. Filling me, fucking me like he suggested. Pounding deep within me so hard I can't help but come within minutes.

God, I really, desperately want that.

My moan seems to knock him out of his stupor and he rears his head back, releasing his hold on me as if I've burned him. Scrambling off the mattress so fast it all happens in a frenzied blur. He's standing on the side of the bed, running his hands through his hair and clutching the back of his head as he looks at me in utter disbelief. "What the fuck just happened?"

Sitting up, I smooth my hair back from my face, wincing when my fingers brush over my bandage. "Don't pretend you don't know what just happened."

He glances down at himself, spotting his erection no doubt, and makes one of those frustrated male sounds he's so good at. "Tell me we didn't . . ."

"Don't worry." I climb off the bed, trying my best to look dignified as I stand before him, knowing I'm failing miserably considering I'm wearing a see-through tank and skimpy panties. I should be embarrassed, but screw it. "We didn't. Like you don't know that." We didn't even get in any tongue action with our kiss and I'm downright desperate to know his taste. To know if we're as compatible as I hope we are when it comes to kissing.

Disappointment settles over me, mixed with a fair dose of irritation. This conversation we're about to have is gonna go south, quick.

"Why are you in my bed?" His gaze drops, drinking me in, and those cool blue eyes of his heat with unmistakable arousal.

"Why am I always in your bed? Why do you think I come to you at least four times a week in the middle of the night and slip beneath the sheets with you? If you're going to pretend like you don't know what's happening here, I swear to God, Colin, I'm going to kick your ass."

He has the nerve to laugh, the jackass. "Did you know you're pretty hot when you're mad?"

"This isn't a joke." Taking a deep breath, I tell myself to remain calm. He's doing his usual thing. Pretending nothing serious just went down, acting like he has no idea what actually happened.

He's a liar. I wonder if he's been playing me this entire time.

"I know it's not." His words practically dare me to explain exactly what's happening.

So I go for it.

"We never talk about it, you know." I take a step toward him, forgetting my lack of clothing, too focused on my anger. "What happens at night between us. What's been building and growing since I moved in with you."

He backs up, his expression wary. "What do you mean?"

"Don't act like you don't know." I take another step closer, his body heat radiating toward me, tempting me. Despite my anger and frustration, I still want him and it's infuriating. "Your bad dreams, me sneaking into your bed and holding you close. Trying to make you feel better. What do you dream about, Colin?"

"I don't remember," he says automatically, but he knows. Just like I know.

"You dream about my brother." Another step, and this time I grab his hand and cling to it. "It's been almost two years. You need to let Danny go."

He jerks his hand out of mine. "I don't want to talk about this."

"We have to. It's like this huge wall that sits between us. And every time I try to scale it, you push me off." I start toward him again, ready to push him, hit him, I don't know what, but he grabs me first. Wraps those big, warm hands of his around my waist and sets me away from him as if he can't stand having me too close.

"I won't do this, Jen. Not now." The expression on his face really says *not ever*.

And that pushes me past my breaking point. I'm done.

"That's why I won't stay here. This place, this entire situation, is unhealthy. Oh, and our so-called relationship? Completely unhealthy. I refuse to stand by and let you pretend nothing is happening when something so is. I'm not going to be the only player in this game." Turning, I head straight for the door, praying he'll chase after me, grab me, kiss me senseless.

At the very least, yell at me to stop, beg me to listen to his explanations. I want that glimpse into his soul, his heart. The wall he's built around it is made of steel, absolutely impenetrable, but I want to be the only one who can bust it down.

Yet he does nothing. Absolutely nothing. Just lets me go, as usual, without saying a word.

So I walk out, never once looking back. It takes everything within me not to look back.

When I finally make it to my room, with the door firmly

locked, the window thrown open to let in some of that deliciously cold night air, I collapse on my bed and cry. Heavy, painful sobs take over my body as I bury my face in the pillow so he won't hear me. Leaving him is the right thing to do, the only thing to do. This merry-go-round Colin and I are on is pointless. My crying over him? It's pointless, too.

As the last sob escapes me, I'm thankful for the cool breeze that dries the tears on my cheeks. Thankful even more for the sleep that slowly but sweetly takes over me.

Colin

I let her walk out of my room and didn't try to stop her. What the fuck is wrong with me? Twenty-four years old and I'm acting like a child. She means the world to me and I keep on letting her go. Keep on pretending what's happening between us isn't real. All for her sake, I tell myself. I don't want to hurt her.

Bullshit. More like I don't want to hurt myself. Taking risks with my career is never a problem. Taking risks with my personal life?

Forget it.

Collapsing on the edge of the bed, I lean forward and hang my head, resting my elbows on my knees. My earlier erection is long gone, replaced by a pile of regret that bubbles up, threatening to choke me. She's right. I lied. I knew exactly what happened between us. How good she felt, how amazing she tasted. How responsive she'd been within seconds of me touching her.

Like a complete asshole, I pushed her away, pretended I didn't know what was going on, and essentially shut her out for the last time. She walked out of my room without looking back once, hot as fuck in a pair of panties that rode up her ass and showed off her firm cheeks, a thin tank top that was see-through, allowing me to make out the color and size of her nipples right before she turned away from me.

They were deep rose and tiny.

"Fuck." I run my hands through my hair again and again, messing it up and not really giving a shit. The dream hadn't been so bad tonight. Danny was beckoning me to follow him through the woods like when we were kids. I'd chased after him, eventually losing him, as usual.

Then flew into a panic when I realized he was gone. When I realized he was never coming back. I've had variations of the same dream for years. We could be little kids, in high school, or even the age we were the last time we were together, but it always ends up the same.

I lose him. I can't find him. And as I search everywhere, I slowly figure out he's never coming back. Danny is dead.

Since Jen moved in with me, she's been there for me without asking any questions, sneaking into my bed, offering me comfort, and I always take it. Revel in it. Then pretend it never happened.

Well, no more. I need to stop acting like a coward and talk to her. Before I lose her forever.

Standing, I stride out of my room and walk with determined steps to Jen's, conscious of the fact that I'm in my underwear and nothing else. Not the best outfit for a serious conversation, but screw it. If I'm lucky, maybe she'll invite me into her bed and we can continue where we left off earlier.

Yeah, right.

The door is shut and locked, but I have one of those tiny keys resting on top of the door frame. I reach for it, feel the cool metal beneath my fingers and grab it, jamming the key into the lock and turning it until the lock springs open. Silently I slip in, not wanting to scare her or worse, disturb her if she's sleeping.

I hope like hell she's not sleeping.

But she is, and disappointment crashes over me. I draw closer to her bed and see that she's on her side facing the window, the covers tucked around her shoulders, her eyes closed and lips pursed. Without thought I settle on the edge of the bed as gently as possible, seeking her warmth. Reaching out, I touch her hair, letting the dark brown strands sift through my fingers. She's the total opposite of me. Dark hair to my blond, chocolate-brown eyes to my pale blue ones, sweet to my bastard-like ways.

I don't deserve her. I push her away because I know it's true. But what would it be like to give in? Just once? And show her how much I want her . . .

Jen rolls over onto her back, a soft sigh escaping her, and I let my hand drop, holding my breath as I wait for her to wake up.

She doesn't.

Following my instincts, I stretch out beside her on top of the comforter, slipping my arm around her waist and pulling her in. I close my eyes and rest my cheek on top of her head, breathing in her scent, absorbing her sweetness. Just having her near calms my racing heart, soothes my agitated nerves. The dream made me edgy. Her confrontation rattled me further, until all I wanted to do was sweep it under the virtual rug and pretend it never happened.

But now as we lie together and I hold her close, a sense of peace settles over me. She snuggles closer, her head resting on my shoulder, her mouth close to my neck. Her breath flutters against my skin, sending a scattering of tingles all over me, and then her lips move, damp and warm. "You won't be able to deny we're in bed together this time," she says in this sexy little whisper that goes straight to my dick.

Fuck. I grab hold of her tight, moving her body so she's beneath me, I'm straddling her hips, and we're right back at square one. Right where we started before this all fell apart.

This time, I'm not going to let that happen.

CHAPTER 4

Jen

". . . and that was it. I said that to him and he jumped me like he was going to, you know, do me or whatever. At the very least, kiss me. But he didn't. He stared at me like I'd grown three heads, and then he climbed off me."

"No."

"Yes." I nod, getting into my pitiful story. But at least I'm telling it to Fable, who understands. Anyone else would probably laugh at me. "Right before he left, he said . . ." Pausing, I take a breath, lowering my voice so I can mimic Colin. " 'You're right. I can't deny it any longer.' Then he bent over, kissed the top of my head, and walked right out of my room."

Fable stares at me, her green eyes wide, her mouth hanging open in disbelief. Any other day, I'd want to laugh. We could probably laugh over this together someday because really, last night had been ridiculous. Surreal.

I'm not laughing now, though. And neither is Fable. She knows how important Colin is to me. How drawn I am to him despite not wanting to be. She gets it. She went through her own turmoil with Drew and they somehow came out the other side. The happy side.

I have the distinct feeling that's not gonna happen for Colin and me.

"So he bailed. He was on top of you in a bed and did

nothing," Fable finally says. "And said he can't deny *it*? What, are you an *it* now?"

Shrugging, I glance down at the table. We're at Fable and Drew's apartment, though Drew isn't home. He's at football practice and her brother, Owen, is at his high school junior varsity's practice. Following in his sister's boyfriend's footsteps, which I can't help but find cute.

"And you let him go. Didn't say a word to him. Just let him leave." Fable sounds completely mystified. I can relate, since I, too, am totally mystified.

And miffed. Totally, completely bent out of shape.

"What could I say to him? 'Hey, wish you'd stay so we can finally do it?' I don't think so." I'm still staring at the table, which is small and dark and perfect. I think they just bought it—I remember Fable telling me they went furniture shopping. There's not a mark on it, not even a fleck of dust.

"If I were you, I would've yelled something like, 'Don't think you're ever getting back in my bed, dickhead. Not with that sort of shit going down.' I mean, the guy needs to be put in his place. He can't just use you and leave you like that. What a jerk!" Fable is all quiet bravado and I admire that. Wish I could yell at Colin and tell him how he really makes me feel.

How much last night's seeming rejection hurt. How he really didn't use me. How I sometimes secretly wish he *would* use me. I went to his bed willingly. I always go to his bed willingly. I can't stand to hear him suffer, hear him cry out. Sometimes he'll say my brother's name. Sometimes, mine.

His pain breaks my heart. It's a pain he stifles in the light of day. That he semi-acknowledged what we have lit a flicker of hope within me.

That he walked away—again—snuffed out the feeble flame.

I do the same thing, though. I'm stifling my pain, my secret. It's easier that way. Still doesn't mean I understand him, though.

"I told him I was quitting, that I was leaving, all of it. He doesn't want me to go but he didn't really say why, either, so . . . it's pointless for me to be here." I finally lift my head and meet Fable's gaze. She looks disappointed in me and I hate that. I've done that a lot in my life—disappoint people. I don't mean to. It just happens.

"I don't want you to leave. Neither does Drew." Fable's voice is soft. I know what she's trying to do. "We'll miss you, and you know I don't say this sort of thing to just anyone. You're the first real friend I've ever had. Drew jokes that you defuse me and he'll pay big money to keep you around."

My heart pangs at Fable's confession, at the humor she's trying to bring to this otherwise serious conversation. She's my first real female friend, too. I was always close to my brother and, yes, Colin. But other girls? Not really. Until I moved here and met Fable and we somehow bonded.

"You're okay with living here because this is where you grew up, and now Drew needs to finish college. And of course there's Owen," I say. Though I wonder what's going to happen once Drew is drafted by the NFL, because the man is just too damn good of a player not to get drafted.

I know Fable doesn't want to leave because of Owen, but she's going to have to make a choice and soon. I don't envy her that.

"There's nothing for me here—can't you see that?" I say. "No roots, no ties. Not that you don't count, but . . . I can't stick around here forever." I swallow past the lump in my throat, pissed at myself. That I can't admit the real reason I won't stick around is because I'm afraid my past will catch up with me and I won't know how to explain it. And that a cer-

39

tain someone won't freaking acknowledge we might have something together. Something real and beautiful and amazing if he would just open his eyes—and his closed-off, made-of-steel heart—and just realize it.

"Men suck," Fable says irritably, making me laugh. She grins in return, and I know that was her intention.

"They do," I agree. "With the exception of yours."

"Oh, please. He's definitely not perfect. On occasion, he sucks big time. But yeah. I'm keeping him." Her cheeks flush the faintest pink and I'm filled with an insane amount of jealousy that I hate to acknowledge, even to myself. I love my friend. I love that she's found such unconditional love from a sweet, gorgeous guy who wants nothing more than to take care of her.

How I wish Colin felt the same. He has no problem with me taking care of him, but heaven forbid I need him for anything beyond a job and a roof over my head.

Ugh. Fable is so right. Men suck.

"Maybe you should just jump him," Fable suggests out of the blue, startling me from my thoughts.

"Are you serious?" I don't know if I have the nerve to just . . . jump him. Despite how badly I want to. I've known Colin for what feels like forever. While I'm willing to walk away from him and his generosity, I'm not quite ready to push my luck and put myself on the line for him sexually. Talk about making myself vulnerable.

What if he rejects me? I don't know if I could take it.

"Hell yes, I'm serious. What better way for you to leave with a big bang than to . . . get banged." Fable bursts out laughing, the sound downright dirty, and I can't help it.

I join right in.

That's how her little brother Owen finds us a few minutes later, the two of us howling with laughter at the table as we trade sexual innuendos, the cheesier the better. I'd just let a ball reference fly when Owen ambled up to the table, a confused expression on his face.

We both stop laughing at the same moment, staring up at him in quiet horror.

Grimacing, Owen shakes his head. "I don't even wanna know."

Fable and I start giggling all over again as Owen moves into the kitchen to get himself something to drink. I watch him out of the corner of my eye, startled by how grown-up he looks. He's only fourteen and a freshman in high school but he's tall, and he's filling out quickly, with broad shoulders and chest.

The girls will love him.

"Your brother is gonna be a complete lady killer someday," I say.

Fable sighs, worry filling her gaze as she quickly studies him. "He already is. Now that he's on the junior varsity team, he's attracting a lot of attention from girls. I don't like it."

She's gone straight into vigilant big sister mode and I love it. She's so fiercely protective, I would never want to cross her. "Don't say anything mean," I warn her, but she glares at me.

"There's no one else to protect him from all those . . . she-devils." I almost laugh but don't dare. The look on Fable's face is downright scary. "I'm serious, Jen. They're all sniffing around him like dogs in heat."

"I heard that," Owen calls from the tiny kitchen.

"I wanted you to," Fable calls back. She leans across the table and lowers her voice. "I had sex way too young, you know? The idea of him doing that . . . freaks me out. I want him to stay a kid for as long as he can."

How could I break it to her that Owen has been far from a kid for years? I think she knows this; she just doesn't want to admit it. Only a few months ago she was complaining to me about finding yet another Baggie of weed in his jeans pocket. Though I don't think he gets high the way he used to, what with being on the football team and following in Drew's footsteps.

"He's so tall," I say, sounding lame but wanting to change the subject. I don't really want to talk about sex and drugs in reference to Owen.

"Almost as tall as Drew." Fable rolls her eyes, but her wistful expression betrays her. "I'm such a shrimp. Those two gang up on me and I'm done for." And she loves the things they do together. As a family. That the two most important men in her life now have a tight bond, as well.

More jealousy flows through me and I shove it down, smiling blissfully at Fable instead. "You three are like a happy little family unit."

She's positively glowing at my statement. "I've never really been part of a happy family unit before," she confesses softly.

I have. And I miss it.

Badly.

Colin

She was off tonight and I missed her. Terribly. I know it's pitiful, but I mirror my schedule to hers as best I can every week. I tell myself it's so I can drive her to work and I don't have to worry about her finding a ride home since she doesn't have a car. Not that she's my responsibility or anything.

Really, I just want to spend as much time with her as possible.

But today I couldn't make it happen. We needed more coverage in the restaurant tomorrow night for a special event, so I had to give her a different night off than usual.

Tonight I worked on the next two weeks' schedule and made sure we'd be working every night together. I have to take what I can get, considering she's leaving me. Forever. She's pissed at me and I can't blame her. I'm the one who had her exactly where I wanted her last night. Half-naked and warm and soft, her body beneath mine in her bed. Her eyes, her entire face, open and full of so much hope, so much want. Seeing all that, spread out before me like the most perfect offering ever created, overwhelmed the hell out of me.

So I gave her some bullshit excuse and walked out.

No wonder she's done with me. If I were her, I'd be done with me, too.

I left work early because I couldn't take it anymore and besides, business was dead. Wednesday nights are notoriously quiet. The college students seem to pretend they're studying that one night a week more than any other. Considering it's still early in the semester, the majority of them probably are. They all start out with good intentions, but it goes south quick. Plus, there are so many weekly events in the downtown area that bring the kids out in droves. Thirsty Thursday is a big one, the kickoff for the entire weekend.

May as well rest up considering the next few days ahead, as usual.

Entering the house, I see there's only one light on in the kitchen, the dim one over the sink. The house is quiet, no TV on, and I glance around pointlessly, knowing Jen isn't there. If she were, I'd sense her. Smell her. Feel her.

She has that much of an effect on me, though I'm not sure she's aware of it. I'm still mulling over everything she admitted last night. How she said she wanted me. Did she really mean that? I know there's something between us, an undeniable sexual chemistry that brews every time we get near each other. I always figured it was one-sided, since she never owned up to it. Ever.

Until last night.

I replay the kiss in my mind, which hadn't been much but had felt like everything. I know I want more. I want to slide my tongue against hers. I want to know the sounds she makes when she's aroused. I want to see her naked, her smooth, golden skin, those long, pretty legs tangled in the sheets. I want to swallow her moans and fill her body and brand her as mine.

Swallowing hard, I go to the fridge and grab a bottled water, tearing off the cap and taking a quick swig before I slam the door so hard the beer bottles inside rattle against each other. I slap my palm against the switch on the wall as I exit the kitchen, killing the light before I start down the hall toward my bedroom.

Frustration thrums through my veins, making me angry—the most pointless emotion in all the land, besides jealousy. Why do I always deny myself? Yeah, I shouldn't fuck around with Jen. Yeah, she's too good for me. Her brother was my best friend and I let him down in the worst way—and then sent him off to his death when I should have gone with him.

Making the promise to Danny that I would always take care of Jen had been easy. Actually making good on that promise proved much more difficult. She ran away. I found her almost a year ago, living in her car, stripping at the sleaziest club in the area, for the love of God. She worked most of the night and slept in her car in the parking lot of Gold Diggers.

I'd found her like that. Desperate and hungry and ready to run from me, though I hadn't let her. I chased after her. Forced her to listen to me, forced her into my car so I could take her home. I'll never forget how she looked. Like a wild animal caught in a trap. Frantically looking for a way to escape.

We'd always been friends. Growing up, we were close. Danny never mocked my connection to his sister, which I appreciated, because what Jen and I had shared was special.

We don't talk much anymore, though. She's keeping something from me and I can't figure out what. Discovering that she danced and took off her clothes had been bad enough. What more could she be hiding?

Who knows? She's not telling me squat.

Now here I am finally doing something right. Finally not being a total selfish prick and giving Jen the opportunities she deserves. I can't hold her back from doing what she wants. It's not fair. If she wants to leave and find her footing somewhere else, I need to encourage her. Lord knows her parents don't. They're too wrapped up in their own problems to pay attention to hers. You'd think they'd be over their son's death and how it affects them, how it's damn near ruined their marriage.

Huh. I have no business talking.

Once I enter my bedroom, I methodically strip off my clothes, leaving a trail behind me as I walk into the master bath. I turn on the shower and immediately step under the icy spray, gritting my teeth against the cold blast. The temperature of the water snaps me out of my shit mood and I stand under it for a bit, soaking my head.

Soaking my thoughts.

I finally turn up the heat, shampoo my hair, soap up my body, and rinse. Grab hold of my cock and jerk off to thoughts of her like a boy harboring an unrequited crush. Jen with me in the shower, her body soapy and slick, her smooth skin gleaming from the water. She'd touch me everywhere, her hands wandering all over my skin as she knelt before me. Her lips would whisper over the head of my hard cock just before she took me deep inside . . .

And as I slump against the slick wall, panting, my muscles trembling from the effects of my orgasm, I close my eyes and press my cheek against the unforgiving tile. Wishing she were with me, naked and eager under the spray, on her knees just as I imagined, ready to take me in her mouth.

Just before I grab her by the shoulders and haul her into my arms, press her against the wall, and fuck her into oblivion. That's what I really want.

But instead, I'm alone. As usual.

"Danny! Damn it, where are you?" I move through the forest, calling his name over and over again.

He's laughing. I can hear him. Maybe he's in a tree, hanging from a branch and watching me as I search everywhere for him. All the while he's laughing at my frustration. Or maybe he's hiding just beyond the trail, behind a bush. I can't figure out where he is. All I know is that I can hear him.

"Danny! Swear to God I'm gonna kick your ass if you don't show your ugly face now," I yell, stopping in the middle of the trail. The sun beats its merciless heat down upon me, and I rake a hand through my sweat-dampened hair. His laughter rings in the distance, infuriating me, and I kick at a rock, pissed that he keeps doing this to me.

I'm sick of his games. All I want to do is talk to him. See him. Insult him. Laugh with him.

Just like old times.

"Fuck you, Wilder. Come and find me!"

He's daring me, as if we're playing some sort of twisted hide-and-seek game, and I trudge on. Ignoring the heat, ignoring how the trail narrows and becomes rockier. More treacherous. I stumble and I hear his mocking laughter, the jackass.

"Don't slow down, follow my voice," Danny encourages. "Don't be a pussy!"

His words anger me and I increase my pace, determined to catch his ass so I can kick it. "Fuck you, Cade," I mutter, and he laughs harder.

"You can't get me. I've always been the stronger one. The better one," he taunts.

Not true.

"The faster one," he continues. "In school, I did better in all the sports. I got the prettier girls. You were always second best, Wilder. Hell, your old man doesn't even bother to come around and see you anymore. Well, he never really did, did he?"

"Fuck. YOU!" I break out into a full run despite the heat, how tired I am, how the sweat literally drips into my eyes. I wipe at them with the back of my hand and see Danny in the distance. Standing there, his hands on his hips, a big shit-eating grin on his face.

I want to wipe that grin off with my fist.

Clenching my hands so tight my fingers ache, I run up on him, ready to reach out and grab his shoulder, but the next thing I know, he's on the ground. Lying flat on his back, his entire body still, his dark brown eyes wide and unseeing. Staring up at me with no acknowledgment of life, they're completely empty.

"No." The sob falls from my lips as I fall to my knees and gather him into my arms. His body is cold. So damn cold and stiff and I hold him closer, his face pressed against my chest, my face against the top of his head. "Don't you die on me now, you motherfucker."

No response.

Tears stream down my cheeks and I shake my head. "I won't let you die." I squeeze him so tight I know he can't breathe and then I push him away from me, staring down into his face with dawning horror as he flops to the dusty ground with a thud.

His eyes are gone, replaced with empty, cold black sockets. He's not Danny anymore. He's a corpse. A skeleton. His body is brittle, his clothes, his fucking skin . . . gone.

Fuck.

A ragged sound escapes me and I leap to my feet, looking around in a panic. Now I'm lost. And if I don't find my way back, I'll soon be as dead as Danny.

"I gotta get out of here," I mutter to myself as I try to retrace my steps. But it's no use. As I continue on, I become more and more lost. Until I've circled back and there's Danny again.

Lying in the middle of the rocky trail, a cold and lifeless skeleton. The goddamn skeleton sits up, his black eyes on me, his voice calm as he lifts his hand. Pointing at me, he says, "It's all your fault I'm dead. I hope you're proud."

Another sob escapes me as I fall to my knees again. Hell no, I'm not proud. If I could switch places, I would. I so would. He didn't deserve to die. Everyone loved Danny, while everyone other than Danny merely tolerated me.

I wish I were the one who died.

"Colin." A soft, sweet voice reaches through the haze and I clamp my lips shut, trying to stave off my cries. "Colin, wake up. You're having a bad dream."

This is no dream. I'm facing my ugly reality every single day. I let everyone in my life down.

Everyone.

"Please, Colin." My body shakes. Her slender hands are

on me, trying to offer comfort. They smooth over my shoulders before she gives me another shake, this one firmer. I had no idea she was so strong. Mentally, yes, the girl can endure anything. I admire her for that.

Love her for that, too.

Love?

Maybe I am dreaming . . .

Blinking open my eyes, I see her. Jen's face above mine, her delicate brows scrunched together, those big brown eyes full of concern. A relieved smile curls her lips and she touches my cheek with delicate fingers. "You're awake." Her voice is so soft, I almost can't hear her, and I wonder if she's talking this way so she won't startle or scare me.

Staring at her, I drink in her pretty, familiar features. The soft glow in her eyes, the way she touches me, makes me realize I need her in my life. I need her to open up to me again, share with me her hopes and dreams and problems. I want to help her. I want her to help me.

There's more between us than friendship, more than our shared history. She means everything to me.

The realization renders me breathless.

I squeeze my eyes shut, then slowly open them again, trying to get her into focus. My muscles are tight, my entire body is tense, and she slips her fingers into my hair, her touch so gentle it sends tingles scattering over my skin.

My very exposed skin, since I'm naked as the day I was born.

CHAPTER 5

Jen

He's trembling in my arms, his electric-blue eyes stark and full of so much misery and pain as they stare into mine. I go with my instincts and draw him fully into my arms, clinging so tight I'm afraid I might never let him go.

His dreams are coming more frequently and I'm worried. They're consuming him. Time is supposed to heal all wounds, not make them worse.

Though time hasn't healed all *my* wounds, I suppose, so why should I expect it would for Colin?

Rolling onto my back, I bring Colin with me, his head nestled on my shoulder, his hair tickling my skin. He slings his arm around me, resting it across the top of my chest, his big hand cupping my shoulder. I don't mind the heavy weight. He feels solid, alive, so incredibly right lying with me like this. He's still shaky, though his breathing is evening out, and I tentatively sink my fingers back into his silky, soft hair, hoping to calm him down.

"Want to tell me about it?" I ask him this same question every single time.

And every single time he ignores it. Still, I have to try.

I rake my fingers through his hair again and again, closing my eyes when he nestles closer, our legs tangling. His skin is hot, the hair on his legs rasps against mine, and he's so incredibly hard . . .

As in I can feel his erection since he's naked.

My eyes fly open and I stare up at the ceiling. I've come to his bed countless times, but he always at least has underwear on. Not tonight. I can feel every blessed naked inch of him against me. Arousal courses through me, trickling through my veins, settling between my legs, and I press my lips together. The temptation to turn toward him is so overwhelming I have to remind myself I can't do it.

Well. I could. But I'm not about to play with fire.

"I was chasing Danny," he finally says, his voice so quiet I have to strain to hear him. I'm stunned he's saying anything. This is a total first. "That's how my dreams always start."

I quietly wait him out. I'm scared to speak for fear he'll shut up. Scared *not* to say anything, too, for fear he'll shut up.

"The scenario can change, but I'm always, always chasing him. Looking for him. Most of the time I don't find him, but when I do . . ." He shudders. "Those dreams are usually the worst."

"Did—did you find him in this one?" I want to know, and then again, I don't. I used to dream of Danny, too. All the time after he first died, some of the dreams sad, most of them happy, though I always woke with an ache in my heart because I missed him so much. Those dreams were more like memories of our past, as opposed to horrible nightmares.

"I did." His deep voice is somber, the sound slowly breaking my heart.

Colin is always breaking my heart. He can smile and laugh, joke and flirt at work, but it's all a mask. At home, here in the middle of the night, this is the real man. The one who deals with pain and suffering and so much damn guilt it has to be paralyzing.

I wish I could absorb some of it for him, but I have my own pain to contend with. If I weren't so worried he'd hate me forever, I'd tell him what I did. How I sold myself to men so easily. My secret shame would devastate him. He thinks he's dealing with a tremendous load of guilt . . .

Mine nearly suffocates me.

He says nothing else and neither do I. We lie there together quietly for so long, his breathing starts to slowly even out, and I know him well enough to know that he's fallen back asleep.

I wish I could sleep, too, but I can't. Not when I'm held captive in his strong arms, his big, hot body pressed to mine. My thoughts race with what he told me, the questions running through my mind. I've known Colin for years, yet in many ways he's still a complete mystery to me.

As I stare at the ceiling, I'm achingly aware of how close he is, our bodies practically entwined. After our kiss last night I can think of nothing else but doing it again. Doing more. Taking our intimate moments further.

Kissing him, doing anything else with Colin, would totally deter me from ever leaving him. Though I'm not stupid, my heart might be, and my body definitely would. It would betray me in an instant. I know I would become addicted to him. We're not even doing anything and I literally crave him. Want to taste him, touch him, run my hands and mouth and tongue all over his skin.

I wouldn't describe myself as a very sexual person. I'm no uptight virgin, but no guy has ever really rocked my world and left me gasping for more. As I grew up with an overprotective big brother and his equally overprotective best friend, boys tended to steer clear of me in my earlier teen years and I couldn't blame them. As I grew older, though, those same boys came chasing after me once Danny and Colin graduated high school, and yeah, I dated a few. Had sex for the first time with my first serious boyfriend on prom night during our senior year.

A spectacularly bad experience for me at least, and Doug Evans and I broke up soon after. Then he took off to college midway through the summer after we graduated, and I never saw or heard from him again.

I had one other long-term boyfriend, but we split right after Danny died. He couldn't take all the mourning and sadness, not that I could blame him. I would have broken up with me, too. Other than that, I've had sex with a handful of guys, but nothing too serious—and what happened when I was at Gold Diggers doesn't count.

But no man has ever rocked my socks off, for lack of a better term. The only guy who makes me want is the one who's lying here with me, sleeping on my shoulder, clinging to me like I might be his lifeline.

He devastates me and he doesn't even know it.

This is absolute, exquisite torture. I need to get out of his bed before I do something stupid. Slowly I try to disengage myself from his hold but he clings tighter, his fingers curling around my shoulder, his weight seeming to become heavier as he lies half on top of me. I thought he was asleep, but he's not acting like he is.

"Don't go." He whispers the words against my neck. I can feel his lips move, their damp warmth upon my skin making me shiver. "Stay with me."

His words, the tone of his voice, render me completely still and I lie there, immobilized. I want more, want to do so much more, but I'm afraid he'll reject me the way he did last night. I played it off to Fable earlier—hell, I played it off to myself—but that hurt, how easily he walked away. How Colin never acknowledges anything that happens between us. It's confusing.

Devastating.

"Colin . . ." My voice drifts off when he touches my jaw, his fingers feather light as they trace my chin, then slip down my throat. His entire hand spans the front of my neck, exerting the slightest bit of pressure, and a wave of arousal washes over me at his possessive touch.

He slides his hand down, settling on my chest, his wide palm pressing against the tops of my breasts, his fingers gently tracing my collarbone. My breath hitches in my throat, leaving me in shuddery little whispers I can't control.

"You want this. I can feel your heart racing." His lips are on my neck, his breath a hot gust on my skin. "You come to me every night always wanting to help me. Never asking for anything. Why, Jen?"

"You're my friend." A shaky exhale leaves me. "I don't like to see you hurting."

Colin remains quiet, nuzzling me with his nose, inhaling deep, as if he's trying to inhale *me*. I've gone completely rigid, stunned by the way he's acting. I like it, I can't lie, but he's also scaring me.

I don't want to get my hopes up.

"Is that all there is? That I'm just your friend and you don't want to see me hurting?" He sounds incredulous, as well he should. After what I said to him last night, how I told him I wanted him?

Yeah. He knows I'm full of crap.

"I . . . I don't know." God, no way can I admit how I feel *again* only for him to throw my words back in my face.

Again.

He moves so quickly I gasp, shocked to find him hovering

above me, his face close to mine, his hand moving to cup the side of my neck. His eyes are practically glowing as they rove over me. "What the fuck are we doing?"

His bold question shocks me further. I have no idea how to answer, and I close my eyes when he presses his forehead to mine. I can't look at him. Everything I'm feeling at this very moment is too . . . much.

Colin Wilder is the epitome of too much.

He shifts closer so that our lips practically touch. "I have no idea," I whisper, my lips moving over his as I speak. His mouth is on mine and then he's kissing me. Soft, heady kisses that make me dizzy, my lips parting with every brush of his, a whimper escaping me when he draws my lower lip in between his and sucks.

He feels so good, tastes even better, and he shifts against me, his erection brushing the very center of me. We're perfectly aligned; he could shove aside my panties and be inside me within seconds.

I want it. I want him so bad my entire body is wound tight, feeling like at any given moment I could shatter into a million tiny pieces.

A ringing sounds in the distance and I open my eyes to find Colin staring into them, his gaze full of questions. No way do I want to stop this. We've only just begun. He can answer his phone later.

But then I realize the ringing is coming from my cell phone in my room. We can hear it through that thin wall we share. Disappointment crashes over me at the same exact time I see it shade Colin's beautiful eyes.

Damn it! I have Colin sprawled on top of me naked and my fucking phone is ringing. And it's the special ring tone that I assigned to none other than my mother, who never, ever calls me. Especially in the middle of the night.

At least in a long time. All of a sudden, I'm filled with a weird sense of déjà vu that leaves me uneasy.

"I-I have to get that." I shove at his broad mountain of a chest but he doesn't so much as budge. "It's my mom."

He leaps off me as if I burned him with the word and I scramble off the bed, running for my room, but I'm too late. I've missed her call. Immediately I dial her number, my heart racing, my head pounding, worry gnawing at my stomach.

"There you are," Mom answers, her voice slurred.

"Mom, what's wrong?" I grip my phone tight, dread consuming me. I don't want to know what's wrong. Maybe something happened to Dad. There's really no one else in our family to worry about anymore. And we've only just started talking again, my mom and I, though it hasn't been easy. After I ran away without a word and then Colin found me, I had a difficult time talking to them. I felt too guilty for leaving.

I still remember the night I left. I'd planned my getaway for weeks. Saved up a little money, sold off a few things. I told absolutely no one I was going, though I really didn't have any friends around who would have cared.

The evening had been cold and my parents stayed up for what felt like forever. Drinking and arguing and crying—yet again—over Danny. I'd put my hands over my ears as I lay on top of my bed. Closed my eyes as tight as I could to drown out their sorrow.

Escaping hadn't been easy, but it had been the right thing for me at the time. I avoided their calls, my mom's texts, until I changed my cell number. I gave them no way to find me, though somehow, they eventually did. I think one of Danny's high school friends saw me at the club.

How embarrassing!

They're still wrapped up in their mourning for Danny, not that they care what I have to say about it. There are so many things I could tell them. Terrible, horrible things, but I know they wouldn't hear me. Oh, they'd pretend they were listening, but my words wouldn't sink in. Besides, my parents don't really talk. My dad works too much. My mom . . . I don't know what she's doing, but I have my suspicions. She's drinking too much. Drowning her sorrows.

I don't know how to help her. I don't want to. It's incredibly selfish of me to think that way, but I can't help it.

"Belinda Lambert called me," she said. "You remember Parker Lambert, right? He was right in between you and Danny, graduated high school the year after your brother did."

Frowning, I try to place him but I can't. Sometimes all those kids I went to school with morph into one big blur. And I went to school with pretty much all of them from kindergarten through senior year of high school. Funny how they're all just a mass of faces now, not a one of them really standing apart. "Why are you calling me in the middle of the night to gossip about local boys?"

She lets loose an irritated sound. I wonder if she's drunk. It's not quite two A.M. Has she been at a bar? I sort of can't imagine it, but then again, I can. She's done this before. And besides, weirder things have happened these last few years. "I ran into his mom at the Buckhorn. Parker died in Afghanistan, ju—just like your brother in Iraq."

Oh God. She's definitely drunk, considering she was at the Buckhorn, the bar where all the locals hang out in Shingletown, where I grew up. "When . . . when did it happen?"

"A few days ago. Belinda's devastated. Just devastated." She hiccups and sobs at the same time and I settle on the edge of the bed, hanging my head as I listen to her go on. Crying over Danny, crying for Parker.

Crying for herself.

She used to call me like this a lot, right after Danny died. I'd worked late-night shifts at one of the diners in the next town over, a real tourist trap where I kept busy, worked plenty of hours, and made great tips. She would call me on my thirty-minute-plus drive home, a little drunk from the wine she consumed too much of at dinner and crying. Always crying over the loss of Danny and how unfair life was.

I'm sick of it. Yes, I miss my brother, but it's been almost two years. Why can't everyone just . . . move on? He would be furious to see everyone act like this, especially Colin. I left home for this very reason, and here I am all over again. Surrounded by sadness and despair. I need a change of scenery. I need to find myself without the dark cloak of my brother's untimely death hanging over me.

As I finally hang up with my mom and crawl into bed without going back to Colin, I realize now more than ever that I need my freedom.

The healing butterfly tattoo on my neck is becoming more and more representative of my life as every day passes.

CHAPTER 6

Colin

We've gone back to the way we were, Jen and I. Those few days after she gave her notice and confessed that she wanted me and I basically refused her, those two nights in my bed . . . all of that's forgotten. We're back to her working, me working, and the two of us living together but never really talking.

It's been a week. She's leaving me in three. To find out what's going on in her life, I eavesdrop on her conversations with others at The District like a desperate loser looking for any glimmer of information. They're all curious as to why she's leaving, and why I'm not reacting. They all think we have a secret thing and we've never really deterred them from thinking otherwise.

More like *I've* never deterred it. I know how hot she is. Guys would be all over her if they thought they had a sliver of a chance. So I glower every time I catch any guy approaching her. Putting all of my past 'I'm a protective big brother, don't touch her' skills from when she was a teen and every dude in her class wanted to bang her.

They all leave her alone and she never protests. Somehow, I still fucked this up.

When people question her about her plans, she's always evasive, offering general answers and with such a pretty smile every single time, I swear my heart seizes up when I see it. I'm surprised I haven't dropped dead of a massive heart attack before the age of twenty-five. Last night had been an eye opener. I want her. Just looking at her makes me feel all growly and possessive. Jen belongs to me.

She just doesn't realize it yet.

Only Fable knows what's really going on in Jen's life and head—at least I figure she knows everything, because she and Jen are so close. Whereas I know nothing, because Jen and I aren't anything close to close.

My employees on shift tonight are all crowded in the bar at this very moment, chatting before the dinner crowd shows up. I don't bother reprimanding them, though I should. I rarely let them get away with standing around and doing nothing while on the clock.

But the restaurant looks good—everything's clean and the tables are properly set for the customers. I like everything to have a certain look, a clean aesthetic that gives us a reputation for being a classy joint, as my father would say, versus yet another dive bar/restaurant where the college students hang out.

Considering I've trained my employees so well that they're actually getting shit accomplished without me having to remind them, I just don't have it in me to yell.

Besides, I'm trying to glean information about Jen, since she's sure as hell not talking to me. They all surround her because they respect her. She's taken it upon herself more than once to help run the place. She has a convincing way about her; corralling my employees and getting them to do what she wants comes naturally for her.

She'd make a terrific manager someday. She's not ready yet but with the proper training, she would be great.

"Do you have a job yet?" Becca, one of my newer cocktail waitresses, is the one eagerly grilling Jen at the moment.

"I hope to go to Sacramento on my next day off for interviews." Jen shrugs, her body language casual, but I can hear the nerves in her voice. "I have a few things set up."

"You're so brave, just leaving like that with nothing lined up." Becca sounds like a borderline idiot, admiring Jen for taking off with no real plan. I thought she had one. She's always been too impulsive. "I wish I had the guts to do something like that."

"Guts? I think she's crazy. There's nothing brave about up and leaving a solid, dependable job and a place where you have great friends who'll be there for you no matter what you need. Why would anyone want to walk away from that? Sounds like the ideal setup to me and she's just . . . bailing." Ah, leave it to Fable to call Jen out for what she's doing. I know Fable is good and pissed at Jen.

"Fable." Jen shakes her head, clearly exasperated. I can only see the back of her head, but I'm sure she's giving Fable the death glare. "Haven't we already had this conversation?"

"Maybe." Fable shrugs. "Can't I be selfish and wish you were sticking around? There's no reason for you to leave."

"There are a bazillion reasons for me to leave. One of them just so happens to be here at this very moment."

Dread sinks my gut to my toes. She's talking about me. And not only is she talking about me, she's doing so in front of a handful of my employees. Employees that get it and suspect something is going on between us. And will now suspect I have everything to do with her leaving.

Fucking great.

Moving away from my perch at the hostess stand I stride into the bar, clapping my hands and putting on my stern boss face. "All right, let's break up this unofficial powwow and get to work. Customers will start trickling in at any minute."

They scramble like cockroaches when a light's flicked

on—even Jen, who shoots me a worried look as she hurries past, headed straight into the dining area. Fable's the only one left, standing her ground, looking every inch the fierce little warrior she is.

"Don't you have something to do?" I ask, sounding like a complete dick and not really caring. I'm grumpy as shit. I've been grumpy since Jen dropped her "I'm leaving" bomb on me.

Fable waves her hand at me, the lights from above catching on her engagement ring, making the diamond twinkle brightly. "Clearly I must, since no one else is doing anything about it."

Before I can say a word she's rushing me, her expression tight as she shoves my shoulder so hard, I take a step backward. "What the hell was that for?" I ask as I rub my shoulder, more than a little pissed.

More than anything, I'm stunned that she would do such a thing. Touch me like that. Looking at me like she wants to kick my ass into the next planet.

"For being such a stupid idiot who won't do anything to stop the girl you care about from walking out of your life forever." Her green eyes blaze fury at me and I take another step back, downright scared of the ferocity I see written all over her expressive face.

"I don't know what you're talking about." Wincing, I jump out of her way when she tries to hit me again.

"You're lucky I missed. You're being a complete asshole." She rests her fisted hands on her hips, positively fuming. "I don't care if you *are* my boss, we're also friends, right?"

"Yeah, but at the moment, I'm officially your boss, considering you're on the clock and all." The minute the words fly, I know it was the wrong thing to say.

Her lips tighten so much they almost completely disappear. "Hey look, there you go being an asshole again."

Grabbing her arm, I silently lead her outside, to the alley behind the restaurant where all the employees hang out during their breaks. Some of them eat, some of them smoke, and all of them gossip. Luckily enough, it's just Fable and me out here. I couldn't take her berating me where anyone could see and hear us. As if I'd let her.

If I wanted to be a complete jackass, I could fire her on the spot. At the very least, write her up and suspend her for a few days. She'd deserve it for the set-down she's giving me. Talk about insubordination!

But I know I deserve whatever she's going to say, so I'm going to take it. It's gonna be ugly, but maybe she can knock some sense into my head. Lord knows I need it.

"If you want to yell at me, do it out here," I tell her once the door is firmly shut behind us. I can hear the music coming from inside the bar, hear the noise level start to swell as the restaurant slowly fills with customers. Like a switch, we go from empty to full, just like that.

"Want me to be brutally honest?"

Jesus, if she wasn't being brutally honest just now, what do I have to look forward to? "Please, be my guest," I say wryly, readying myself for the blow.

"She's in love with you."

Fuck. I hadn't expected that. I flinch, as if Fable's words physically hit me.

"Don't say a word, because you're just going to ruin it. Or make me madder. I warn Drew not to say anything when I talk to him like this because he always, *always* makes it worse. Men." Fable shakes her head but she doesn't look that angry. She loves Drew Callahan more than life itself. Lucky fucker. "Don't you see the way she looks at you? She keeps your every secret, deflects it when everyone, and I do mean *everyone*, flat-out says to her face that she's fucking the boss. She defends you always."

I say nothing, because what is there to say?

Fable's on such a roll, I wouldn't be able to get a word in anyway. "I don't understand what's going on between you two, so who am I to judge? But I'm not sure if she understands it either. All I know is she believes you don't feel the same way she does. And that's why she's leaving. She can't take it anymore."

"Can't take what anymore?" I finally ask, my voice cracking. I almost sound like I'm ready to break down and cry.

"Jen can't take being in love with you when you don't feel the same." She peers at me with those all-seeing eyes. I don't know how Drew can stand it sometimes. Her unconditional love knows no bounds for him but Fable's gaze is damn near penetrating and I want to squirm where I stand, like a little kid caught doing something bad. "So. Do you feel the same? Or are you just stringing her along?"

"I—"

"If you say 'I don't know,' I swear to God, I will knee you in the balls."

Swallowing hard, I realize my voice has up and disappeared. I don't doubt Fable's threat for a second. My balls are shriveling up in fear at this very moment, for the love of God.

"I know I'm crossing the boss-employee line but you need to hear this, Colin. And I think you get that, too. That's why you're not saying a word. Why you're not getting pissed at me for being such a rude little bitch and calling you out on your shit." Fable steps closer, scaring the hell out of me, but I stand my ground, bracing myself for the next round of physical blows.

But she delivers it with words instead.

"If you don't want Jen to leave, then you need to find those balls you're so afraid I'm going to demolish, man up, and tell her. Don't let her go. Tell her how you feel."

Ah, she makes it sound so easy when it's so . . . not. "She's already looking for another job," I protest weakly. "She wants to go apartment hunting this week. Roommate hunting."

"Excuses." She waves a hand, dismissing my words. "But hey, if you're willing to let her go that easily, then by all means, go for it. Encourage her, then. Help her out—make it easier for her and get her out of your life once and for all." Fable rolls her eyes and laughs, though there's no humor behind it. "Don't you ever wonder why you can't let her go? Don't you realize how you eventually chase after her no matter what she does or where she goes? Always trying to snare her into your net? If you want to give her all that freedom she's so desperate to find, escort her right the hell on out of here."

Before I can finally come up with something to say to defend myself she walks away from me, opening the door and slamming it behind her with such force, the sound rattles both the building and my bones.

Leaving me alone with my thoughts, my feelings. They swarm me, overwhelm me, and I know there's no way I can stand out here dealing with all this shit.

So I follow her inside and hide away in my office.

Hide away from Jen.

CHAPTER 7

Jen

"Don't I know you?"

Glancing up, I find a man probably in his mid-forties standing before me on the other side of the hostess counter, staring at me.

Hard.

The restaurant is packed. The staff has been scrambling all evening. I should be on my break but instead I'm helping out at the front desk, handling payments, greeting customers in between checking up on my tables when the hostess is off seating others. I do this sort of thing whenever it gets a little crazy, and no one protests. Tonight, though, is extra busy, proof Colin needs to hire more people, and that makes me feel guilty for leaving.

Seeing this man is reminding me why I need to go. I don't want to know him but I do. He's a bad memory I don't want to deal with, especially here.

I smile faintly through my sudden nerves, wishing I could tell him to screw off. I don't like the way he's looking at me. He hands over his credit card and his dinner bill, and I automatically take it. "Are you a regular customer at The District?" We have lots of them, though they're usually younger than this guy. I know he's not a regular. Not here.

"Not at this place. My wife convinced me to take her here

tonight for our wedding anniversary." He sounds irritated, and I wonder how in the world I got stuck taking his credit card and running it. Wasn't he Fable's customer?

"Congratulations," I offer weakly, guilt assuaging me. Of course he's married. Weren't they all? "Did you enjoy your dinner?"

"A little overpriced," he huffs out, sounding irritated.

I ignore him, tapping my fingers on the screen, waiting for the credit card approval. It doesn't come fast enough and when the receipt finally prints out, I tear it off and hand it to him, practically shoving a pen into his hand.

"I know I've seen you before," he says, signing his receipt and pushing it and the pen back across the counter toward me. I don't dare look at him, and he seems to know I'm hiding from him.

"Thanks for coming. Hope you have a good evening," I say as I give him his copy of the receipt. Chancing a glance at him, I see the way his gaze drops to my chest, raking over my body in an overtly intimate way.

A shiver runs down my spine. Yeah, this is definitely one of the guys who I . . .

"Did you ever work at Gold Diggers?" He's lowered his voice, leaning toward me over the counter, and I step back, furiously shaking my head.

"I don't know what you're talking about," I start, but I clamp my lips shut when he smiles lecherously, pointing his finger at me.

"You did. I remember you." The smile grows, and my heart sinks to my toes. "I think you might've helped me out after hours one night, too." He pauses, his eyes lingering on my lips. "No man forgets a mouth like yours."

Holy. Shit. I can't believe he just said that. Panic races through my veins and I glance around, looking for an out.

"Ready to go?" A woman approaches, going right to the man's side, curling her arm around his. Clearly she's his wife, and I wonder what she might do if she knew I'd taken money from this man in exchange for a blow job.

Because that's how he knows me and the shame that threatens is so overwhelming, I'm tempted to run. I blanked out most of the men, never paying too much attention to their faces or bodies. Not wanting to know any details, trying to make them seem inhuman. It's easier that way to pretend they're not real.

But this guy is real—and so is his wife.

"Yeah, honey." He sends me a pointed stare, as if I'd blab where I knew him from or something crazy. He shouldn't worry. I don't want any trouble. "Thanks," he says to me gruffly and I nod in answer, surprised by the way the woman glares at me over her shoulder before they leave the restaurant.

Exhaling loudly, I sag against the counter, rubbing my forehead with the tips of my fingers. If what just happened isn't an indication I need to get out of here and quick, I don't know what else is. This is the second time in as many weeks that an encounter like this has happened.

Why now? Why all of a sudden are the scumbags who frequented Gold Diggers finding me? I don't get it. It's like the universe is trying to tell me something.

"Are you all right?" A warm hand settles on my shoulder and I whirl around, a gasp escaping me at the too intimate touch.

But it's just Colin. As his hand drops away from me, I see the concern and the caring in his gaze but I try to ignore it. "I'm fine," I say, swallowing hard.

"You're pale." He steps toward me, touching my cheek,

and I flinch. Again, his hand falls away and like an idiot, I miss his touch.

"Tired." I offer him a wan smile, wishing he'd leave me alone. Also wishing he'd whisk me out of here and rescue me for good. Maybe we could run away together. He doesn't want to face his problems and I don't want to face mine. We could avoid everything. Together. Alone. Naked . . .

Yeah. That sounds like my every dream come true.

"It's been a busy night. You should go take a break," he suggests, reaching out to touch me. Again. I let him this time, pressing my lips together when he tucks a wayward strand of hair behind my ear. He's so gentle, so sweet. Does he know how torturous this is? How much I want him?

We deny each other what we both want. I'm starting to wonder if we're both out of our minds.

"Everyone still needs help," I tell him, the breath catching in my lungs when he steps closer. He's invading my personal space, helping me forget what just happened with that horrible customer. "I'll take my break in thirty minutes. It should slow down by then."

"Take care of yourself. I don't like to see you looking so rattled." His gaze drops to my lips and I part them, wishing he would kiss me. Which is crazy considering we're in the middle of a very public restaurant.

"I'm okay. Really." I offer him a bigger smile and he returns it, the sight of that familiar, heartbreaking crooked smile making me want to throw my arms around him and never let him go.

"I miss talking to you," he confesses, his voice low.

I'm stunned by his words. "I miss talking to you, too," I automatically say in return.

"Before you—leave, let's try to do that, okay?" When I

don't say anything, he continues. "Let's try and talk? Catch up with . . . everything? I feel like I don't know you anymore, Jen."

He doesn't. There's too much I don't want him to know. That's why we don't talk.

"Sure. We can catch up. Sounds great." I sound flippant and I see the hurt in his eyes, but I ignore it.

We're always hurting each other rather than facing the truth. It's just easier that way.

"So you're going to Sacramento on your day off?" Fable asks the question innocently, but there's a motive behind her words. She wants to know if I'm really going through with this.

And she's ever so hopeful I'll back out and say I'm staying. Too bad I'm going to disappoint her. After what happened earlier, I know my leaving is the right choice. I'd rather be anonymous than deal with those sorts of confrontations.

Offering her a firm nod, I steadily count out my cash tips. It's our nightly ritual, where we all sit around a few tables and tally up our take for the night, then each of us puts in enough for the busboys and the hostesses. "That's my plan."

"How are you getting there?" Another innocent question, and this one I don't have an easy answer to, since I don't own a car.

Yeah. I really need one. It's the first thing on my list of what I need to function when I'm on my own. "I was hoping I could borrow Colin's car."

Fable bursts out laughing, the wench. "Yeah, right. He doesn't want you to leave and you really think he's going to let you drive his fancy-schmancy car alone to Sacramento? You gotta be kidding."

"I have my license. I know how to drive a freaking car," I

say grumpily, stacking up the one-dollar bills. Tonight was good, the tips were plentiful, and I'm thankful for every dollar I count.

I need all of them, since I'm going to be living on my own and paying all the bills that come with independent living.

"In the big city? Come on, small-town girl. You'll probably freak with all the traffic. And isn't that car of Colin's his precious baby?"

For a person who tried her hardest to plan this move thoroughly, I'm looking like a complete idiot right about now. "Fine, you can drive me."

"I work that day. I already checked the schedule." Fable shrugs. "And I don't own the truck, Drew does. We only have one vehicle and if I'm not using it to run Owen over to practice, Drew's driving to his practice or dropping me off at work or going to school or . . . whatever."

Crap. I'd love to do this by myself. I don't want to be dependent on someone else. I wish I could rent a car but I don't have a credit card and there's all these rules about using your debit card and you have to have a certain amount in the bank account. It's too complicated and not like I always have extra money floating around in my account. I'm saving to get out of here, not blow it all on a rental car. "I wonder if anyone else would take me . . ."

"Seriously? I thought you had this all planned out." Fable turns to look at me, her expression incredulous, and I immediately feel about two inches tall.

"I never thought about a car and that's such a huge expense . . ." My voice drifts and I'm overcome with embarrassment. I'd been living in my car when Colin found me, but it took a total dump right after I moved in with him. He helped me sell it for parts and I made a whoppin' two hundred bucks.

What the hell was I thinking, giving Colin my notice so soon? I mean, I know what I was thinking. He'd pissed me off so bad that I blurted out I wanted to quit, which I'd been planning to do all along but with at least a little more finesse . . .

God, I really screwed it up. To come to him now and say, "Hey, give me a few more months, I need a better plan" would be way too humiliating.

But how am I really going to make it on my own?

"Hell yeah, it's a huge expense. You spent money on a tattoo yet you didn't think of saving money for a car? I don't get it." Fable shakes her head, her disapproval ringing clear.

I reach for my neck, rubbing at my mostly healed tattoo. She's making me feel like a complete failure at life. And all of her criticism is also making me quietly furious. Since when does Fable have the right to judge me? "We make our own choices, you know? Not all of us know how to take care of ourselves perfectly." *Like you supposedly do,* I wanted to say.

But those last four words are certainly implied. By the shocked look on Fable's face, she knows it, too.

"I never said I know how to do things perfectly," she says defensively.

"You don't have to." I toss my money for the hostess and busboy that were on duty tonight into the center of the table and stand, ready to get the hell out of there.

"Jen, wait," Fable calls, but I ignore her. She's got her shit together, has her perfectly gorgeous boyfriend/fiancé, a decent job, and a brother who's on the right track. Yeah, so her mom sucks and her dad is invisible. Yeah, so Drew has his problems, but come on. He's a star football player probably on his way to the NFL, he's loaded, and he's madly in love with her.

I'm alone, living with a man who won't admit there might be something between us. Or worse, he feels absolutely nothing for me and this thing I think is happening is totally one-sided. Oh, he lusts for me. I know that. But there's nothing else.

Nothing. Else.

Now I'm stuck having to leave when I'm not close to being prepared. What if I don't find a job? What the hell am I doing?

Whose fault is this anyway, you moron? That's right—go look in a mirror and check out your reflection.

I exit the restaurant through the back door, ending up in the alley. No one's out there and I plop down on an old chair, tilting my head back with a low sigh so I can check out the brilliant night sky.

Colin will be waiting for me either in his office or out front. Everyone else will leave through the main doors as well. I can find a few minutes of peace by myself.

Or mull over my absolute failures in life at the mere age of twenty-two. Could I be any stupider? It's one thing to dance and strip on a stage for a living. Letting men stuff dollar bills down my G-string, trying to cop a feel—it was horrible, but I did it for the money. Lots of women do.

Then I got desperate. Moving in with a fellow dancer was my first mistake. She associated with unsavory people who stole all my money. Next thing I knew, I was meeting guys in the backseat of their cars and taking cash for making them come with my hand. Or my mouth.

I never took it any farther than that. I might have, though, if it had gone on longer. I don't know. I was desperate. Scared. Colin came along at the right time and saved me.

I owe him everything. Yet I'm leaving him without an explanation. It's bad enough that he watched me strip. Worse that he caught me in a car with a guy, though nothing had happened. That's a moment we don't talk about.

Letting my head fall back farther, I slump in the chair,

thunking my skull against the wood once. Then I do it again. Maybe I can knock some sense into my stupid brain if I keep it up. Maybe I could work up the courage to actually talk to Colin again rather than avoid the real issues.

"Are you trying to hurt yourself?"

Great. I close my eyes. If I can't see him, then maybe he's not really there, right? "Go away."

He ignores my demand. "I've been looking for you." Of course he has. He's always looking for me. Then he never does anything once he has me. I'm the brave one all of a sudden, which blows my mind.

His voice is the stuff of dreams. Deep and melodic, full of promise even when he says something completely benign, like "Have a nice day." Girls fall all over themselves to hear him utter those words. Any words.

"Maybe I don't want to be found." As in, catch a clue as to why I'm back here when no one else is.

"Fable's worried that you're mad at her."

I'm so tempted to open my eyes at that remark, but I squeeze them closed. "She has reason to worry because she's right. I'm totally mad at her."

"Why?" He sounds shocked. After all, we've been great friends pretty much from the moment we met. People think we're cute together, how in looks we are total opposites. I'm tall. She's short. She's blond. My hair is dark brown. We look sorta funny together and everyone eats it up, which is silly. This isn't a sitcom. This is our life.

And right now, my life and everyone in it is irritating the crap out of me.

"I don't want to talk about it," I mutter. I'm sure that's the last thing Colin wants to hear, but too bad. I'm not in the mood to share all my secrets with him. He's always so damn close-lipped, so right back at him, you know?

"Well, I'm about to lock up." He lets it go, which I appreciate. And it also drives me crazy. He would push, try and get more out of me, if he really cared. Right? "Everyone's left." He pauses and I wonder if he feels as wound up, as unsure, as I do. "You ready to go?"

I want to say no, but that's so stupid. He's my ride home. We live together. How else am I going to get to the house? Walk in the middle of the night? His neighborhood is pretty far from downtown and it would take forever to get there. Besides, who knows what sort of creeps I could encounter? In the middle of the night, the downtown area is crawling with them.

Not bothering with an answer, I stand and walk past Colin, going through the still open back door. He follows behind me without a word, his silence making me edgy so I decide to offer him the same treatment. Usually I'm the one who feels the need to fill the quiet. I'd rather talk about nothing than endure even a minute of uncomfortable silence.

Tonight, I'm too weary for even that.

Colin

She climbs into my BMW, the car I indulged in as my reward after I opened The District. It's a sweet ride, but I rarely use it beyond the drive-to-work, drive-home route. How fucking boring am I?

Her scent fills the interior, sweet and sultry and so uniquely Jen, my entire body reacts the moment she's inside. Her shoulder brushes mine as she locks in the seat belt, her hair snagging on my shirt for the briefest moment before she settles into her seat.

It's the same ritual every day. I breathe deep when we're on our way to work. And I breathe deep when we're on our way home. Trying to calm my nerves, tell myself I don't really want her.

More than anything, I'm trying to inhale her. As if I could lock in her scent and never, ever let it—or her—go.

I'm going to miss this. Miss her. For once I was brave, asking her to open up to me. There was a motive behind my request. I saw her earlier. The customer telling her he knew her from Gold Diggers, the pure panic that washed over her pretty face. I wish she'd told me about that. I should have pushed harder for the real answer when I asked what was wrong.

"Can I ask you a question?" she says out of the blue, her tone extremely neutral. Too neutral.

"Uh, go for it," I answer, wondering where she's going with this.

"Would you ever . . . let me borrow your car?" She's trying her best to sound like it's no big deal. I'm not buying it.

"Why do you ask?" I glance at her out of the corner of my eye.

"I don't know. Just wondering." She shrugs, which means there is way more motive behind it than she's letting on.

"I seem to remember you being a shitty driver." She'd wrecked her brother's car when he taught her how to drive. He'd raged over that for weeks, if not months.

"If you're talking about Danny's stupid Bronco, then fine, yes. I suck. I'm a terrible driver." She pauses for only a moment. "I was freaking fifteen, what do you expect?"

I chuckle, surprised I can still do it. Laugh. It's been tense around here lately and I hate it. "He never let you live it down."

"He probably still wouldn't." She clamps her lips shut, as if she doesn't want to say anything else, and I remain quiet, not willing to talk anymore about Danny either.

It's too damn painful.

Everything had been left hanging between my best friend and me. We'd argued about my not joining the military. I told him he was stupid to do it without me. I'd been so angry that he'd lost the chance to come with me and start a business together, I hadn't even bothered to see him off when he left. Only after he was gone did I have the balls to email him and tell him I was sorry. We'd chatted, we'd emailed, but it had never been the same. In one of our last conversations, he made me swear to watch over his sister if anything happened to him. I promised I would.

Soon after, he was gone.

"You haven't answered me." Pausing, she worries her lip with her teeth. I'd really love to worry that sexy, pouty lip with *my* teeth. *Shit.* "Would you let me borrow your car?"

"Well, is it an emergency?"

"Um . . . sort of?" Now she sounds way too unsure for me to believe her.

"A planned emergency? Because there's no such thing." I slow and turn right onto the street that leads into my neighborhood, my gaze drifting across the rows of beautiful houses, the perfectly manicured lawns, the expensive cars sitting in the driveway or parked out front along the curb. I love this damn neighborhood. It's one of the better ones in town and nothing like the place where I grew up.

This is the sort of neighborhood you see in commercials, on TV, in the movies. I used to live on a dirt road when I was a kid, my mom's little house nothing more than a shack. The roof was full of leaks and the floor was all uneven, with creaky floorboards and torn linoleum, and the one bathroom was no bigger than a closet and had a shower, no tub. No real yard, freaking chickens wandering around among the dirt and the weeds, crapping wherever they wanted. The very definition of rustic. I'd hated it.

Got the hell away from it, too. Never went back, much to my mom's irritation. Last time I talked to her, she accused me of behaving exactly like my father.

I could only silently agree. Then I immediately felt guilty and mailed her a check the next day. Put her in a new house, too, a few years ago, one she complains about frequently. She missed the old house, the one she grew up in, so it must have had sentimental value.

Personally, I wanted to mow it down with a giant tractor, but she wouldn't let me. So it sits empty. Probably overrun with mice, squirrels, and raccoons by now.

"Fine." She huffs out a sigh, full of irritation. "I need a ride to Sacramento. Not that I can ask you for one because that would be beyond tacky. So I was hoping I could borrow your car for the day."

She's insane. Like I'd let her drive my car in an unfamiliar area. And her asking to borrow my car *is* tacky. I know where she's coming from, but I want to hear her explain it. "Why can't you ask me to drive you there?"

"Um, because I'm essentially ditching the home and the job you've so generously offered me for the great, wild unknown?" She laughs, sounding almost . . . manic.

Clearly, she's stressed the fuck out. I'm ready to join her club.

"I'm still your friend, Jen. You've done so much for me. It's the least I could do for you," I say quietly as I turn onto my street.

More laughter comes from her, though there's not much humor in the sound. "I've done so much for you? Who are you kidding? You sacrifice everything for me. Always. You're my knight in shining armor, running to my rescue. What do I ever do for you?"

You're just . . . there. Holding me in my bed when I wake

up shaking and crying from my shitty nightmares. Never judging me, never asking too many questions. I wish I could tell you this. I wish I were brave enough to tell you how I really feel. More than anything, I wish I could tell you all my secrets.

I shake the words from my head. I can't say them now. I can't say them . . . ever.

"I'll take you to Sacramento." I hit the garage door opener as I pull into my driveway, easing into the garage and shutting off the engine like I do every other night.

But tonight, it's different. Tonight, Jen's looking at me as though I've lost my damn mind, those pretty dark eyes of hers eating me up. Probably wondering what the hell's wrong with me.

I wonder what the hell's wrong with me, too.

"You shouldn't."

I turn to face her straight on, my gaze clashing with hers. "Why? What's the big deal?"

She licks her lips, making them shiny and drawing my attention to them. Fuck it all, I want to kiss her. Forget the past, forget the present, forget the scary-as-hell future—I just want to lean over the center console and press my lips to hers. Steal her breath, steal her thoughts, steal her heart.

Like she's done to me.

I don't do any of that. I sit there calmly, my car keys in the palm of my hand, my body tense and ready for flight. She says the wrong thing and I'm outta there. She says the right thing and I'm jumping her in my car, in the garage, like a teenager trying to score before curfew's up.

"The big deal is that the only reason I'm moving to Sacramento is because I want to escape you," she admits softly. "This place, everything that's happened here . . . the memories aren't good, Colin. I can't stay. It hurts too much."

Her words slice my heart in two, not that they're unexpected. After seeing the way she looked when the man asked her if she'd worked at Gold Diggers, I think I know why she wants out of here. Away from this town, away from me.

So I do what I predicted. I get the hell outta there, leaving her alone in the car, in the garage.

While I barricade myself in my room.

CHAPTER 8

Colin

I can hear the music playing from within the large, nondescript building. It's loud, with a throbbing beat. As I draw closer to the entrance, the enthusiastic yells coming from the men inside are hard to ignore.

Whoever's on the stage must be putting on quite the show.

Entering the building, I pay the cover fee and walk inside, my eyes adjusting to the darkness. The music has stopped and the stage is dark, the men quiet as they wait anxiously at their tables.

I sit at one, ordering a beer when the cocktail waitress approaches. She flashes me a sultry smile, her blond hair cascading down her front, though not disguising her ample breasts on display.

She doesn't interest me. I'm too caught up looking for the girl I lost track of. The girl I disappointed.

A single spotlight suddenly shines on the stage and the curtains part, revealing a woman straddling the back of a chair, long, bare legs spread, feet clad in stiletto sandals. Her head is bent forward, her dark hair falling over her face, concealing her identity.

Recognition rises within me, making my spine tingle. I know who she is.

The music starts, slow and sensual, and she grips the chair back, tossing her head around, her long, dark hair flying. She stands, kicking the chair away with a thrust of one sexy leg, and the men start to cheer as she struts out onto the catwalk, a saucy smile curving her ruby-red lips.

Jealousy flares and I rest my clenched fists on top of the table, overcome with a wave of possessiveness. That's my Jenny up on that stage, wearing a fucking G-string and a bikini top that barely covers her breasts. I've never seen her like this. Moving to the beat as if she was born to dance, her hips shimmying, her arms above her head, fingers running through her hair. She's pure seduction and I feel like I've been sucker-punched in the gut.

The men around me yell and whistle, chanting her name. They call her Janey, and relief fills me that at least she withheld her true identity from the crowds of strange men who come to watch her dance on a nightly basis.

I know who she is. I know the real Jennifer. Or at least . . . I thought I did.

The music ends quickly and I stand, making my way to the door that leads backstage. A bouncer stops me. The guy is huge and broad, with arms as big as my goddamn head, and I try to push past him. Tell him that I'm Janey/Jenny's brother.

He doesn't believe me and sends me packing.

I linger. I search. I ask questions. But I don't see her. No one knows her. They're all lying, protecting her, from what I don't understand. Frustrated, I leave the parking lot. I notice a lone car parked away from the others, the windows steamed, the vehicle rocking slightly from whoever's moving around inside it.

Like a man possessed I run toward it, yanking open the driver's-side door to find Jenny inside with a man. A strange man who has his hand on her breast and her hand is on his crotch. I don't fucking know what's happening, but next *thing I know I reach inside and yank her out. Toss her over my shoulder and carry her to my car, ignoring her protests, wincing against the punches her hands are pounding against my back.*

"Put me down! Go away, Colin! I don't need you. I've never needed you!"

She's angry, but I don't care. I'm angrier. Disappointed. In both her and myself. What is she doing? It's bad enough she strips on a stage every night. Why the hell was she in that man's car, letting him touch her like that?

I don't want to know. I'm in fucking denial.

It's easier that way.

I sit straight up in bed, my body covered in sweat, my head roaring, the blood rushing in my ears, drowning out all other sounds and thoughts. Thrusting my hand through my hair, I grab my cell phone and check the time, see that it's just past three in the morning.

A shudder runs through me and I flop back onto the mattress, staring up at the ceiling. For once, there's no Jen in my bed to offer me comfort, holding me in her arms after my nightmare.

Fuck. That one had been a doozy.

Rarely do I dream about Jen, and I figure that's because she's such a part of my day-to-day life, I don't need to see her in my dreams. Well, I have the occasional sweaty sex dream, where I imagine her naked and me thrusting deep inside her welcoming body. Unfortunately, that particularly fantasy is all too rare.

This last nightmare scared the hell out of me. Finding her in the car, her hand on the guy, him groping her . . .

The way she looked at me, the things she said . . .

Go away, Colin! I don't need you. I've never needed you!

Jesus.

Breathing deep, I throw my arm over my eyes, trying my best to block out the words. Instead I concentrate on slowing my heart rate, willing myself to fall back asleep, but I can't.

All I can think about is the damn dream. Jen. Jennifer Cade dancing on a fucking stage like some sort of sex goddess—for other men. Since when did I want her to be my personal sex goddess?

Longer than you ever realized, asshole.

Right. I've turned into an angst-ridden asshole that can do nothing but mope and push a girl away. The kind of man who could probably turn his life into something pretty amazing, if only I would let her in. If only I could drop my walls.

Women have moved in and out of my life. Nameless faces, pretty bodies, girls I've used for physical release and nothing else. Relationships are nonexistent. I've never wanted one. Never thought a woman would want one with me. I'm just like my father. I can't settle down. Dad tried but he left, keeping Mom on a string. A string she happily lets herself stay attached to.

I don't get it.

I think of pissed-off Fable and wonder if her boyfriend would give me any advice. Chuckling, I roll over on my side and close my eyes. Yeah, we're sort of friends and we get along all right, but come on. I'm older than the guy, though not by much. I've actually lived my life, whereas he's been shuttled from one school to another by Daddy's money, never having to work a day beyond perfecting his throw and submersing himself completely in football.

Yeah, I have money, too. Now. Dad always had money since he inherited a fortune from my grandpa a couple of years after I was born, but for the most part, he made me work for mine, the motherfucker. He'd given me the restaurant just like his father had given him one long ago when I was a baby, when he left Mom, and after extensive training, I was left to my own devices. He'd come back into my life time and again, wanting us to work together, and I reluctantly agreed.

We're so similar, it's hard working with him. We clash constantly.

My mom took what he gave her, always muttering to me what a cheap jackass he was, though I know that's not true. I don't understand them, don't understand how they fell in love and decided to marry in the first place. The two of them—especially now—make zero sense together.

They're still freaking married, for Christ's sake. I think she secretly wishes he'll come back to her. I think he likes knowing that she's there, waiting for him. Their relationship is sick and twisted. The push and pull between them. The arguments. No wonder I don't want a relationship. Look at the example I've been given.

Yeah. My life is completely different from Drew's. But maybe the guy could help me. It might not hurt to have a different perspective.

At the very least, Drew could help knock some sense into me because he seems like a sensible guy. He has to be to deal with Fable on a day-to-day basis. That woman is crazy. Crazy beautiful, crazy protective, crazy opinionated, crazy all of the above and then some, but the most loyal girlfriend I've ever witnessed.

You're just irritated with Fable because she called you out on your shit.

True. She made me face things I really didn't want to see.

I still don't.

"So what did you want to talk about?"

I take a swig from my beer, glancing at Drew. "What makes you think I want to talk about something specific?" My voice is falsely jovial, as is my smile. We're at a bar downtown, one not even close to my restaurant, a place where the college kids really don't hang out. It's geared more toward the older local guys who get out of work and are looking for a drink or two before they gotta go home and face reality. I chose the location on purpose, didn't want any distractions.

"I guess we're—friends, but it's not like we hang out." Drew frowns. "I don't think you've ever asked me to meet you at a bar and have a few beers. We usually have the girls with us as a buffer."

He's right. We always have Fable and Jen with us.

"Fable's angry with me," I say, changing the subject. Slightly.

Drew nods, his expression grim. "I know. She'll get over it. I told her she can't tell everyone what to do."

I'm shocked that he knows, but then again, I'm not. Those two tell each other everything. There are no secrets between them from what I can tell. "I think she's mad at Jen, too."

"She was, but they hashed it out or whatever earlier, and now everything's fine."

Well, hell. I had no idea. Of course, I haven't seen or heard from Jen all day long. I'm sure she's avoiding me. I can't freaking blame her.

"I'm guessing everyone getting pissed at each other has to do with you and Jen?" Drew raises a brow, waiting for my answer, which he already knows.

I nod, feeling glum. "I should apologize."

"It would help, I'm sure," Drew says wryly.

Damn it. This is not how I envisioned myself, acting like

a mopey jackass over a woman. I'm a take-charge kind of guy. I see something I want, I go after it. Usually. But for whatever reason, I deny myself when it comes to Jen.

Women are good only for some occasional relief. I don't care about them or their feelings. I don't have time to nurture a relationship. Whatever a woman wanted from me, I only gave her my physical self. My emotions, my thoughts? Those were always mine.

It's so easy to fall into bed with a woman. Have sex, give each other pleasure. It's the aftermath that scares me. That's why I can't chance it with Jen. She's my friend first, and she fucking *matters*. I know I'd ruin it between us. Jen would want more than I could give. I'd disappoint her and she'd break it off with me. For good.

I can't risk it.

"I plan on taking Jen to Sacramento tomorrow to help her look for an apartment, take her to a few job interviews she has lined up," I say, keeping my gaze locked on the beer bottle in front of me, watching the neck sweat with condensation.

"And why the hell would you do that?"

I try not to react to the level calmness in Drew's voice, but damn. The way he's talking unnerves me. Being here, supposedly asking for his advice, sets me on edge. What the fuck am I doing?

"If I can't keep her here with me, I may as well take her where she wants to go and help her," I say quietly. Ice-cold shock washes over my skin at my admission. It's one thing to have all of these thoughts bottled up inside me. It's quite another to actually hear myself say the words out loud.

"Huh. I never figured you for a complete pussy." Drew slouches over the counter, gripping his near-empty beer bottle and spinning it between his fingers.

Turning, I glare at him in disbelief. "What did you just say?"

Drew flicks his gaze at me, then looks away. "You heard me. I thought you had more balls than that, man. It's one thing to let her walk out of your life. It's a whole other thing to be the one behind the steering wheel, driving her the fuck out of here. No wonder Fable's pissed at you."

"I don't understand why either of you would really give a shit," I mutter, irritation flowing through my veins, firing my blood. He's insulting my manhood, for the love of God. He called me a pussy and said I had no balls.

Fuck that noise. I'm outta here.

"I am the absolute last person to give you advice," Drew says just as I'm sliding off my bar stool. He knows I'm ready to bail, that I don't want to hear what he has to say. "After all, I'm the idiot who ran from Fable when I should've been running *to* her."

I pause, listening despite wanting to tell him to eat shit.

"If I could do it all over again, I would've been honest from the start. I would've told her what she meant to me. I would've never run, never pushed her away. I would've pulled her into my arms and never, ever let her go."

Tilting my head, I keep my back to him, absorbing his words, the pain behind them. Those two suffered, I know that much. When I first hired Fable, I thought Drew was a bad influence on her. I thought he was some slick-talking asshole ready to slide into her life, mess with her head, and then dump her.

Turns out he was the best thing that ever happened to Fable. They're good for each other. Balance each other out. I would never say this out loud, but . . . I'm jealous of their relationship. They love each other fiercely, are so damn protective of each other.

I want that. Most likely I could have that. With Jen.

Could you? Could you really? Or have you already ru-ined it?

"I'm an asshole." Slowly, I turn to face him, crossing my arms in front of my chest. "Is that what you're trying to tell me? Because I'd have to agree."

Drew smiles. "That's not all I want you to take away from this, but yeah. Stop being an asshole. And stop denying your-self what you feel. Go with it. Be with her. You *want* to be with her, don't you?"

I offer the tiniest nod in answer but can't make a sound. Just the idea of confirming that I want Jen with actual words to another person chokes me up.

Having Jen means I need to open myself up to her com-pletely. The thought of that is scary. What if she doesn't like what she sees? What if I disappoint her? It could happen. I disappoint everyone in my life. My mom, my dad, Danny.

It's easier to pretend she's only my friend rather than admit I want more. The idea of her rejection scares the hell out of me.

"Then tell her. At the very least, show her." He pauses. "She deserves it, after what she's suffered. With the loss of Danny, and . . ." His voice trails off and I wonder what else he's talking about.

Probably me, and everything I've done to her to let her down.

"I've done her wrong." My voice cracks and I clear my throat. "I did her entire family wrong. I've broken promises I've made to her family throughout the years again and again."

"What sort of promises?" Drew asks, interrupting me.

I stop and stare at him. "What did you say?"

"I asked what sort of promises did you break? I'm curi-ous." He holds his hands up in front of him when I send him a thunderous glare. "I know it's none of my business. You don't have to tell me if you don't want to."

I swore I would stand by Danny no matter what. And when I didn't do that, I promised my best friend I would take care of his sister. I promised their parents I would take care of the both of them. I lost Danny and wanted to save Jen—and I did so. But I broke that promise, too. I swore nothing bad would happen to her. Terrible, awful things happened to Jen when she was at Gold Diggers.

I failed on all counts.

"I promised Danny we would join the military the same day together and I bailed." Just saying the words aloud fills me with regret.

"Why didn't you sign up?"

"My dad made me an offer I couldn't refuse. He gave me a restaurant to run, my very own business that would belong only to me, with the potential for more." What kid wouldn't jump at that opportunity?

"What else?" Drew prompts, pushing me, and I cave willingly.

"I promised Danny I would take care of his sister. I failed at that, too." Big time. "I—I don't deserve her."

"You really believe that?" Drew asks quietly.

I hate how calm he looks, how sure he is of himself in this very moment, while my emotions are all over the damn place. *I'm* the confident one. I'm the one that never lets anything bother him, who can take care of every situation and make it all right once more.

With the exception of the entire Cade family. I screw them over again and again.

"Yeah," I finally answer.

"Then prove yourself wrong, man." Drew shakes his head. "Prove yourself wrong."

CHAPTER 9

Jen

"Rise and shine, sweet cheeks."

I snuggle closer into my pillow, squeezing my eyes shut against the early morning sunlight streaming into my room. I know I didn't leave the blinds open before I went to bed. I must be dreaming. And no way is Colin in my room calling me *sweet cheeks*. I mean, what the hell?

"Jennifer Lynn Cade." He gives my shoulder a shake and I shrug his hand off, totally aware of the heat from his touch on my skin. "If we want to make it to Sacramento at a decent hour, you need to get up and get ready."

Okay. Something is definitely wrong with this picture. First, Colin is most definitely in my room. Usually I'm the one in *his* room trying to wake him up from yet another terrible dream that tends to send him deeper into this downward spiral of self-hatred.

Second, Colin sounds downright affectionate. What the hell?

"Lazy," he murmurs just before he slaps—yes, *slaps*—my ass. "Come on, sweet cheeks. Let's do this."

I scooch my sweet cheeks away from where I can feel him sitting on my bed. Cracking my eyes open, I find him right next to me, wearing jeans and a dark blue T-shirt that stretches across his shoulders and chest in the yummiest way. The man is as big as a mountain and I'm ready to climb him. "Did you just call me what I think you called me?"

He smiles, and it's like a billion tiny daggers straight to my heart. I can practically feel it cracking in my chest, he's so damn beautiful. "Considering your ass is hanging out of those tiny shorts you're wearing at the moment, I think I can say on proper authority that your cheeks are pretty damn sweet."

"Oh my God." The cheeks on my face are so hot my skin feels like it's going to catch fire as I jerk the blankets back over me. I didn't even realize I was only half-covered by the comforter and that he could see the tiny shorts I wear to bed. Sans panties.

How freaking mortifying.

His mood doesn't fit. Lately he's been so somber and sullen and Mister Downer, I'm surprised to see the smile still pasted to his face. I shouldn't say "pasted" because it looks genuine and I have to admit, I like seeing it. I like seeing him happy and carefree. It reminds me of the past, before all this heavy, awful shit happened.

"Like I haven't seen your ass before." He stands and stretches, lifting his arms high above his head, making a rough sound in the back of his throat that's undeniably sexy. His shirt rises with the movement, offering a glimpse of his flat, toned stomach, and I'm filled with the urge to lick him there.

God bless America, what is wrong with me? I'm sitting here gaping at him like some sort of shell-shocked war victim. I can't think about licking Colin's perfect abs. I need to concentrate on getting the hell out of here before I do something incredibly stupid.

Like, you know, attempt to lick Colin's abs.

"You've got ten minutes to get those sweet cheeks into the shower and get ready. Then we're hitting the road," he commands as he drops his arms to his sides, his voice full of that aggressive authority I would never admit arouses me like nothing else.

Sometimes I really love it when he bosses me around.

"Hitting the road where?" I ask, my gaze following his right hand. It reaches beneath his shirt, scratching his belly lazily, lifting the hem so I catch another peek of all that tempting skin. Dark golden hair trails from beneath his navel, a path that, yep, I want to follow with my tongue. See where it takes me.

Hmm, I know exactly where it'll take me and I so want to go there.

Closing my eyes, I thunk the back of my head hard as hell against the headboard, irritated with my train of thought. Am I horny? Was I having an amazingly realistic sex dream, or what? Having him here in my room, on my bed, I can't stop thinking about him. What I'd like to do to him. Naked. With my mouth and my tongue and my . . .

"I'm driving you to Sacramento, remember?"

I open my eyes to find him watching me, one brow cocked, his hands on his hips. He looks . . . gorgeous. Good enough to eat. Irritated with me, too—I can see it in his pretty crystal-blue eyes. But there's amusement flashing there as well, so he's not that pissed at me.

Only sorta.

"Don't you have stuff planned today? In Sac? You know, looking for a job, an apartment, all of those important things a girl needs to do to move on with her life?" he prods.

It's all coming back to me now. God, my brain is a foggy mess, especially when I haven't had my first cup of coffee yet. "I have two job interviews later today. Both of them not till this afternoon, though."

"I'm sure you'll find a job pretty quick." He sends me a look, one that's all business. "If you need a reference, don't hesitate to put my name down on the application. I won't sabotage this for you, Jen. I hope you know that."

"Of course you wouldn't," I automatically say, but really? I'm not too sure. I'm suspicious of his mood. He's been protesting my wanting to leave since I made the announcement and now he's going to be my first-class, sexy-as-hell escort into my new life? I don't get it.

More than anything, I flat-out don't get *him*.

"I'd love to stand around and chat, but we're wasting time. You need to get ready." He grabs the end of the comforter and yanks it right off me, making me shriek. Damn it, I'm in nothing but a thin white tank top and no bra, plus the shorts that bared my ass to him already.

I may as well be naked.

Scrambling for the comforter, I try and grab it, but he keeps it out of my reach. "I'm practically indecent," I tell him, giving him a meaningful stare.

He doesn't pick up the hint. "I've seen you in less," he drawls.

My cheeks warm with embarrassment. "Yeah, when I was eight and you caught me skinny-dipping in the creek. That totally doesn't count."

"Actually, you were nine. And it definitely counts." He smirks. I hate it when he smirks. Makes me think he's turning into a big ol' douchebag, though really, I know he's not. He's just so damn cocky sometimes and it bugs me, because he has reason to be. The man is almost perfect. "You've come to my bed wearing the same exact thing. What's the big deal?"

"You're really going to go there?" I'm shocked. This is the last thing I want to do, discuss his scary dreams and bring our mood down. I much prefer the happy, carefree Colin. I can't remember the last time I saw him like this.

"There are lots of places I'd like to go with you, Jen. I just haven't told you about them yet." With that, he turns and leaves my bedroom, quietly shutting the door behind him.

I slump against the headboard the second he's gone, breathing easy once more. What did he mean by that? He makes me nervous. The whole butterflies-in-the-stomach, I-can't-eat, I-can-hardly-think-or-talk type of nervous that no other guy has ever been able to make me feel. I love it. I crave it.

It also scares the shit out of me.

"So how were you going to get here?" Colin asks over three hours later as we're driving around Sacramento, looking for a place to eat close to my first interview. We'd already scoped out the building, Colin overly attentive in making sure it was in a safe, clean neighborhood. He doesn't want me working in a bad area, he already told me on the drive down. He gave me a fifteen-minute lecture on safety and checking my surroundings wherever I'm at and blah, blah, blah.

At any other time the lecture would have bugged me. Now, I kind of appreciate it. It means he cares. For a man who has a hard time showing his feelings, I cherish this little glimpse. Does that make me lame?

Maybe, but I don't care.

"What do you mean?" I'm not really paying attention to what he's saying to me, because I'm so focused on trying to find a decent restaurant before my stomach starts to growl loudly.

"You never did tell me if you arranged a ride with someone else." He sends me a quick look. "Who was it?"

Oh. Yeah. I did arrange for someone to take me, but I canceled via text message after Colin left my room. "Jason."

I shrug. He's one of the waiters at The District. Great guy, going to college, cute and smart. I could be interested if someone weren't so busy screwing with my head.

Or my heart.

"Jason as in my waiter, Jason?" Colin's voice is tight. He almost sounds . . . jealous.

Yeah, right.

"I don't know any other Jasons, so that's the one." I keep my gaze purposely averted. No way do I want to look at him, see all the curiosity and speculation. Should I let him think something's potentially going on between Jason and me? A little jealousy doesn't hurt. Besides, I don't need to tell him Jason already has a girlfriend and they're madly in love. He's a quiet guy who doesn't talk much about his private life at work, but when he heard me talking about needing to go to Sacramento for job interviews and not having a ride, he offered. And I accepted.

Colin also doesn't need to know that Jason's girlfriend, Kim, would have accompanied us.

"Was he mad you turned him down at the last minute?"

I finally dare to look at him. He's staring straight ahead, which is a good thing considering he's driving. His jaw is clenched, and his hands grip the steering wheel so tight his knuckles are white.

Oh yes, he's definitely jealous. I can't freaking believe it.

"He was cool. He offered to take me out of the kindness of his heart, not because he already had plans to go to Sacramento or anything. I offered to pay for his gas and the trip would've eaten up his entire day off. I'm sure he's glad I canceled." That way he could spend the day with his girlfriend doing whatever the heck they wanted, instead of being my personal chauffeur.

"I doubt that," he mutters, shaking his head. "He probably wanted to get in your pants."

Such a jerk thing to say—and completely unwarranted. I sorta love it, though. His jealousy is another glimpse of emotion from Colin. "Nope." When he looks at me once more I offer him a bright smile. "He has a girlfriend."

"Big deal."

"Not everyone's a player." *Like you,* I want to say, but I hold my tongue. "He told me he'd bring Kim along. We've been upfront with each other since he offered to drive me. We're just friends," I stress. Why I need to explain anything to him I have no idea. It's not like he's my keeper. He sure acts like it, though. "You're the only one who's being so shady."

"How the hell am I being shady?" He turns into the crowded parking lot of a popular chain restaurant.

Let me count the ways. "I tell you I'm leaving and you flip out. Try to convince me to stay. We argue. We don't really speak to each other for a couple of days, which is something we never do. Now you're all agreeable and wanting to help me, no questions asked. Acting jealous when I mention another guy's name." I cross my arms in front of my chest, slumping in my seat as he pulls the car into a slot and cuts the engine. "To me, that's all shady behavior."

He turns to look at me, leaning forward so he's dangerously, deliciously close. I can smell him, feel his body heat radiate toward me, and I'm tempted to burrow in like an idiot. "First of all, I know Jason has a girlfriend. So when you mention he's the one who was going to bring you here, I'm suspicious. I can't help it. He's a good guy, but hey, even good guys have bad intentions."

"Not everyone is a jerk." I raise my brow.

"Are you saying I'm a jerk?"

His earlier jovial, nothing-bad-has-ever-happened-between-us mood set me on edge. I'm the one who should be suspicious here, not him. And he's too damn close. I have to spend the rest of the day with him, driving around in his car. Looking at him. Smelling him. *God.* "You don't have the best reputation when it comes to women," I say primly.

"So you're holding that against me." His gaze cuts to the windshield and he looks at the restaurant, lost in thought.

I become lost in thought, too. I'm a confused mess of emotions when it comes to Colin. Mad, sad, frustrated, aroused—I'm experiencing all of that at this very moment. It's the craziest thing. All my anger dissipates the longer I look at him. Studying his beautiful face, that firm jaw I long to trace with my lips, his perfect mouth I yearn to kiss . . .

"I want to prove you wrong." His deep, determined voice breaks through my clouded brain, startling me. "I can't take away my past. I can't fix the things I've done to you and your family."

Frowning, I shake my head. "Things you've done to me and my family? What are you talking about?"

"I promised them I would take care of you. I promised your brother." Grimacing, he waves a hand, dismissing my question and his way-too-vague answer. "You want to start a new life and I'm not going to stop you. You deserve happiness, Jen. And if being where you are now doesn't make you happy, then you need to go out and find that happiness. You deserve it."

I press my lips together, foolishly overcome by what he's said. We're sitting in the parking lot of a lame restaurant having this profound conversation and it feels surreal. Makes me wonder if I'm making a huge mistake, leaving him. Leaving everything I know behind so I can forge a new start in life for . . . what? A change? A challenge? To escape my past?

My past is creeping up on me and bleeding into my present more and more. That's enough to make me want to run and hide.

Reaching behind me, I rub my nape, brushing against the healing scabs on my butterfly tattoo with my fingers. Touching it grounds me, reminds me that I'm changing my life for the better. I've been thinking about Danny a lot lately. How he wouldn't want to see me miserable. How he wouldn't want to see Colin miserable, either.

It makes me wonder if spending so much time with each other is exactly what's making us so miserable . . .

"Let's go get lunch," I say softly, desperate to change the subject before I say something really stupid. "I'm starving, and my interview's in little over an hour."

Without looking at me, he reaches for his door handle. He's just about to open the door when I touch him, my fingers curling around his forearm. "Thank you," I murmur.

He turns to look at me over his shoulder. "For what?"

"For encouraging me." I don't want to let him go. His arm is pure muscle and sinew, and I can feel the soft hairs tickling my fingertips. Dropping my gaze, I study his big hand, those long, capable fingers.

"I'd do anything for you, Jennifer." I jerk my head up when he calls me by my full name, my startled gaze meeting his. "Someday I hope you'll realize that."

CHAPTER 10

Jen

"So you're currently a waitress." The woman glances over my application, her mouth screwed up in distaste.

I sit across from her, a narrow table dividing us. The interview is for a personal assistant to the vice president of an advertising agency. We're in a tiny meeting room of some sort and I swear their air conditioner is broken. The air in the room is practically stifling and I'm tempted to fan my face for some sort of relief, but I restrain myself. "I am."

She switches to look at my résumé, the one I'd agonized over for hours a few days ago, when I lined up these interviews. Fable helped me with it. Even Owen made a few contributions; the kid is surprisingly good in English and he spotted some mistakes.

But she barely looks at it, lifting her head to pin me with an assessing stare. "Almost all of your work experience is in the food industry."

"It's what I know, yes, but I'm more than willing to learn." I lean across the table, ready to launch into the speech I'd practiced in my head during the drive here, ready to bust out all of those impressive words that will no doubt push her into hiring me on the spot. At least, I hope. "I'm new to the area and am looking to line up a position with potential to grow. I'm a quick learner and I really need this jo—"

"Do you know Microsoft Office?" she interrupts.

I press my lips shut, swallowing my speech. "Some." It's an exaggeration. Well, I can use Word, but nothing too fancy.

"Specifically Excel? I'm in constant need of spreadsheets." She smiles, but it's not genuine. She knows she's got me. "How about PowerPoint? We give a lot of presentations here."

"I . . . I can take a class," I offer weakly, wincing. Local community colleges offer those sorts of courses all the time and I'm dying to go back to school. Once I can afford it . . .

"I appreciate the offer." The smile turns condescending, just like that. *Ouch*. "We'll be in touch."

That's it? I watch her stand and I do the same, pushing away from the table and bringing myself to my feet as if I'm in a daze. I shake her hand and she practically shoves me out of the building.

And I thought the last interview had been bad. At least that man had given me a solid ten minutes of his time, listing the duties of the receptionist position I was interviewing for, his gaze straying to my breasts every few seconds, which kinda creeped me out.

Okay, fine, it really creeped me out.

It's not as if I'm dressed indecently or anything. Straight black skirt and heels, a white, sleeveless shirt with a delicate lace collar and pretty little pearl buttons that run down the front. My hair is pulled into a sleek ponytail, and the pearl earrings my grandma gave me for Christmas when I turned thirteen dot my ears. Respectful, earnestly-looking-for-a-job clothes, and the guy still leers at me.

I can't win for trying.

Breathing deep, I walk across the hot parking lot, the heat from the sun seeming to radiate upward from the asphalt in waves. I head toward Colin's car, determination filling my steps. I refuse to get upset, but talk about disheartening. Every interview I've had today, including the spontaneous one I'd stumbled upon while at the restaurant waiting to be seated, ended badly.

I'd overheard the man in the restaurant saying he needed a marketing assistant and I'd barged right into his conversation, turning it into an appointment so we could talk more after I finished eating. I'd had the interview not even an hour ago with the gentleman, who ran a marketing firm, and it turned into a bust.

A complete and total bust—like I am.

"That was quick," Colin says when I slide inside the car. I breathe a sigh of relief at the cold air blasting on me from the vents and I lean forward, letting the air wash over my heated skin. "Tell me they hired you."

"I can't, because that would be a lie." Tilting my head back, I close my eyes, a little sigh of relief escaping me. I had no idea how hot and sweaty and worked up I'd gotten during that stupid, waste-of-time interview.

"You're kidding me." He sounds incredulous, and I sorta love him for that. I need someone on my side at the moment. I'm feeling like a total failure.

"No one wants to hire someone who has zero office experience to work in an office." I settle into my seat, my eyes still closed. I wonder if he'd be offended if I napped the entire ride home.

"How do you get office experience if no one will hire you to work at an office?"

"That's my point exactly." I sigh again because it feels good. It also feels good to kick off these killer high-heel shoes I'm wearing, so I do that, too. I swear my toes just sighed with happiness along with me as I stretched them out. "The woman was rude. Condescending. Looked down her nose at me and asked if I had Excel or PowerPoint knowledge. Of course I don't, and she knew it."

And I didn't even mention my work experience at Gold Diggers. Not that I ever would. That's no one's business but my own.

"Want me to go in there and kick her ass for you? I totally would." He sounds so hopeful I can't help but laugh.

"I know you would and I appreciate that, but no. She'd call the police on you and that would end up ugly." I shake my head. "This was such a wasted trip. Let's go home." I don't even catch myself using the word *home* until it's too late. The word had already flown out of my mouth.

But Colin doesn't acknowledge it, thank goodness. "I thought you wanted to look at apartments, too."

"What's the point if I can't afford them? I don't have a job here. I'll probably have to settle for a waitressing position at some shitty restaurant and make it work." The thought alone depresses me and I squeeze my eyes shut again, trying to block out the dismal possibilities. I've messed this all up, but there's no going back now. "I'll tell myself it's temporary, but we'll all know that's a lie. I'll be a waitress my entire life. Oh my God, that's so depressing!"

"Hey." He reaches for my hand, giving it a squeeze. "You'll figure this out. I know you will. So you've hit a couple of bumps in the road. This won't be the first time or the last. You're smart. You can make this work."

"Sure I can. Says the girl who has nothing lined up, who gave you her notice and has nowhere to go in a matter of a few weeks." I shake my head. "I'm a complete dumbass."

"No, you're not. You're just anxious to really start living the life you want to live. I get that. I totally get that." I crack open my eyes just in time to watch him bring my hand up to his mouth, brushing the softest kiss across my knuckles. My skin tingles from the contact and I curl my fingers around his, wishing we didn't have all of this . . . past blocking us. He's somehow put me on a pedestal and believes the two of us can never work out.

Wouldn't he just die if he knew the truth? Talk about falling off the pedestal! It's bad enough he knows I was a stripper. How would he feel if he knew I was basically a prostitute, offering hand jobs and blow jobs for quick cash in the Gold Diggers parking lot?

God, that sounds sordid and disgusting!

"Take me home, Colin," I whisper, my mouth going dry when his hot gaze meets mine. I see all the heat and want swirling in the pretty blue depths of his eyes, all of it directed at me, rendering me speechless.

It's so ridiculous, what we're doing. Why can't we give in to this? I'm leaving. For all I know, I'll never see Colin again. So what's wrong with a little sex between friends until I move out and far away from that shitty little college town I keep calling home as if I secretly want it to be?

So scary, but the only time I feel safe, the only time I feel like I'm at *home*, is when I'm with Colin.

Colin

I like how she told me to take her home, though it took everything in me not to acknowledge that little slip. I like even more the way she sneaks looks at me as I drive. She thinks I don't notice, but I do. Everything she does, I notice.

Drew's advice has lingered in my brain all day long, so I've tried my best to keep it light and prove to her that I want her, yet instead I made her suspicious and questioning. I guess I can't blame her. But it had felt damn good to flirt with her this morning when I first woke her up. God, what a sight she'd been . . .

I can still see the curve of her ass peeking out from those indecently tiny shorts. How she'd looked in her sleep, her long hair down and spread across her pillow, lips parted, eyes closed as she lay on her side. One leg slung on top of the comforter, which was pushed down to her waist. Revealing the tank top she wore, which did nothing to hide what she looks like when she's not wearing it.

It made me want to dive under those warm, soft covers with her and touch her. Run my hands over her skin and slowly wake her up until she's a moaning, writhing, needy mess beneath me.

Yeah. Didn't happen.

We're quiet during the drive back home, but it's not an uncomfortable silence. Before we even left Sacramento, I turned on the satellite radio I'm addicted to and scrolled through the channels until I found a decent station. The drive isn't bad, just about ninety minutes, and thankfully traffic isn't too shitty. Jen falls asleep relatively fast after the occasional glance toward me and I leave her alone, thankful we don't have to make pointless small talk.

My mind wanders as it usually does when I drive and of course, I think of Jen and what happened today. Is it wrong for me to be glad her interviews didn't go as well as she'd hoped? It's not that I don't believe in her. The girl can do anything she sets her mind to and she's smart as hell.

But I don't want her to leave me. God, I'm a selfish prick.

Then prove yourself wrong, man. Prove yourself wrong.

Drew's words ring in my head, the jackass. I wonder if he realizes how much our talk affected me. I'm running, just like he did before he realized his mistake. Or more like, I'm pushing her away. Doing my best to make us not happen, and now she's on board with that thought, too.

This proves I'm also an asshole.

The minute we reach the outskirts of town I turn the radio up, hoping to wake her. She stirs, murmuring something unintelligible, and I chance a look at her.

Big mistake.

Jen's slouched in her seat, her shoes kicked off, her shirt untucked and a few buttons at the top undone, offering me a teasing glimpse of creamy, golden skin. The tops of her breasts, the white lace of her bra—just seeing that delectable hint of her body makes me break out in a sweat.

I reach over and turn up the air, desperate for some relief.

"I'm freezing," she murmurs.

I glance in her direction, catch her shivering as she wraps her arms around herself, a weak defense against the blast of cold air. Yeah, she's wide awake now. "Close the vent," I suggest, not willing to turn the air conditioner down. I need it to cool down my too heated thoughts.

She does as I tell her, then settles back in her seat. "I can't believe I slept through practically the entire drive."

"You were tired."

"More like stressed." She curls up in her seat, tucking her legs beneath, her and I'm tempted to tell her that position isn't very safe, but then I'll just sound like a naggy old man so I hold myself back. "I can't believe I have to start this process all over again."

I stay quiet for a few minutes, navigating the familiar drive through town toward my house. The twilight sky is purple and black, with tiny white stars just starting to twinkle, and all the streetlights flick on, illuminating the road as I speed toward the subdivision.

"You know, I could help you," I finally say nonchalantly

as I turn onto my road. "I plan on opening the Redding location soon. I'll need someone to assist me and work in the office while I'm gone."

"No." Her answer is vehement, downright hostile. She shakes her head. "No way."

What the ever-loving fuck? "Why the hell not?"

"I refuse to take your handouts any longer." She sits up straight, uncurling her legs and shoving her feet into those damn sexy high heels. "We've had this discussion a million times, Colin. No."

"And we'll probably have it a million times more." I pull into the garage once the door finishes opening and cut the engine, turning to face her. "I don't know why you won't take my help any longer. I want to be there for you, Jen. I'm your friend. Let me do this for you."

"I'm not your charity case, okay?" The words explode from her, shocking the shit out of me, and I lean away from her, my back pressed against the driver's-side door. "I won't take your little scraps of help because you feel some sort of twisted guilt over what happened to my brother. Danny's been dead for two years. Two freaking years. You act like you're the one who threw the bomb that killed him and I don't get it!"

I open my mouth, ready to say the same old shit in defense, but she cuts me off, calling me on it.

"I don't want to hear it. It'll just be the same thing you always say. That you don't mind. That you do it for my family, that you do it because of the guilt you carry, which is ridiculous. Save it for someone who'll actually believe you."

"I broke promises. To you, to your parents, to your brother. I don't want to break any more," I say, but she's not listening.

Jen pushes open the door and climbs out of the car without another word, slamming the door so hard it reverberates through the garage, rattling the metal doors.

Without thought I climb out of the car and follow her inside, my head pounding, my blood roaring hot and fast through my veins. I try and help her out and she throws my generosity in my face. I'm sick of it. Hell, I'm sick of myself.

I find her in the kitchen, her hands curved around the edge of the granite countertop, her back to me as she hangs her head. She's kicked off those sexy heels but she's still tall. I can hear her breathing, feel the tension radiating off of her in palpable waves, and I want to touch her. Comfort her. Draw her into my arms and never let her go.

"You're not my charity case," I say softly. Her shoulders tense at my words. "I . . . care for you, Jen. I want to protect you. It tears me up inside when I think about what happened to you, when no one knew where you were."

She says nothing, just keeps her back to me.

"When you're hurting, I want to make it better," I admit. "But every time I open my mouth, I seem to make it worse."

She releases a shuddering breath before she turns around to face me, her expression unreadable. "You're not honest with me, that's why you make it worse. You hold yourself back."

"I sometimes think you're not honest with me either." I clamp my lips shut, unable to go on. I can't call her out when I hide from her as well. If I were honest, I'd tell her how I really feel.

I've done things I'm not proud of. I've pushed aside those I care about to strive for more with my career. I fear I've turned into my father.

And no one likes my father.

"Fine. You're right. I'm not honest. I have my own secrets. That's why I'm leaving. I'm running away from it all. Not a

very responsible, grown-up thing to do, but it's all I've got."
She approaches me slowly, her eyes shimmering with unshed
tears. The sight of them nearly undoes me but I straighten my
spine, stiffen my upper lip, and pretend I'm a fucking statue.
"I'm not sure you can handle my secrets. But despite them, I
want you, Colin. All of you—your faults and your strengths,
the good and the bad, it doesn't matter. I want it all."

Her words wash over me like a soothing balm and I feel
everything within me loosen. All that tightly coiled-up tension, the anger, the frustration, everything that's been pent up
inside me for what feels like a century just melts at first sight
of the glow in her eyes. Those tears are for me. Her pain, her
emotions, they're all for me, and like a complete ass I've
stomped all over her these last few months.

Hell, the last few years. Ever since I've known her, really.
I've been protective to a fault. Guarding her, watching over
her. Losing her . . .

Wanting her. Not allowing myself to have her. Pushing her
away, hurting her. Every single damn time.

She deserves better. A man who would have rescued her
right away instead of letting her continue to work at a place
that dragged her down farther every single day she went there.

"I'm out of here in a few weeks. There's no going back."
She lifts her chin, determination written all over her sad face.
"My leaving is going to happen whether you like it or not. I
will make it happen despite all of these recent . . . obstacles.
So why can't you give me a little bit of yourself? That's all I
want, Colin. And then I'll walk away from you before it gets
too complicated. It's what you want, right? I know you don't
do complicated."

I don't do complicated because I saw what happened between my parents, and they're the worst kind of complicated.
No one understands them, least of all me.

Yet with Jen, it's already complicated before it's even begun. That's how bad I have it for her. Once I have her, will I be able to walk away?

I don't know.

"You're going to turn me away yet again, aren't you?" she asks when I don't say anything. The irritation in her voice rings clear as her entire body goes tense. "I can't believe it. I offer myself up to you with no strings attached and you're trying to figure out how to let me down easy. God, I am *such* a moron!"

Unable to hold myself back, I rush toward her, angry that she would insult herself. Panicked that she really is going to walk away and I'm going to lose my chance. Thinking too much sucks. I need to just let it happen. Take this opportunity that she's presenting me.

And let her go when our time is up.

"You're not a moron," I murmur, reaching for her. I cup her face in my hands and position her so she has no choice but to meet my gaze. I skim my thumbs across her cheeks, feel her shudder at my touch. "You make an offer like that and a man needs to process it first."

The unshed tears still glimmer in her eyes and one escapes, leaving a damp trail across her skin. Leaning in, I stop its descent with my lips, tasting the salt, hearing the catch in her breath. "We do this and it's not going to be some half-assed thing, you know," I whisper.

She closes her eyes, her tears tangled in her long, thick lashes. "What's it going to be, then?"

"A discovery." I nuzzle her nose with my own, breathing in her scent, her very essence. God, I could devour her! It's taking everything within me to keep calm and not unleash all over her. "An exploration."

"That sounds like . . . research." Her breath hitches in her throat when I drop a tender kiss on the tip of her nose.

Chuckling, I shake my head. "It's the farthest thing from research." I drift my lips across her cheek, blazing a hot path on her petal-soft skin. "You're right when you said I don't do commitment. The closest thing I've ever been to commitment is . . . what I share with you."

She tentatively places her hands on my hips, her fingers curling into the waistband of my jeans. Having her hands on me sends little darts of fire throughout my insides, making me harden in an instant. She has no idea what sort of effect she has on me. How much restraint I'm using at this very moment not to throw her over my shoulder like an oversexed caveman and cart her off to my bedroom.

"But it can be no more than friendship with added . . . benefits." I lift my head so I can look into her troubled gaze. She doesn't like what I have to say and I don't like it either, but I have to be honest. Stringing her along and making her believe this is something more is a mistake.

The two of us together would never work. I'm too damn selfish. I'd disappoint her. I'd hold her back when she needs her freedom. I'm not worthy of her. She's everything sweet and good in my life, where there's little sweet and good remaining.

I've kept her—and our relationship—as pure as possible even after all of these years. With the realization that she's leaving me, that we'll never be together again, I need to take my opportunities where I can.

Jen bites her lip and drops her gaze. "I can handle that."

Her body language is more than telling me she doesn't really want to handle that, but I can't worry about it now.

I want her too damn much.

CHAPTER 11

Jen

What Colin is offering me is exactly what he offers every other woman who's flitted in and out of his life. A temporary affair, something meaningless and conveniently disposable, since that's all he can handle.

I'm the one who offered first. I have no one to blame but myself. So for once, I'll take what I can get and screw the consequences. I want him, any way I can get him. The constant fight, the push-pull between us, has grown old.

My new mantra floats through my mind again and again. *Be free. Let go.*

Bracing my hands on his hips, I lift up on tiptoe and brush my mouth against his. The kiss is soft, as chaste as can be, and he holds himself completely still. Almost as if he fears I'll pull away from him if he makes a sudden move.

But that's exactly what I want him to do. Make a move. Show that he wants me, anything to get this started between us. It's been building for so long I'm not quite sure how to approach it.

I sometimes wonder if he pushes me away because I was a stripper. And that's not even the worst of it. So I must work my hardest to keep my secret to myself. Even Fable doesn't know the worst of it. No one ever will if I have my choice.

I push all negative thoughts of my recent past aside and

kiss him again, my lips moving over his in gentle exploration. They're soft, full, and damp, and he tastes like absolute heaven. He grabs hold of my waist when I wobble toward him, our chests brushing, and I hear his quick intake of breath. That tiny sound, the way his body tightens completely beneath my grip, fills me with a rush of power that's positively heady.

He reacts to me. He wants me. Maybe just as bad as I want him.

Without saying a word he grabs hold of my waist, and I gasp when he picks me up and deposits me on the countertop. I'm above him now, though not by much considering he's so tall. I stare into his eyes, winding my arms around his neck, my fingers sliding into his silky, soft hair. Those gorgeous blue eyes look back at me and I lean down, kissing him again. Groaning when his tongue swipes along my bottom lip, then nips at it with the edge of his teeth. A jolt moves through me at the deliciously sensual contact and I'm instantly hungry for more.

So much more. More than he'll ever be able to give me. But I can deal with that.

"Open up, Jenny," he whispers against my mouth, his voice husky and full of promise. No one calls me Jenny anymore. I put a stop to it when I was in the eighth grade, but hearing him say it sends a thrill running down my spine. "Let me in."

I part my lips at his command and he slides his tongue against mine, the kiss turning instantly hot. Deep. I cling to him as he steps closer to the counter, my knees bracketing his hips, his arms circling around my middle. He splays his big hands across my back, holding me firm as his mouth consumes mine.

This is exactly how I imagined it would be between us.

Hot. All-consuming. Overwhelming. I hear muffled whimpers and realize I'm the one who's making them. An ache has started between my legs while he skims his hands all over me, his mouth fused with mine. I want more. More touching, more kissing, more skin-on-skin contact. We're trying to get close, closer and closer, and I slide my hand down the wide expanse of his back, slipping my fingers beneath his shirt so I can touch bare, smooth skin.

He tears his mouth away to break the kiss, panting against my cheek as if he needs the break. I know I do. My emotions, my everything, are a jumble in my head, though I wouldn't have it any other way. "Tell me to stop right now," he says, his voice harsh. He's out of breath, looking so completely worked up I can't help but be pleased knowing I'm the one who did that to him. "And I'll walk away."

If he walks away I'll kill him . . .

God, look at me. The man toys with my emotions so bad he's pushing me to violence. "I don't want you to stop," I say, shaking my head.

His hands shift so they're in front of me, his fingers toying with the tiny pearl buttons of my shirt. "I've waited for this moment for what feels like forever."

I swallow hard, overcome by his admission. *God, so have I,* I want to say, though it's much harder for me to confess. That we wanted this all along, together, is enough to make me want to ask him why we wasted so much time when we could have been together.

But I don't. Because I know that's not what he really wants. To be with me on a permanent basis, in a real relationship. That's just too much for him to bear.

"Please don't stop," I whisper because I'm still afraid he might. And I can't have that. Not again.

"Good. Because once I have you naked, kissing you everywhere . . ." He pauses, his mouth pressed to my ear. "I won't be able to stop."

"I-I'm okay with that." He's reduced me to stuttering. My brain, my entire body, is on overload at having him so close. His hands on me, his fingers slowly undoing each button that runs down the center of my shirt. He's undressing me, his fingers brushing against my stomach, my bra, the tops of my breasts, until the shirt is completely unbuttoned and hanging open.

Pulling away slightly, he pushes the shirt from my shoulders so that it falls down my arms and puddles behind me on the counter. He studies me unabashedly, his eyes lit with dark, needy lust. "You're so damn beautiful," he says, his voice gruff.

His words make my cheeks flush with embarrassment but still I sit up straight, my breasts thrusting out with the movement. The bra I'm wearing is made of white satin and trimmed with lace. I'm not very well endowed and it dawns on me that the bra also has some major padding, making me appear bigger than I really am. Guys kinda hate that. I had the misfortune to discover that a few years ago with a real jerk I'd been dating who'd been sorely disappointed when he took off my bra. So I try to avoid wearing this sort of bra when I'm on a date.

Damn it, I wish I'd worn something else.

"Pretty." He traces his index finger across the tops of my breasts, close to the delicate lace, and I clench my thighs together but it's no use. I feel his touch as if he's slowly stroking me between my legs, setting my entire body on fire. "We should take this off, though. I bet you're even prettier without it on."

I wait breathlessly as his fingers go to the center of my bra, undoing the front clasp with ease. The cups spring apart slightly, exposing me, and I press my lips together, overcome with worry that he'll be disappointed. Or worse, call me out as a fake.

The women I've seen him flirt with are nothing like me. They're curvy and blond, with huge breasts and tiny waists, whereas I'm tall and thin, with slight curves and small boobs. The total opposite of every girl I've ever seen him show a glimmer of interest in, I can't help but wonder why he's attracted to me.

But then he touches me and I forget all about my worry, my insecurities. All I can do is feel.

Colin slides his big, warm hands beneath the cups of my bra and pushes them aside, his palms brushing against my hard nipples. I hiss in a breath at the delicious contact, closing my eyes as I feel his weighted stare directed at my chest. His fingers tug my bra straps down my arms and I hold them out, feeling the bra fall away from me. I'm bared completely to him.

"Christ, you undo me." Without warning he leans in, pressing his mouth to my breasts, his lips drifting across my nipples as they race across my skin. "You taste so good," he whispers, just before he circles his tongue around first one nipple, then the other. I open my eyes to see his hands are as busy as his tongue. One of them skims over my knee, up my thigh, moving beneath my skirt. His fingertips brush the front of my damp panties and I suck in a harsh breath, spreading my legs as best I can to accommodate him, but the skirt's hindering my movement.

"Here." He pushes my skirt up my thighs and I lift up to help, until the fabric is bunched around my waist and I'm completely exposed. Colin rests his hands on the inside of my thighs, spreading me wider, his gaze zeroed in on my pale pink cotton panties. I lean back, my hands braced on the cold granite counter, and it chills my heated skin.

His smoldering stare makes me feel beautiful, desirable. Just the way he looks at me leaves me almost embarrassingly wet. I squirm when he strokes a single finger down the center of my panties, holding my breath when he pushes firmly against my most sensitive spot.

I press my lips together to stifle the moan that wants to spill and suddenly he's right there, his face in mine. "I don't want you to hold back," he says, his voice firm. "I've waited this long; I'm dying to see you fall apart."

He never looks away from me as he slips his fingers beneath the front of my panties, touching bare, hot, wet skin. I sink my teeth into my lower lip as I groan low in my throat, closing my eyes so I can lose myself to the sensation of his sure fingers touching me in all the right places. As if he knows exactly where I want him, how much pressure he should exert, how gentle he should be. He's perfectly attuned to my body and I can already feel the wave hovering on the edge, just ready to wash over me and sweep me away.

"Open your eyes," his deep voice commands. "Look at me."

My eyes flash open, my chest heaving as I meet his gaze. Without looking away from me he tugs my panties from my hips, pulling them down my legs until they become tangled around my ankles. I kick them off, realizing that he's completely clothed while I'm naked save for the skirt still bunched around my waist.

I feel vulnerable yet sexy, especially when his appreciative gaze rakes over me from head to toe.

"I want you to know who's about to make you come," he murmurs, his eyes hooded, his arms coming around my waist so he can grip my butt and haul me to the edge of the counter. Kneeling before me, he turns his head and presses his mouth to the inside of my thigh, and I moan at the hot path his lips blaze over my skin.

I can't believe he just said that to me, as if I wouldn't know it's him. Colin. More than that, I can't believe he's down on his knees in front of me, about to place his lips between my legs and most likely drive me out of my mind in a matter of seconds.

"You're so hot. And wet." His mouth settles over the very center of me, his tongue darting out for a quick lick. I jolt so hard I almost fall off the counter.

But he's got me. Those large hands are wrapped around my hips, holding me in place as he continues to lick me, his tongue teasing, searching, his lips sucking. My belly tingles, my entire body is quivering, and I throw my head back, lifting my hips so I can get closer to that decadent, devious mouth as he works his magic on me.

"Look at me, Jenny." He says it again, adding my name to get my attention, and I snap my head back up, staring down at him to find him watching me carefully. "You're close, aren't you?"

Nodding frantically, another whimper escapes me. I'm teetering right on the edge, ready to plunge into the depths of what is looking to be a monster orgasm. And he knows it.

"Tell me what you want. Tell me what to do to take you there." His voice is dark, his gaze heated, as he tries to prompt me into talking.

I'm not one for dirty talk. Truly, I'm not one for talking during sex period, but this is Colin. And he's always been rather persistent.

"Um . . ." I moan when he sucks my clit hard between his

lips, slipping a long finger inside me, slowly sliding inside my welcoming body, in and out, building the tension that's coiled within me with a few thrusts of his finger. "Oh God, yeah, that. Do that. All of it," I choke out, barely able to form words.

I feel him smile against my sensitive flesh and a shiver runs down my spine. He starts to stroke deep within me, adding another finger, increasing his pace as he continues to suck and lick between my legs, his eyes never leaving me. Ever.

It's the most intensely intimate moment of my life. Our gazes locked, his mouth on me, his tongue, his fingers inside my body. I feel connected to him, more than I've ever felt to another person before, and I close my eyes, overcome with sensation. Emotion.

Too much emotion.

And just like that, the biggest, most intense orgasm takes over me completely. I'm trembling, gasping his name, scared I'm going to slide right off the sleek granite, and his hands grip my ass so tight I think I might have bruises.

I don't care. I want him to mark me; it makes me feel like I belong to him. And I want to belong to him, despite my acting like I'm perfectly fine with a temporary affair.

The shudders still consume me, making my limbs shake, my heart race. My orgasm leaves me dizzy, breathless. I don't think I've ever come so hard in my life.

Colin

That was a fucking beautiful sight, watching Jen fall apart like that. Talk about unromantic, throwing her up on my counter, stripping her almost completely naked, and going down on her in the middle of my kitchen.

Damn, it was worth every minute, though.

I gentle my lips against her wet, quivering flesh, giving her one last slow lick before I stand back up. She's a sweaty, shaky, out-of-breath mess, her once sleek ponytail now a complete wreck with hair everywhere. Her lips are swollen from my kisses and her chest and cheeks are flushed.

She's gorgeous. And now I'm going to take her to my giant bed, strip naked, and fuck her into the mattress for the rest of the night.

My every dream come true.

"You okay?" I ask just before I kiss her, long and deep.

Jen doesn't even flinch, though I know she tasted herself on my lips. I break the kiss first, entranced by her swollen, delicious mouth. "That was . . . intense," she murmurs.

"It was. Beautifully intense. And you're amazing." I kiss her again, because I can't *not* kiss her. She's so damn pretty and sexy as fuck sprawled across my counter. Her body is gorgeous, all long limbs and slender curves. I can only imagine those endless legs wrapped around me while I fuck her senseless.

My dick gets harder just thinking it.

Reaching for her, I pick her up, and she automatically wraps those long legs around me, anchoring herself. I grip her butt, my fingers sinking into her flesh as I haul her toward the hallway that leads to my bedroom.

"Where are you taking me?" she asks, her lips right at my ear, as if she doesn't know. Her arms are wound around my neck, her fingers buried in my hair at the back of my head. She starts kissing and licking the spot just behind my ear, as though she knows how much that drives me wild.

"To my room," I say gruffly. "So I can fuck you properly in my bed."

Her lips go still on my neck and she shifts so she can look at me. "You have such a dirty mouth."

"I think you like that dirty mouth, especially when it's on your—" Jen places her fingers on my lips to stop me from saying it and I can't help but laugh.

"No guy has ever talked to me like that," she admits, her voice soft as she drops her fingers away from my mouth.

Jealousy grips at my chest and I try my best to ignore it. "Ever?"

She slowly shakes her head. "Never."

"Glad I'm the first, then." I increase my pace, striding into my bedroom and depositing her on the bed so she lands with a little bounce. I watch in fascination as she reaches behind her and unzips her skirt, then shimmies out of it, tossing the wrinkled fabric onto the floor so that she's finally gloriously naked.

So beautiful and all mine, at least for tonight. For the next few weeks, if we hold true to the promise we've just made. I want to hold to it. But will she? Orgasms between friends rarely work out in the long run.

If I weren't so ready to get naked with her, I might find that thought amusing.

"Do you always talk like that?" she asks.

"Talk like what?" I shrug out of my shirt, then start undoing my jeans.

"Say such dirty things while having sex." Her eyes practically bug out of her head when I shuck my jeans and underwear in one tug, my cock on blatant display just for her. "Uh . . ."

Smiling, I stride toward the bed and join her, lying on my side nestled close to her warm, fragrant body. I rest my hand on her stomach and stroke upward, slowly sweeping over the valley between her breasts. I like that I've rendered her at a loss for words. "What I just said to you was positively mild," I drawl, laying it on extra thick.

She turns her head toward me, her sweet-smelling hair getting in my face. "You're not what I expected."

I brush the silky strands away from my eyes. "And what did you expect?" Leaning over her, I drop little kisses along her collarbone, her breasts, those pretty little hard nipples. She's not what I would consider amply endowed and typically I'm drawn to women with large breasts.

I love everything about Jen's body, though. Wouldn't change a damn thing.

"I don't know," she whispers as she places her hand on the back of my head. The subtle pressure she exerts shows she likes what I'm doing, so I draw her nipple into my mouth deeper, savoring the taste of her skin. "That feels so good."

Soon we're both touching and kissing and licking each other's bodies, our legs entwined, Jen's fingers curled around my cock. I'm desperate to sink deep inside her warm, welcoming body, to pound my way to orgasm while getting lost inside her, but I'm taking it slow. Easing up to this because she deserves nothing less than the very best that I can give her.

I can only hope I don't disappoint her.

"I want you inside me," she whispers when we're long minutes into this agonizing torture. She crawls over me, her face in mine, her fingers still gripping my erection.

Smoothing my hands down her back, I caress the soft, plump flesh of her ass. "Grab a condom out of the drawer."

She glances toward the bedside table and reaches out, pulling open the drawer and withdrawing a condom wrapper. Moving away, she opens the condom, kneeling in front of me as she holds the tiny rubber ring poised in front of my cock. "Can I put it on?"

"Hell yeah," I mutter, entranced by the look on her face, the glow in her eyes. She leans over my erection, her hair shielding her face since I removed the band and set her pony-tail free only minutes earlier. Her fingers dance along my length, tracing the tip before she settles the condom over the head. She slowly rolls the condom on, stroking me as she does, and my eyes threaten to roll back in my head, it feels so damn good.

We're teasing, tormenting each other like we've done for so many years. Instead this time, we're naked, wrapped around each other and trying to drive the other crazy with wanting. Until I can't take it any longer and I roll her over so she's beneath me, her long legs spread, my hips nestled in between her thighs, my cock thrusting toward the very center of her.

Sweat beads my brow as I study Jen, my hands braced on either side of her head. Her dark hair is spread across the pil-low, her velvety brown eyes slumberous, that plush, sexy mouth swollen from my punishing kisses. She runs her hand down the center of my chest, my stomach, her fingers teasing my navel, then drifting farther south to trace the trail of hair that leads to my aching erection.

"You say I'm beautiful, but you're the beautiful one," she whispers, her gaze locked on my chest, seemingly entranced. "I could touch you like this all night."

"And drive me out of my ever-lovin' mind," I mutter, earning a big smile for my comment.

"Oh, we can't have that." She slips her hand around my hip, pulling me in, and then I'm sliding inside of her body, my cock enveloped by her hot, wet depths. I slowly sink deep, deeper, until I'm fully embedded inside her. Our bodies are perfectly aligned, chests pressed together, hips nestled close.

I close my eyes. Clench my jaw. It's taking everything

within me not to let loose and come like a geyser at this very moment, like some sort of inexperienced teen who can't keep it together. She wraps those long-as-hell legs around me, sending me deeper, and I groan, the familiar tingling already starting at the base of my spine.

No. I refuse to come now. I gotta make this first time good for her. For us.

Watching our connected bodies, I slide out of her almost completely before I push back inside. Again and again I enter her, keeping my pace slow, intoxicated by the sight of my cock disappearing inside her body again and again. Her hips arch as she tilts her head and bows her back. She closes her eyes as she moves with me, her hips circling, tiny little whimpers sounding in the back of her throat.

I could thrust in her hard once, maybe twice, and I'd blow, no problem. But she seems to still be working for it. No way am I going to let go before ensuring that she's come again. "Touch yourself," I whisper.

She stills, her eyes flying open, dark and fathomless as she frowns. "What?"

"Touch yourself, Jenny. Make yourself come with me inside you," I encourage, wanting to see her do it. My skin gets hot and tight just thinking about her fingering her clit, making herself come all over my cock.

Sinking her teeth into her plump lower lip, she reaches between us, her index finger brushing against her clit, the tip nudging against my cock. I groan and start to pump harder, noticing that she keeps the same pace as she glides her finger over her clit. Until we're both straining toward it, reaching for it . . .

An agonized groan falls from my lips in the sound of her name as I thrust once, hard as hell, sending me so deep I'm afraid I'll rip her apart. But she clings to me, her entire body shaking, my name being whispered again and again, so I let go. Let loose.

Let my orgasm take over me completely.

Now we're clinging to each other, only the sound of our loud breathing filling the room. My skin is covered in sweat, as is hers, and I start to move away from her but she tightens her arms around me, her fingers digging into my back as if she doesn't want to ever let me go.

"Stay for a minute," she murmurs against my chest, her lips tickling my skin, making me shiver.

"I'm crushing you," I start, but she cuts me off.

"I like it. You feel good, crushing me," she admits, her voice soft and sleepy-sounding.

Fuck. I don't know what to say. What to do. In the aftermath I'm usually the one who's hopping out of bed, getting rid of the condom, and hustling my ass out of there. I never bring women home. I made the mistake of that once long, long ago when I was successfully running my first restaurant in Southern California. The woman took one look at my decent apartment near the beach and decided she was ready to set up and play house permanently.

Had to nip that in the bud real quick. That one terrifying moment made me swear off ever bringing a woman back to my place. And now I have one living with me. One who wants to leave while I'm desperate for her to stay.

Everything's different with Jen. We have a history. An intricate past that I don't want to ruin with a relationship destined to end. She's leaving and I won't stop her. It doesn't matter if the sex between us is phenomenal. She wants out.

So I'm letting her go.

Finally, she releases her hold on me and I head into the bathroom, tossing the condom in the trash, glancing at myself in the mirror. I don't look any different, though I definitely feel it. I see the same ol' pretty face looking back at me that I sort of hate if I'm being truthful. This face gets me into trouble. It's easier to get what you want when you have a pretty face, right? And I don't need any help with getting into trouble. I can do that on my own, thank you very much.

I'm curious, though. What does Jen see when she looks at me? Someone she cares about? Someone she can easily forget? Both options scare me.

So I don't know. I'm not sure I want to know what she sees. How she feels.

Turning off the bathroom light, I walk back into my bedroom and slip into bed, pulling the covers up over us. She scoots closer to me without a word, her back to my front, and I wrap my arm around her middle, holding her close. She feels damn good. Snug and warm, and fitting perfectly against me. I never want to let her go.

Pulling away from her slightly, I smooth the hair away from her neck, my gaze locked on the tattoo. The blinds are cracked open and the dull glow from the streetlight outside filters into the room, helping me see the delicate, colorful lines of the butterfly.

I trace it, sweeping my finger across her skin, feeling her shiver beneath my touch. Leaning in, I kiss her there, my lips lingering, and she moans softly.

"There's meaning behind this, isn't there." I dart my tongue out for a lick, absorbing her salty-sweet taste. I can't get enough of her.

"I like butterflies." She sighs when I squeeze her closer to me. "And yes. There's meaning."

"What is it?"

"It represents my wanting to break free of my past." Her voice hitches and I frown, pressing my chin into her shoulder. "I've done things I'm not proud of, Colin."

"I know. I wish you could let them go. No one's judging you." I hate what she's done but I can't hold her actions against her. She'd been in a tough situation. Confused and alone and damn it, that was partially my fault.

"May—maybe someday I could learn to let them go." She pauses. "Not yet, but I'm close."

Damn. My life has been completely changed by this one beautiful, amazing woman that I've known since we were kids.

And I'm not sure what to do about it.

CHAPTER 12

Jen

"You're glowing."

I swat Fable's arm as I walk past her. "I am not." Crap, I probably am, not that I'd ever admit it, especially to her.

But that's what happens when you experience an amazing, outrageous all-night sex fest with a man who can't seem to keep his hands off of you. Or his fingers or his lips or his tongue . . .

A shiver moves through me at the delicious, forbidden memory.

"You so are. That can only mean one thing."

Stiffening, dread slithers down my spine. I know she's my best friend and I've told her everything that's happened between Colin and me up until now. But she doesn't know about this latest chapter in our lives, and I really don't want to tell her.

She's never approved one hundred percent of Colin as being the one for me and I don't want to hear her warnings. She thinks he's too slick, too much of a charmer to really want anything serious. I've always agreed with her. I can't help but wonder if I'm having a momentary lapse in judgment.

Besides, what happened between Colin and me feels too

new, too fragile, to share with anyone but us. I still need to cherish it, process it.

Enjoy it. Alone.

"You found a job, right?" she asks when I don't say anything.

Relief replaces the dread and I shake my head, trying to hide my smile. I shouldn't be smiling. I should be incredibly depressed, because how the heck am I going to get out of this stupid place filled with dirty memories that haunt me? I'd forgotten about the shitty interviews from yesterday, my all-night excursion in Colin's bed wiping out all unpleasant thoughts.

They're all coming back with a vengeance now.

"I didn't," I finally say as I start to wander around the restaurant, lighting all of the candles that sit in the center of the tables. "None of them wanted to hire me."

"Are you kidding?" She sounds indignant, just like Colin had yesterday. A warm, fuzzy feeling starts in my stomach. Everyone believes in me but me. Maybe I should start paying attention and believe in myself for a change. "Why not?"

I shrug, sticking the long lighter into the glass candleholder and clicking the ignite button. "I'm tired of working as a waitress, so I'm aiming for an office job. Problem is, they want someone with office experience and I don't have any."

"But you're . . . *you*. You're awesome. Surely you had a kickass interview and impressed the hell out of them. You're smart. You look the part. Who wouldn't want you working for them?" Fable looks completely perplexed and I love her for it.

"I guess I'm not kickass enough, considering they didn't offer me a job. No one even seemed that interested." I move from table to table, Fable following behind me, setting the tables with silverware. The two of us are at the tail end of dinner service prep. We've been working together so long we've established a perfect rhythm.

"So what are you going to do now?" Fable asks after we finish up the last table.

Great question. One I don't have an answer for. "I guess it's back to . . . plan A." Whatever plan A is.

"And that is . . . ?" Her voice trails off as she raises a brow.

The girl can make anyone sweat with one lift of an eyebrow, I'll give her that. Poor Drew. And poor Owen. Neither of them stood a chance in a fight with Fable. "Um, back to the job hunt. And the apartment hunt. I'm checking out the roommate options on Craigslist."

"You're going to room with someone you don't know? Are you crazy?" Fable shakes her head. "What if they're a serial killer looking for their next victim and you fit their profile?"

"You worry too much." I sigh. I can't stress about that shit and besides, I'll find someone, a girl who's close to my age and maybe a college student. I've been scanning the listings the last few days and stumbled upon a few good possibilities that I already contacted. I haven't heard back from them yet, though.

Maybe I'm the one who looks and sounds like a serial killer . . .

Ha ha. I'm funny.

"But Jen . . ."

"Look, Fable." I round on her, stopping her in her tracks. I'm not angry, but I'm tired of everyone trying to tell me what to do. "I know what I'm doing. It may look risky but I'm not that stupid, trust me. I'm taking all of the proper precautions."

Fable scrunches her eyebrows together. "I never said you were stupid. I just . . ."

"You're worried about me. Yeah, I totally get it. I'd be worried about me, too. But I'll land on my feet. I always land on my feet. I'm like a cat."

"A cat who's always eventually caught and set on her feet by a certain someone named Colin Wilder," Fable mutters.

I part my lips, ready to say something sarcastic right back, when I realize he's nearby. I feel his overwhelming presence. He's standing behind me—I can smell his intoxicating woodsy clean scent, feel the heat of his body penetrating mine as he steps even closer. I swear his hand brushes against my backside in a discreet caress and a wave of desire crashes through me.

"Someone say my name?" He sounds amused. His deep voice causes tingles to sweep over my skin and I press my lips together, almost afraid to turn and face him.

Afraid I might melt if I see that particular gleam in his eyes. The one that says he knows exactly what I look like naked and he can't wait to get me in that state again.

"Speak of the devil." Fable flashes him a saucy smile. "Your little waif here was telling me she didn't find a job yesterday when you two went to Sacramento."

Did she really just call me a little waif? If anyone's a waif it's Fable. She's so short it's ridiculous.

"Unfortunately, the people who interviewed her were idiots." Colin moves so he's standing beside me, his arm brushing mine. I press my lips together so I don't gasp at the contact, because wow. I felt that simple brush right down to my toes. "They didn't see her full potential."

Fable looks from me to Colin then back at me again, both eyebrows raised now. *Damn it.* "And are you saying *you* see her full potential, boss man?"

He laughs and shakes his head. "I do. I've always seen Jen's potential." We both happen to look at each other at the same time. Big mistake. Is that adoration reflected in his gaze? I look away before Fable reads too much into it, but too late. Her eyes are narrowed and she's smirking at me. I'd know that sly look anywhere.

And it is the absolute last thing I want to deal with.

"Time to get to work, girls," he says, reaching out to squeeze my arm gently before he walks away. "I'm opening the doors now."

I watch him go, my arm still tingling from where he touched me, my eyes focused on his perfect butt encased in those perfect black trousers. I had my hands all over that butt last night. It's solid, rock-hard muscle and I loved feeling it flex as he pushed deep inside me . . .

"You banged him, didn't you."

Fable's soft voice breaks through my dirty thoughts and I turn to her, ready to protest, but she shakes her head.

"Don't bother denying it. You two are so obvious. Oh my God, no wonder you're glowing." She steps closer to me, lowering her voice. "You had sex. With Colin. Holy. Shit!"

"Stop." I grab hold of her arm and steer her out of the dining room, which is filling up with employees and dinner guests fast. I take her to the back hallway that leads out to the alley. "Don't say anything, okay? I don't want it to get out and I don't want Colin to know that you know, either."

"I'm not going to tell anyone. You can trust me. I'm the best secret keeper around. Ask Drew." She purses her lips and shakes her head, a mysterious light filling her eyes for the briefest second. Sometimes I can't really figure her out. But I can't worry about it at the moment. "And why don't you want Colin to know that *I* know you two are having sex?"

She hisses the last word out and I roll my eyes. I can't believe I'm having this conversation. We're closer than I've ever been with another friend before, but I am definitely not one to talk about my sexual escapades. I'm a very private person, especially when it comes to sex. The good and the bad kind. "Stop saying it like that."

"Stop acting like it's a bad thing." Her easy acceptance fills me with relief. "I can't believe you two finally caved and did it. It's about damn time." She nudges me. "So. Is he any good?"

My cheeks heat as I remember the way he buried his face between my legs in the freaking kitchen and made me come so hard I yelled out his name, nearly falling off the counter.

"Don't bother answering. Your face says it all." Fable laughs. "He's pretty damn good."

He's amazing, but I don't want to kiss and tell. Not yet. Maybe not ever.

I'd rather keep all that amazingness to myself.

Colin

I try my best to ignore her but it's fucking hard. Or more like, *I'm* fucking hard, watching Jen while she works all night in that short, clingy black dress that's the standard uniform for the waitresses. Somehow, she's the sexiest thing in this place, in that dress. Her legs look a mile long, what with those black stiletto sandals she's wearing. She pulled her hair into a high ponytail, showing off the delicately beautiful butterfly tattoo that graces her nape. The tattoo that represents her need for freedom from her past, freedom for her future.

The tattoo both fills me with resentment and makes me want to trace every fragile, colorful line of it with my finger. And then with my tongue.

Jesus. I need to get a grip.

She repeatedly catches me staring and I don't bother looking away. Sometimes she drops her gaze, her cheeks turning pink, which is cute as hell. Other times she blatantly stares back, a wicked smile curving those lush lips I'm desperate to kiss.

More than once she just laughed and shook her head, as if she found my uncontrollable need to keep my eyes glued on only her amusing. But I catch her watching me, too. A lot. She wants me just as bad.

And later tonight, after we're through with work, I'm gonna bury myself inside her so deep, it'll be a wonder if I can ever come back out. Just knowing I have that to look forward to leaves me as hard as a damn rock.

I finally lock myself away in my office so I'll quit looking like a lecherous ass. I don't know how Jen feels about it, but I don't want anyone else who works here knowing what we've done. Their whispered speculation is bad enough. Though I've never denied it, I don't want to give them confirmation that it's actually happened between us.

So I throw myself into my work. I glance over the construction reports from the Redding location. I plan on going there in the next couple of days so I can see it in person. Construction is coming along nicely and all seems according to schedule. The restaurant is slated to open in less than eight weeks, and we're pretty much on track for making that happen.

Jen won't be with me then. That realization feels like a solid punch to the gut.

Pushing the reports aside, I turn to my computer and start going over the upcoming orders. Check out The District's Facebook page. Tweet about the happy hour special we have every Thursday.

I'm so distracted I don't hear my office door open, and not

until it clicks closed quietly do I glance up to find Jen standing there, leaning against the door, a shy smile on her face.

"Hey," I say, letting my gaze blatantly roam over her. Again. She's gorgeous, looking a little unsure, a lot sexy.

"Hi."

"On your break?"

She nods and pushes away from the door, approaching me slowly. "Can you take a break with me?"

I push my chair away from the desk, leaning back in it. "What did you have in mind?"

"Oh, I don't know." The shy smile turns instantly wicked. "What would you like to do?"

Everything I can accomplish in what, ten minutes? I bet I could slip my fingers between her legs and get her off in less than five. Maybe she could get down on her knees and suck me off.

Yeah. We could get a hell of a lot done in ten minutes.

"I'm up for whatever you've got in mind." I fold my arms behind my head, my fingers interlacing across the back of my neck. "Tell me what you want."

"This." Before I can even think, let alone say another word, she's on top of me, straddling me on my chair, her mouth on mine, her hands in my hair. The kiss is instantly hungry, our tongues tangling, turning the kiss deep. Deeper. I grip her waist, slide my hands up her sides so I can map her curves. Cupping her breasts, I give them a firm squeeze and she whimpers against my lips.

"You looking for a quickie?" I ask with amusement when she breaks the kiss first, moving to slide her lips down my neck.

"Maybe," she murmurs against my throat, her tongue drawing a heated path along my skin.

I close my eyes and let my hands drift down, playing with the hem of her skirt. "You've been driving me crazy all night."

"Right back at you," she breathes, lifting her head so she can meet my gaze. "It's like you can't stop staring at me."

"I can't." I dive my hands beneath her skirt and skim my fingers along the soft skin of her upper thighs and higher. Her ass is bare, she's wearing some sort of lacy thong, and all I want to do is tear it off of her. "You're trying to drive me absolutely insane, aren't you?"

Her smile turns wicked again, the sight of it taking my breath away. I'm used to a feisty Jen. A friendly Jen. I've seen almost all of her moods, every little facet of her personality, or so I thought.

But a sexy Jen is almost too good to be true.

She licks her lips, shifting on top of me so her lower body rubs against my erect cock. Leaning in, her mouth is at my ear, her damp lips brushing it when she speaks. "I want you to fuck me in this chair."

A bolt of lust shoots straight to my cock. I squeeze her ass, pulling her in as close as she can get. "Yeah?"

"Yeah." She nods, her teeth nibbling my earlobe. "I've been wet for you since you interrupted Fable and me talking earlier, all bossy and demanding. God, it turns me on when you act like that."

Okay, she is seriously blowing my mind. I had no idea she had it in her, not that I'd ever given her an opportunity to act like this with me in the past. "Well, let me see if you're right." I slip my fingers between her legs from behind and discover that she is most definitely wet. And hot. She moves against my fingers, her teeth sinking into her lower lip, lids at half mast, looking like the sexiest thing alive, and all I can do is watch her, too captivated to do anything else.

"Oh God. I'm going to come," she murmurs when I slip two fingers deep inside her. She lifts her hips, riding my hand, getting herself off with my fingers, and then she's shuddering, my name falling from her lips, her hands curled around my shoulders as she clings to me like she might tumble off my lap if she doesn't hold on tight.

Just as I imagined, I got her off in what? A minute? Maybe two? Fucking unbelievable.

"That was the hottest thing I've ever seen," I whisper, kissing her lips softly, reverently, my fingers still moving slowly inside her body.

She releases a shuddering breath, slipping out of my hands, off my lap. I'm momentarily confused until she kneels before me, her hands resting on my knees. Clearly indicating her plans without saying a word.

This is like my every fantasy come true. I would have rather fucked her in my chair, but having Jen on her knees in front of me after I just got her off with a few thrusts of my fingers? Amazing.

And yeah, I'm all for a blow job, but is my office door locked? If anyone can just walk in, it's going to happen when my cock is in Jen's mouth because come on, that's the sort of luck I have. Shit would hit the fan and the gossip would be rampant.

"Is the door locked?" I ask, nodding toward it. The last thing I want to do is break this magical sexual spell that's fallen over us and get up to go lock the door. Talk about spoiling the mood.

"I locked it when I came in." She reaches for the button on my pants, undoing it with ease. "So don't worry, no one can walk in on us. It's just me. And you."

I hold my breath when her fingers brush against my stomach. She slides the zipper down on my pants, then spreads the fly wide, exposing my cock straining against dark gray cotton. She curls her fingers around me, squeezing gently, her gaze locked on my boxer briefs.

Conflict ripples through me. I want her to be quick and get to it, yet I also want her to take her sweet time so I can savor this sexy-as-hell moment between us.

"You're big," she whispers, her gaze lifting to meet mine.

Smiling, I reach out and cup her cheek, pleasure sweeping through me when she turns and places a kiss to my palm. "Every man appreciates that type of compliment."

Jen rolls her eyes and I drop my hand from her face. She grips the waistband of my boxer briefs at my hips. "It's true, though. You're definitely the biggest I've ever seen."

I barely contain my scowl. Damn, I hate when she talks about other guys, which she seems to do quite often, and so casually, too. I know I'm a total commitment-phobe, but I'm starting to realize she is, too. I don't recall her ever being with anyone in a long-term relationship. Not even in high school.

I'm both curious to know her sexual history and not interested whatsoever. Only a glutton for punishment would ask her such a thing.

So I let it alone.

"My break's over in less than ten minutes," she says, a saucy smile curling her lips, her fingers teasing my abs. "And my boss is kind of a hard-ass, so I don't want to make him mad."

"Is he now? And what will he do to you if you're late coming off your break?" I sit up straight, lifting my hips when she starts to pull my underwear down. I'm left sitting before her in my shirt with my pants and briefs in a heap around my ankles, my erect cock pointing directly at her.

"I don't know. Fire me?" She laughs as she strokes my cock with feather-light precision, her delicate fingers dancing over my sensitive skin, my belly, the insides of my thighs. Anticipation curls through me, driving me fucking insane with every pass of her fingers, and finally, she leans in, brushing her mouth across the head of my cock.

If I could, I'd keep her on hand as my personal sex slave. Because damn, her touch, her mouth, her everything feels so fucking good . . .

I lean back in my chair, closing my eyes at the sensation of her lips slowly taking me inside her mouth. Her tongue licks, her mouth sucks, and soon she's bobbing up and down on me, her hands gripping my thighs, her lips tight and hot and working me into a frenzy in a matter of seconds.

She hums in pleasure around my cock and I jerk in her grip, ready to come, not embarrassed at how quick she made that happen. We've both been riding the edge all night. The past few hours out in the restaurant have been nothing but torturous foreplay.

Lifting her lids, her gaze meets mine, hot and dark and completely unreadable. I want to say something, anything, ask her what the fuck she's thinking, what the hell is she doing to my head since I'm not thinking the way I usually do. She's a trip. The two of us together, we're a complete trip and I want it to continue.

So what's stopping me?

Pushing all negative thoughts from my mind, I concentrate on Jen. What she's doing to me with her skilled lips and tongue, how much she seems to enjoy pleasuring me. She slowly releases my cock from her mouth, her tongue darting out to tease at the tip, circling around the flared head, not missing a spot.

And still her gaze never leaves mine.

Fuck, that's it. I can't take it. I'm coming, all over her lips, her tongue. She drinks it in, her mouth back on me, easing me through my orgasm, and when it's finally over I slump in my seat, shocked at the exhaustion that settles over me. My body's languid and I feel drowsy, completely spent.

Wiping her mouth with the back of her hand, she stands, smiling down at me. "Was that okay for you?"

Okay is the understatement of the century. I can hardly form words, let alone lift myself out of the fucking chair. "Uh . . . yeah. It was fucking amazing, Jen," I manage to choke out.

Her smile grows and she tilts her head. "So I guess my work here is done."

"I'll say," I mutter as I lean over and grab some tissues from the box on my desk. I clean myself up, then stand and start to pull my clothes back on.

Laughing, she turns away from me, heading toward the door. "I need to get back to work before my boss punishes me for taking too long of a break."

Her choice of words is certainly intriguing. "All this talk of being in trouble makes me wonder. Do you want to be punished?" I ask.

She pauses at the door, her hand gripping the handle fiercely. She keeps her back to me. "What are you talking about?"

"Are you into that 'I'm a bad girl, please punish me' type of thing?" I'm really not. I've always preferred to be the dominant one in the bedroom. I enjoy taking command. Sometimes I'll even get a little rough, though nothing too extreme. Pull hair. Bite plump, sweet skin, then devour all that wet, hot flesh.

Just thinking about doing all of that and more to Jen has me growing hard again. Unbelievable.

"I never thought I was," she admits, slowly turning to face me. She smiles, her eyes wild with desire and some other foreign emotion I don't recognize. "But I could be. With you."

Well, fuck. That confession just filled my overactive imagination with all sorts of ideas.

CHAPTER 13

Jen

The shackles of my recent past have slowly been loosened, allowing me to be free with Colin. I can almost forget all of the shameful things I did during such a scary, desperate time. A time I'd rather push from my memories forever, but I still can't, no matter how hard I try. Stripping for a living gave me a sort of freedom I've never experienced before. I felt powerful, at least at first.

Giving myself to men in the backseat of their car for fifty dollars had left me feeling powerless. The contradiction had been . . . confusing.

But nothing filled me with so much power as when I was with Colin. I am on a sexual high and I have no regrets over what I've done with him. It's liberating. Funny how I thought leaving Colin would bring me the escape and freedom I needed. Maybe I was wrong.

Having sex with Colin, finally letting down my guard and showing him all the many things I want to do to him? How I feel about him?

That's beyond liberating.

Not that I can tell him how I feel about him with words, no way. That would just freak him out, the very last thing I want to do. But I can show him. Oh, how I can show him! Which I've done. Repeatedly. I worried it might be awkward between Colin and me after the first time we had sex, but, um . . . no. It is definitely not awkward.

Hot and amazing, most definitely. We're insatiable for each other. Being with him at the restaurant last night, watching him while he worked, turned me on so much I could hardly function. All I could think about was him. Having his hands on me. Having my hands on him. I was so aroused I had to sneak into his office on my break and give him a blow job.

What a rush that experience was, despite my past momentarily tarnishing the moment. Reminding me of what I've done, that I'd taken money for an act that should be sacred and between two people who care for each other.

But I was able to overcome it pretty quickly. It's different between us. I care about him, more than I ever thought possible.

I loved how out of control I made him, how quickly he came. I could see how bad he wanted me, could feel it in the clutch of his fingers when he thrust them into my hair, tugging on it. The pleasurable pain had coursed through my veins, pushing me toward my second orgasm in less than ten minutes, which is just . . . insane.

Colin Wilder makes me absolutely insane.

It feels so good, knowing that we are equally invested in this. That we're dying to get naked for each other every time we're in the same room. Heck, when we're breathing the same air. I've felt so alone with all of these feelings I've had for Colin for far too long. And now we're in it together.

At this very moment, though, I'm alone. Sitting outside in Colin's backyard next to the small built-in pool, laid out on a lounge chair and enjoying the late summer sunshine. September doesn't equal fall in Northern California. It's still hot as hell most days, this one being no exception. A heat wave has settled over the area, the high today predicted to hit near one hundred.

The late morning air is still cool enough but I can feel the heat coming, the sun shining directly on me. I'm wearing my favorite two-piece swimsuit and desperately wishing Colin were home so he could see me like this. The bikini is skimpy, a bright turquoise, with string ties at my hips and two slivers of triangle fabric covering my breasts. I can get away with this sort of swimsuit since I'm small-chested and kinda skinny.

I'd always wanted the blond hair and gigantic boobs that Colin tends to go for, but I've become incredibly comfortable with my body these last few days. Comfortable in regard to how Colin sees me. He thinks I'm beautiful. Sexy. He makes me feel confident in my own skin, something I've never experienced before. I love the fact that he's so appreciative of my curves, my breasts, that he doesn't make me feel cheap.

When we got home last night he stripped me naked without giving me a chance to say a word, not that I was protesting. He laid me out on his bed and proceeded to map every single inch of my skin with his mouth. And when I say he kissed me everywhere, I mean *everywhere*. Even in embarrassing places no man had ever attempted to kiss me before.

I came three times last night. I can feel myself growing wet just remembering what he did to me, how far he pushed me out of my comfort zone.

How much I liked it.

Sighing and with a little squirm, I try to push thoughts of Colin out of my head and concentrate on the fashion magazine in front of me. I flip through the pages, bored with the clothing, the endless ads full of gorgeous, smiling women who exude confidence. The entire magazine is full of articles along those lines. About creating a confident you and finding the perfect career you're destined to have. How to have the best sex of your life—already found that, thanks bunches—the best clothes, the best everything. I know reading these articles is supposed to inspire me. But instead with every article I skim, I become more depressed.

And full of doubt.

Is leaving really the right decision? Now that I have Colin's unwavering attention, should I just up and walk away from him as I originally planned? Of course, the reason I might have his attention is because he knows it's temporary. It's easier to commit to something that won't last, that has a deadline. A finite ending.

Right?

The fact that I have no real plan is scary, too. I did find a possible roommate via an online ad site whom I spoke to on the phone earlier. She's a year younger than me, a junior in college, and works part-time. She just lost her old roommate and is trying to do everything all on her own, and she's failing miserably. Drowning in the endless bills that come with being a responsible adult, a roommate would totally ease her financial burden. And mine, of course.

She sounded ideal, so I committed to her and sent her the deposit money via PayPal not even an hour ago. Then I ran into the bathroom and immediately threw up. I'm so freaked out over whether I'm doing the right thing I'm making myself sick over it.

This is by far the toughest decision I've ever made in my life.

Tossing the magazine on the tiny table next to me, I readjust the lounge chair so it's pretty much flat and lie down, closing my eyes. I should not be soaking up the sun with skin cancer being prevalent and all, but I slathered myself in sunscreen before I came outside. The heat feels good on my mostly bare skin and deciding to be daring, I untie my bikini top, letting the strings drop so I won't have tan lines across my chest.

One wrong move and the top goes bye-bye, but who's going to see? I'm alone out here. The people who live on either side of Colin both work, so there are no stay-at-home moms hovering, no little kids running around in their backyards. I could sit out here naked and skinny-dip in the pool. No one would be the wiser.

Deciding to go for it, I sit up and untie the string that stretches across my back, flinging the top onto the ground. I sigh with satisfaction as I settle back down onto the lounger, adjusting my sunglasses and closing my eyes to the too-bright sun.

Just for a few minutes, I tell myself. I'll lie here for a little bit and let the sun warm skin I don't normally expose at all. It feels good, almost . . . sexual. Well, everything these last few days has felt sexual what with the constant state of arousal I've been living in.

I've been with other men, too many of them probably, though I keep my numbers to myself. Then there are the ones no one knows about, the ones that don't count. The ones who paid me money for a quick good time, money I'd desperately needed.

Not that Colin will ever, *ever* know about those men . . .

But no one, and I mean not a single one of them, made me feel like Colin does. One smile from him and I want to melt. He can touch me in the most casual of ways and my knees threaten to buckle. And when he kisses me, I swear I lose a few brain cells every single time.

Arousal trickles through me at the thought of his drugging, delicious kisses. My nipples bead almost painfully and I'm tempted to touch them. To ease the ache that's slowly but surely building inside me . . .

"Well, well, well. Now *this* is a pleasant surprise."

Tingles sweep over my skin at the sound of Colin's velvety deep voice. Lifting my head, I open my eyes to find him standing on the other side of the pool, near the back door that leads into the house. I can't believe I didn't hear the door open or shut.

I wonder if he thinks I'm out here like this just for him.

"I didn't expect you home," I say, rolling my eyes behind my dark sunglasses. Such a lame reply but he doesn't seem to mind, not if the grin on his face is any indication.

"You lie around outside half naked all the time then? I should be staying home in the morning more often." He starts toward me, the epitome of mouthwateringly delicious, wearing jeans and a simple white T-shirt. The way his shirt stretches across his shoulders and chest make me itch to tear it off him.

Shrugging, I struggle for nonchalance, though inside anticipation curls through me, making me burn . . . everywhere. He's moving with a predatory grace that makes my mouth dry, his gaze never leaving me. Suddenly nervous, I look around for my bikini top, spotting it on the concrete right next to the lounger, and I bend down, snatching it up, ready to tie it back on. Or at the very least, cover myself. I'm feeling exposed. Silly for lying around half naked like this.

"Oh, no you don't." He's at my side in an instant, pulling the swimsuit top from my fingers and tossing it far out of reach. His smug grin is downright wicked as he settles on the edge of the lounger, his hip nudging my side, the denim of his jeans rough against my bare skin. He takes me in, his greedy gaze raking over me before landing on my chest, and my nipples literally ache for his touch. "Enjoying the sun?" His husky voice twists my insides, making me breathless.

I lick my lips, sitting up so my face is close to his. "Yeah." Leaning in, I brush my open mouth against his, lingering, tasting. His tongue darts out, teasing mine with gentle flicks, and I moan softly.

"Fuck, you're trying to kill me, aren't you?" His large hands graze my breasts, his palms brushing against my nipples so lightly I can almost believe I'm only imagining he's touching me.

But he's real. His hands on me are real. Hot and seeking and knowing exactly what I need to fill me with uncontrollable desire for him.

"I swear I had no idea you would come home. You're usually gone in the mornings," I say in my defense. He goes into his office when it's quiet and he can get paperwork done. Phone calls made, emails answered, whatever it is that he needs to take care of. He's been extra busy lately what with the new location opening soon. "I thought I had a morning to myself."

"Tell me." He kisses me, a quick, sweet kiss though his mouth lingers, barely moving away from mine. "Were you going to touch yourself out here, Jenny? Have a little fun while I'm gone?"

"No." I shake my head, biting the tip of his finger when he reaches out to trace my bottom lip, making him softly yelp. He doesn't remove his finger from my mouth, though. "But I was thinking of you."

"What were you thinking about?" His voice has gone tight, a sure indicator he's aroused, and I smile.

"How much I miss you." I kiss him again and he cups my face with one hand, holding me, his mouth coaxing mine open before I break away. "How much I wished you were here. Touching me."

His smile grows. "Well, your wish is about to come true."

Colin

My wish is about to come true, too. Hell, it already has. What man doesn't want to find the woman he's obsessed with lying half naked in his backyard in the middle of the morning? Looking like my every teenage wet dream come to life in a skimpy bikini and no freaking top, her breasts bare and skin gleaming in the sun. Her hair is in a high, sloppy ponytail, big black sunglasses shadow her eyes, and she's . . . beautiful. Sexy.

Just having her like this makes me painfully aroused, and I take a deep breath to calm myself and slow my roll. Swiping her sunglasses from her face, I place them on the table next to her chair before I settle both of my hands on her breasts, taking their gentle weight in my palms and cupping her. Her hard nipples stab my palms and I roll them between my thumb and index finger, pinching slightly, making her cry out.

She likes it a little rough, just like I do. I fucked her last night from behind, pulling her hair, giving her one of many spectacular orgasms. She's so responsive, so unbelievably into it, into me, and I feel the same exact way.

I can't get enough of her.

"Are you wet for me?" I ask gruffly. She likes it when I talk dirty to her, too. There are so many hidden depths and secrets to this woman, she's like a constant puzzle I'm trying to figure out. And once I believe I have her solved, something new pops up, making me realize that she might forever be a mystery to me.

And I like it.

"Why don't you check and see?" she teases, a hint of laughter in her voice.

Sounds good to me. "Lie back, Jen," I demand, using my extra-stern boss voice that for whatever reason seems to arouse her, too. Jesus, it's ridiculous how downright combustible we are together.

She does as I command, lying back on the cushy lounge chair, her legs spreading the slightest bit. I notice—I notice everything about her. The smell of her skin, her uniquely sweet fragrance mixed with the distinctive scent of sunscreen. Stray tendrils of hair brush her cheeks, the elegant length of her neck, and the delicate gold chain she's wearing, a tiny floating heart dangling from it.

Leaning in, I slip my finger beneath the thin chain, playing with the little heart. "I gave you this," I say, startled to see her wearing it.

Nodding, she swallows hard. I see the movement of her throat. "Yes, you did."

It was for her high school graduation and I'd been so damn proud to give her something of value back then, even if it was less than two hundred bucks. She'd been so thrilled when I presented the tiny wrapped box to her, hugging me tight after she saw what was inside. Her whispered thank you close to my ear had sent a strange feeling spiraling deep inside me. The way her body fit, nestled so close to mine, tripped me up, too.

No way could I ever forget that night. It was one of those moments that's burned into my memory forever.

The night I realized I saw my best friend's little sister as something more than a pesky girl trailing after us. The moment I realized that she was an attractive, desirable woman. Funny, how I immediately declared her off limits in my brain. I couldn't fuck around with my best friend's baby sister.

And look at us now.

Pushing the worrisome thought from my mind, I trace her collarbone, my gaze lingering on the necklace. "I like that you're wearing it."

"I like that you gave it to me." Reaching up, she touches the necklace as well, our fingers colliding.

Before I say something completely out of hand, I lean in and kiss her, hot and hard and punishing. She yields to me as she always does, her tongue circling mine, her arms going around my neck, pulling me in closer. I swallow her soft, needy moans, touching her all over her body, touching her breasts, her flat stomach, skimming over her curves, until my hands are resting at her hips.

I toy with the skimpy strings that supposedly keep the bikini bottoms on her body, tempted to give them a tug. Pulling away from her, I sit back, watching her. Her breathing is shallow, her chest rising and falling, her skin glistening with the faintest sheen of sweat mixed with sunscreen and lotion and whatever else she's rubbed on.

Damn, she's pretty. I want to eat her up. Keep her locked inside my house for hours, days, weeks. Lose myself in her again and again until I can think of nothing else. Only Jen. Jenny. Jennifer.

She's all three of those women to me.

Reaching out, I brush my finger over her hip bone, tracing it gently until I'm toying with the knotted bow that rests there. Slowly I undo it, watching the string unravel until it's completely untied. I do the same to the other side, then slowly peel the front of her bikini bottom away, revealing her to me completely.

Sweat beads my brow and I lick my lips. I could eat her up, right here, right now. She spreads her legs some more, revealing pretty, pink glistening flesh, and when I lift my gaze to her face, I find her watching me. Her eyes almost black with desire, her lips parted as if she might be having trouble breathing.

I know I sure as hell am.

"Like what you see?" she asks coyly.

I don't answer. Merely settle my hand over her, my palm brushing against her scant pubic hair, my fingers sliding in between her wet folds. She's drenched for me, she's always drenched for me, and the little whimper that escapes her at my touch sends an electric current straight to my dick.

I'm hard as fuck and can't do anything about it. I glance around, knowing the neighbors on both sides of my house work. There's no house behind us since my fence butts up to the street. Yeah, there's a two-story home two houses over with a stay-at-home mom of three who's always there, but she wouldn't be paying any attention to my backyard, would she?

Maybe. But it's a risk I'm going to have to take.

"I'm going to make you come," I whisper, my fingers delving deeper, slipping inside her body. "I want to watch you."

A hint of a smile curves her lips. "You always want to watch me."

True. "I've never seen you come outside. In the sunlight."

The smile grows, a soft sound of pleasure passing from her lips when I slip another finger inside her. "Is it your personal goal to see me come in as many places as possible?"

"How'd you guess?" I kiss her again before I say something really stupid. Like how much I don't want her to leave me. How much I'll miss her when she's gone. How unnecessary it is for her to go because I'm slowly starting to believe we can make this work. If she'd only let me in.

I think I'm more than ready to let her in.

CHAPTER 14

Colin

Within minutes she's moaning, writhing against my hand, her teeth sunk so deep into her bottom lip I'm afraid she'll draw blood. She's circling her hips against my fingers, my thumb plays with her clit, and then she's falling completely apart, her orgasm sweeping over her and taking over completely.

I'm transfixed by the flush of her skin, the way her breasts heave with her labored breaths, how the inner walls of her sex contract around my fingers as the orgasm consumes her. Her pleasure gives *me* pleasure. With other women in the past, I was always eager to get off, too busy chasing my own orgasm. Rarely concerned if the woman I was with had come or not. So selfish, I know, but I've never denied that I'm a selfish guy.

With Jen, I want to make sure she's coming. Always. And that I'm the only one who can make it happen for her. Who can make it so good, she won't want anyone else.

"Every time I think it can't get any better, it does," she whispers, reaching for me. "I didn't think that was possible."

Neither did I. I feel the same.

I go to her, let her wrap her arm around my neck and haul me in as close as possible. She kisses me, her other hand resting on my chest. She slides her fingers down to skim across my stomach, drawing dangerously close to my stiff cock.

"Take me inside," she says, and I slowly shake my head, making her frown. "Why not?"

"I'm going to fuck you right here." I kiss her. "Right now."

"No." She's the one shaking her head now, all those stray strands of hair brushing against her neck. "No way. I'm not putting on a show for your neighbors."

"Hate to tell you this, but you already did, not that anyone's watching." Smiling, I kiss her when she tries to dodge me. "No one's going to see, Jen. Trust me."

"But . . ." Her voice trails off as her gaze meets mine. "I don't know."

"You're the one who was lying out here half naked in the first place. You started it," I point out, laughing when she slaps my shoulder.

"I already told you I didn't think you were coming home."

"So it's okay for you to lie around with your top off but it's not okay for me to want to have sex with you out here." And I am so fucking her out here. She might try to keep up the protest, but I won't let her. I'm already itching to shed all my clothes and get this party started.

I sound like a cheesy asshole even in my head. This is what she's reduced me to.

She sighs, a soft little sound that goes straight to my dick. "I do want you to." She kisses my lips, my cheek, along my jaw, down my throat, before she moves back up to kiss me right behind my ear. "Take your clothes off, Colin."

Fuck. Excitement rolls through me as I pull away from her and stand, shedding my T-shirt, jeans, and underwear as fast as possible. I don't have a fucking condom, which really messes with my game, and her knowing gaze catches mine, saying she gets exactly what I'm thinking about without her saying a word.

"I'm clean," she murmurs, dropping her gaze so she can study her hands. "I've never had unprotected sex in my life. And I'm on the pill."

I'm shocked. And pleased. I want to be a first for her in at least some way. "Really?"

She lifts her head so our gazes meet once more. "Really."

Well. We have this one thing in common. "Neither have I." Meaning I've never, ever had sex without a condom either. I'm too fucking scared I might become a father to ever take that sort of risk. Look what happened to my parents. They weren't supposed to get married. They weren't even in a serious relationship when my mom got pregnant with me. She roped my dad in, and then they were stuck with each other.

With Jen, for whatever crazy-as-hell reason, I want to say fuck it and toss all worry to the wind. I want to know what it feels like to be inside her with absolutely no barriers. Skin on skin.

A shiver moves over me at the thought.

She eyes me, her gaze wandering down the length of my now nude body, and then she's standing, all that delicious, lean nakedness on display right in front of me. I love her body. Damn near worship it, really. Three days in and I'm ready to fall on my knees in front of her like some pussy-whipped asshole.

For once in my life, I don't really care.

"Sit." Sounds like she's the one who's in command now and I gladly give in, letting her take the reins for the first time. I'm curious to see what she wants. How she wants it.

No matter what, I know I'll like it.

I do as she says, settling on the lounger in the dead center, straddling it as I face her. I'm naked and hard as steel, my cock anxious for her to join me. And then she is straddling me, her knees on either side of my hips, her hands clutching my shoulders. I can feel her, my cock is brushing against her wetness, and I'm desperate to thrust up inside her, drive in deep.

She moves over me, teasing me, smiling when I groan. "Ssh," she whispers as she slowly lowers herself onto my cock, taking me in, inch by excruciating inch until I'm completely embedded inside her body. "Oh God, you feel so good."

My eyes threaten to cross when she starts to move. Slow and hesitant at first, I grip her hips, guiding her onto me. Setting the pace, keeping it leisurely at first, sliding her up and down the length of my cock, going a little deeper with every down thrust. Until we're picking up the pace, both of us lost to the rhythm of our bodies. She's snug and wet and warm, the sensation of her clenching tight around my cock threatening to send me straight into oblivion.

"I'm going to—to—come," she stutters out when I thrust deep with an almost manic pace. And then she is coming, shuddering all around me, pushing me straight into my own amazing climax.

We cling to each other as we try to calm our frantically reacting bodies. We're a shuddering, quivering mess, our panting breaths loud in the otherwise quiet of the late morning. I hear a bird chirp, the not-so-distant sound of a car door slamming, and that sound is the one that snaps her out of it, reminds her that yes indeed, we are a part of the land of the living and for a brief moment, we decided to close ourselves off to the world going on around us and do whatever the hell we wanted.

But now real life intrudes and I'm bummed as fuck.

"We should go inside," she whispers close to my ear, her

warm, shuddery breath making me harden all over again. She feels it, too, I can tell by the way she shifts against me. Trying to get me deeper.

"Take a shower with me." I kiss her. We haven't done that yet. Taken a shower together. I'm suddenly desperate to run my hands all over her soap-slick skin.

"I don't know . . ." Her voice trails off and I lean away from her, seeing the mischievous smile curving her lips.

Without warning I climb off the chair and hoist her into my arms, ignoring her shriek, her hands slapping against my chest demanding I put her down. I carry her all the way into my bathroom, where I deposit her in my shower and crank on the water, slipping inside the glass enclosure so I can join her.

Where I proceed to wash every inch of her.

Jen

I shouldn't have taken a shower with Colin. Now I'm sleepy from the warm water, his warm, searching hands, and my third orgasm of the day. It's barely noon and the man is some sort of lethal weapon. I don't think I've ever had this many orgasms in such a short amount of time.

We're lying in his giant bed, our clean, naked bodies entwined around each other. He's dozing, and I'm wide awake with my head resting on his chest, listening to the steady beat of his heart. It calms me, soothes me, and I wish I could lie here like this with him forever.

But I can't. I haven't worked up the nerve to tell him I found a roommate yet. I don't want to ruin the mood. My news will probably make him cranky and I'm just not ready to deal with that.

So I lie here like a liar, pretending everything is fine between us when it's so not. I knew this would happen. Having sex with Colin is just as good as I knew it would be. Maybe even better. We already share a past, a connection, and now that we've pushed our relationship further, that connection has gone even deeper.

At least for me. For him? I'm not sure.

What's amazing is that I've never felt this way about a man before. Sex was always a means to an end. It's an act that could almost bore me if I was with the wrong type of guy. And I was with plenty of wrong guys . . .

Resting my hand on his chest, I let my fingers drift down to skim across the muscular ridges of his stomach. We have to go to work in a few hours but I'd rather not. I'd love to stay here in this bed, naked with Colin, talking and laughing and having sex for however long we want.

"Everything okay?"

His deep voice breaks through my thoughts. I lift my head to find him watching me, those clear blue eyes locked on my face, pensive and seeking.

"I thought you were asleep," I say.

"I was. But you're tense." Reaching out, he touches the side of my face, his fingers tracing down my cheek, along my jaw. "What's bothering you?"

That he knows something is bothering me shows just how well he understands me. I wonder if he even realizes it. "I have some news," I say, ready to get it over with.

Now he's the one who's gone tense. "What is it?"

Taking a deep breath, I decide to just blurt it out. "I found a roommate."

His expression doesn't change a bit. He doesn't even bat an eyelash. "Really."

I nod, nerves eating at my insides. "The apartment looks nice and is pretty central to everything. It's in the area I wanted to live in. I checked out the complex site online. She's in college, she's a year younger than me, and she works part-time at a clothing store in a mall nearby."

"You haven't met her."

"Well, I've talked to her on the phone. Sent her my deposit earlier this morning, too."

He's still studying me with that eerie, immovable expression. I can't tell if he's happy, sad, pissed, irritated, whatever. "So it's for sure. She's your roommate. You're moving in with her."

"Yeah."

"And you've never met her in person."

"Well, no. Of course not." I throw my hands up in the air, irritated by his seeming nonreaction. "It's not like I can ask you to drive me back and forth to Sacramento all the time, right? I don't have a car and I have no other way to get there."

He ignores what I say. "Don't you think that's kind of risky?"

"What? Handling all of this over the phone and inter-net?" I take a deep breath. This is turning into a fight, which is the last thing I want. But when is anything easy between Colin and me? The sex so far has been incredibly easy, but that sort of thing always comes with a price eventually. "I have no choice."

"So you're still leaving?" He sounds incredulous now. Looks it, too, which just makes me want to punch him.

"Yes. I'm. Still. Leaving." I say each word carefully, wanting him to get the message. I'm out of here—but he can change that with a few simple words. He may not know everything that happened while I was at Gold Diggers, but he knows a lot.

I need to hear him say it doesn't matter. That he won't judge me. I need to hear him say he cares only about me.

Holding my breath, I wait for him to say something. Anything. I don't want him to beg me—I know that's not his style. But if he just said one word. One simple word is all it would take and I wouldn't go.

Stay.

"I'll hire you a moving truck," he says, crawling out of bed completely naked and heading toward the bathroom. My gaze falls to his perfect butt like always.

Right about now, I'd really like to kick it.

CHAPTER 15

Colin

I'd come up with the perfect plan and I came home in the middle of the day to tell Jen, hoping like hell that she'd be receptive. Why wouldn't she be? Last night we had the most amazing quickie non-fuck of my life in my office with a packed restaurant on the other side of the door. The way she was the one who sought me out, hot for me, coming all over my fingers, then giving me a most enthusiastic blow job, will be one of my favorite memories ever.

Finding her almost naked in my backyard earlier today felt like an all-time fantasy come to life. Sex outside by the pool, sex in the shower . . . yeah. Everything between us is fucking amazing.

Then the magical moment was ruined by her announcement that she'd found a roommate. And like a dumbass, I said nothing. I offered to rent her a moving truck like some unfeeling asshole. That was my answer. That's how I treated what was really a delicate situation. I'm a hopeless prick.

She hasn't spoken to me much since. Not that I can blame her.

Why is she so hell bent on leaving? I know she craves independence. But I offer her stability. Maybe too much stability, but still. She doesn't have to worry about finding a job or paying rent or buying a car. I provide all of that for her and more.

Maybe that's the problem, asshole. You completely take care of her, almost like you're her sugar daddy.

Running a hand through my hair, I let out a grunt of frustration. She's into me. I'm into her. I'm offering her a better-paying job that's in another town but still close enough that we could see each other. So what's the big deal?

Don't forget her need for freedom.

Freedom. More like she's running away.

I shove the nagging voice in my head to the back of my brain. I don't need to focus on that shit tonight. I want to keep Jen in my life for at least a little while longer. A great job at a different location would give her a new opportunity, a chance to grow, to reach toward that freedom she's always talking about, but still keep her close. Close enough that we could see each other on a regular basis. As in a real relationship.

For once, that thought doesn't freak me out. I'm eager to tell her. Spend time with her. Lie down in my bed at night and hold her, talk to her. Just be with her.

Does she want to be with me? Does she miss me like she did last night? No surprise visits in my office so far tonight, which is a damn shame. I'd planned on bending her over my desk and fucking her fast and furiously until I had to clamp my hand over her mouth to stifle her cries when I brought her to orgasm.

Jesus, she fucks with my head. She's dangerous and doesn't even know it.

Business has been intense tonight. Two unexpected large dinner parties came in, keeping the girls hustling all evening. Thankfully, Jen had taken charge and managed the floor, impressing me yet again. She has so much potential. The things we could do together with my business. How we could take it further . . .

The bar is still in full swing when I finally go looking for her around midnight, ready to get us the hell out of there. I find her in one of the private party rooms, where she and another waitress are cleaning up the mess left behind by the dinner-goers.

"About ready to leave?" I ask, keeping my voice neutral, though it's difficult when Jen's standing there, her back to me as she bends over to clear the table. If Mandy hadn't been in the room, I'd push myself against her. Smooth my hand over her ass. Haul her in close and let her feel exactly what she does to me. Live out that bend-over-the-desk fantasy that has kept me going all night.

Instead I try my best to look casual, my hands shoved deep inside my pockets so I won't do something stupid like grab her and make an ass of myself in front of Mandy.

"Almost." Jen flashes me a small smile over her shoulder. The knot that had formed around my heart earlier slowly unfurls, easing all that tension I've carried with me the entire night. Looks like she might not be angry with me any longer. "Give us a few minutes and I'll meet you at the car? Out in the parking lot?"

"Sure. Sounds good." I leave the room, nodding at Mandy when she gives me a smile. The dining area is dark and quiet but the bar is still in full swing. I wave and call goodbye to the bartender, Steven, then exit the building. I head toward my car, my head bent against the sudden wind that has come up. It holds a hint of fall in it, cold and sharp and making me shiver.

Crazy, considering it's been hot as hell these last few weeks.

I climb into the car and wait, my gaze locked on the front door of the restaurant as I lean forward and turn on the radio. Long minutes pass and I check my email on my phone, answer a few texts that I didn't realize had come through. I've been so damn busy for weeks. Months. Once the new location is complete, I'm taking a fucking vacation. Disconnecting from the entire world, leaving my phone at home if I can get away with it. I need the break.

I want Jen by my side when I take my break, too. Maybe we could go to Hawaii together. Or the Caribbean. Somewhere hot and tropical where I can watch her lounge on the beach in that tiny bikini she wore earlier, her skin golden from the sun, all that golden skin on display just for me. Just to drive me out of my mind . . .

A shrill yell breaks through my dream vacation thoughts and I sit upright in my seat, reach for the door handle, and scramble out of the car to see what happened. Who needs help.

I run across the parking lot, scanning to the left, then the right, but I see nothing. Panic makes my heart race when I realize it's been at least fifteen minutes since I left Jen back in the restaurant. No way would cleaning up the private dining room take that long.

I see a woman crumpled on the ground, her dark head bent over as she rocks back and forth. I increase my pace, running at a full sprint toward the woman sitting there, and when she looks up at me, the relief written all over her familiar tear-streaked face, fear grips me so tight my vision blurs.

It's Jen.

Jen

I stayed a little too long chatting with everyone still working, trying not to look too obvious that I wanted out of there, though I was still a little angry with Colin for what he'd said to me. Offering a moving truck, how freaking generous of him!

So I talked, I gossiped, and we laughed over silly stuff, my gaze constantly going to the clock on the wall above the bar. Fable kept sending me questioning looks and I know others noticed, too. They had to. I felt like everyone was watching me.

I'm afraid they're all extra suspicious that I'm fooling around with the boss. It's one thing when they say you're doing it and you're really not. I'm scared out of my mind they'll figure us out, which means I'm probably becoming more obvious.

So stupid. I'm just nervous. I don't want to be discovered. I don't want everyone pointing fingers at me saying I'm fucking the boss.

I know people think it, but until recently the rumors were unfounded. Fable's been great about trying to dispel them in that no-nonsense way of hers. But now it's the truth. It'll be hard to face them if they find out I really am doing the boss. I want my coworkers to respect me, not think I'm easy or getting special treatment.

Finally I extract myself from them, after refusing what feels like endless offers to stay and have just one drink. I glance at my phone, surprised to see almost fifteen minutes have passed, and I hope Colin isn't mad that I kept him waiting.

Knowing I've been angry with him all night, he will probably let this one slide.

Stopping at the front door, I frown, staring out the window at the darkened parking lot. He won't be mad. He's never mad. Indifferent, yes, but not after what happened last night.

Or just a few hours ago.

I shouldn't be mad either. He's just keeping his word, right? An easy no-strings affair is what we're having. I'm leaving in less than two weeks. He'll miss me, I know it, just like I'll miss him. But I need to remember that what we're experiencing right at this very moment is nothing more than a fling. A fling that will turn into fond memories later on down the line.

Yeah. I really need to remember that. Forget I'm anxious to see him.

Scanning the parking lot, I wonder where the security guard is. A few of the streetlights that illuminate the lot are out, shrouding certain pockets of the space in total darkness. I'll have to walk across one of those dark spots to get to Colin's car.

Should I text him and tell him to meet me at the door? He'd do it. I know he would . . .

Nah. He'll think I'm a total wimp if I do that. I can run across the lot. It's no biggie. He's just right there.

The minute I walk outside the wind hits me, chilling me to the bone. I duck my head against it, my shoulders hunched as I dart across the parking lot. Glancing up, I see Colin sitting in his car, his head bent, the glow from his cell phone illuminating his face. I smile, my belly filling with tiny, fluttering butterflies at the realization that this beautiful, sexy man is mine, at least temporarily.

Out of nowhere a bulky figure comes at me, knocking me off my feet. I fall onto the asphalt with a cry, hitting the ground so hard the wind is knocked out of me. I curl into myself for protection, my arm feeling like it's being tugged right out of its socket.

"Come on! Gimme your purse, bitch!" The guy towers over me. I can't make out his face since the shadows are cast over it, but he sounds young. Possibly even younger than me.

I hadn't realized I was gripping my tiny purse so tightly. Loosening my hold, I let him take it, then watch in stunned disbelief as he tucks it under his arm like a football and takes off across the lot, rounding the corner and disappearing from view.

I'm panting, left sitting sprawled on the asphalt. Icy shock washes over me as I glance about the parking lot. My throat is dry, I can't manage to form a single word, and I swallow hard. Trying to stand, my legs wobble and I stumble, falling down on my knees, wincing at the pain that lances through me when I make contact with the ground. I look down, see that my knees are scratched and bloody, and that's when I find my voice.

And scream bloody freaking murder.

Within seconds Colin's there for me first, with a few people from the restaurant surrounding me soon after. Someone, I don't know who, calls 911. Colin has his arm around my shoulders, his face in mine, his voice a mixture of concern and cold, calm anger.

"What happened, baby?" He leans into me and whispers this in my ear, his hand smoothing over my hair in a comforting gesture. "Who did this to you?"

I press my head against his strong, solid shoulder and close my eyes for a moment, refusing to cry. I won't let this upset me. That jackass who took my purse—and all of tonight's tips with it—isn't worth crying over. I've endured worse. Much, much worse. This is no big deal. "I was walking toward your car and this guy ran into me, pushing me onto the ground. He—he stole my purse." My voice wavers and I sniff hard, willing the tears that threaten to disappear.

"Shit." Colin sounds furious as he lifts his head and looks around the lot. His jaw is tight, I notice the tic in it he only gets when he's super mad, and his eyes blaze with angry blue fire. "Anybody see him?"

"None of us were out here except for you." Steven says this in the most antagonizing tone, one I hope Colin will ignore, but . . .

He doesn't. Worse, he rises to the bait.

"Are you saying this is my fault, Harper?" Colin's voice is low, full of quiet fury, and the look on Steven's face says he definitely notices. And thankfully backs off.

The police show up quickly and question me, but I don't have much to say. The female officer informs me that there have been a rash of robberies just like this over the last couple of months and I was lucky I didn't get hurt worse. That a woman who was robbed a few nights ago walking across her apartment parking lot had been hit upside the head with a gun—and was still in the hospital because of her injuries.

That bit of information sends a cold ripple of fear down my spine.

Colin urges me to go to the emergency room so they can at least check me out and make sure I'm okay, but I refuse. I just want to go home, crawl into bed, and go to sleep. Forget this ever happened to me.

"You need to call your bank and cancel all your credit cards," Colin suggests on the drive home. The police had finally let us go, the female officer giving Colin a stern lecture about replacing the burnt-out lights in the parking lot and making sure the security guard he usually has on duty is actually . . . on duty.

Her chastising had pissed Colin off, not that I could blame him. He already feels responsible enough.

He always feels responsible, especially for my well-being. I wonder if he's sick of it yet.

"I don't have any credit cards," I say wearily, earning a surprised glance from Colin.

"A bank card at least?" he asks. "I'm guessing the guy

was looking for cash, but you never know what he might try. Credit card fraud is such a huge problem right now."

"Yeah. I'll call my bank in the morning to report it and get it replaced." I close my eyes, my mind replaying over and over again the way the man rammed his big body into mine, sending me sprawling onto the ground. What would I have done if he'd actually used his hands on me, like what happened to that woman a few nights ago? Would I have fought back? Or just lain there and let him hit me?

"You really should call when we get home," Colin continues. "Or you could borrow my cell phone and make the call right now."

"I just . . . I can't worry about that right now, Colin," I whisper, wishing he would stop talking. The last thing I need right now is a lecture. And I can feel one coming on, along with a massive headache. "Please just let me sit here and be quiet for a little bit."

"Fine," he bites out, sounding irritated but I don't care. He's not the one who was just robbed. I know he's worried about me, but I wish he would just . . . lay off for a second.

I know I should be appreciative of him going into his usual protector mode but for whatever reason, I'm beyond irritated, sick of him always running to my rescue, always trying to tell me what to do.

I'm probably being completely irrational, but seeing him yet again trying to take care of me, take over me really, only proves how badly I need to get away from him. Despite the connection we have, the amazing sex . . . it won't last. He doesn't stick.

And neither do I.

The rest of the quick drive home is quiet, and I escape into the house from the garage as soon as he cuts the car's engine. I have no purse, which means the jackass who took it stole a bunch of my makeup, Colin's house key, my cell, and my wallet. And again, I can't help but remember how fat it had been with my night's tips.

I know Colin is right and I should at least call my bank, but I'm too exhausted to even scrub the makeup off my face, let alone make an actual phone call.

I can barely think and act like a normal human being. I'm in full-blown zombie mode as I move through the house, my brain blank, my body taking me where I need to go like I'm on autopilot.

Entering my room, I flick on the lights and stare at my reflection in the mirror that hangs over the dresser. My cheeks are streaked with mascara-stained tears that I don't even remember crying. My face is swollen, my eyes are bloodshot, and I look terrible.

Great.

Looking down, I see that the hem of my dress is torn and my knees are still bloody and scraped. With a sigh, I head into the bathroom to clean up my wounds, but Colin is already in there, searching through the drawers until he comes up with antibiotic cream and Band-Aids.

I watch him from where I stand in the doorway, both loathing and appreciating his effort to take care of me in every way he can. I should be touched that he would do all of this, as though he's my big brother or something. My champion, my knight in shining armor coming to rescue me on his mighty steed.

"Let me help you," he says the moment he notices me standing there watching him. "Come here."

I walk inside the small bathroom and sit on the toilet seat, my skirt rising up and revealing my bloodied knees. He finds a clean washcloth in a drawer and dampens it with cool water under the faucet, then gently presses it to my left knee.

Wincing, I hiss in a breath, surprised at how much the scrape hurts. Colin dabs at my skin, his brows furrowed as he studies my knee.

"You have bits of rock in this one," he says as he reaches out with his other hand and carefully flicks them away. "Doesn't look serious, though."

"It hurts," I murmur, hating how pitiful I sound.

"Sorry." He flashes me a tight, sympathetic smile. "Your knees will look like hell for about a week with the bandages on them, but hey, maybe you could start a new trend." He's trying to joke, to lighten the moment as he dabs the antibiotic cream on my knee and then places a Band-Aid on the wound, but it's not working.

"What sort of trend would that be?" I ask once he starts in on my other knee. *"Hold-up chic?"*

He shoots me a look but never lets up on his tending of my other knee. His touch is so gentle, the look on his face equally so, and watching him fills me with both pleasure and sadness. It makes no sense, the confusion swirling in my brain. Why do I resent Colin for wanting to take care of me? I should be appreciative. I should hug him and thank him for being there for me in my time of need.

Instead, I say nothing. Because I always seem to have a time of need. And he always seems to be right there for me. Saving me.

I'm starting to hate it.

This knee isn't as bad as the other one and he takes quick care of it, bandaging me up and declaring me fixed with the tiniest smile.

I don't have the heart to tell him I feel more broken than ever.

CHAPTER 16

Jen

"I'm firing the security company," Colin announces the moment I shuffle into the kitchen.

Stopping short, I study him through bleary eyes, deciding it's a crime for a man to wake up first thing in the morning looking so damn good. Wearing nothing but a pair of black-and-gray flannel pajama pants that hang indecently low on his hips, revealing all that smooth muscled skin I'm itching to touch, he's making coffee and acting super efficient.

"Why are you firing the security company?" I ask as I sit at the small kitchen table, my movements careful. My body aches and my knees still hurt. As I inhale deeply, the scent of rich, fragrant coffee slowly wakes up my murky brain.

He keeps his back to me, his pants falling even lower when he reaches into the cabinet above him and pulls out two coffee mugs. I see a tan line, and immediately think of how I had my hands all over the area south of it just yesterday morning. My cheeks flush hot with a mixture of embarrassment and arousal, and my body's tingling in all the right places.

Needless to say, nothing happened between us last night. I'd gone to sleep in my bed, and he'd gone to sleep in his. I woke up in the middle of the night to hear him yelling something unintelligible, but I didn't go to him. And the yelling stopped as soon as it started, so I can only hope the dreams weren't too bad.

I felt like a jerk not going to him, but I have to break myself of this habit. I can't keep trying to rescue him. Just like he can't keep trying to rescue me.

God, we're a pair, aren't we?

"There was supposed to be a guard on duty until two A.M., but he left early without consulting anyone. This isn't the first time, either. I want him fired. The company's at fault, so I'm terminating our contract with them first thing when I head into the office."

"Maybe he had some sort of emergency," I offer weakly. My head slowly starts to pound. I'm so not in the mood to fight or discuss what happened last night. It's too early for this sort of discussion.

I just want to forget.

"Come on. I've texted Steven and a few others at the restaurant. They said this guy left early a lot, which pisses me off. And even if what you're saying is true, I really don't care. He should have at least let someone know. They're in breach of contract. Makes it real easy for me to end this relationship. Though now I need to find another security company stat. Preferably tonight." He finally pours each of us a cup of coffee, preparing them before bringing mine with him as he walks to the table and drops into the chair across from me. He slides the steaming mug toward me with a nod. "Here you go. Just the way you like it."

He knows how I like my coffee, heavy on the creamer. "Thank you," I say gratefully, taking the cup between both hands and bringing it to my lips, breathing in the rich, delicious scent before I take a sip.

"So did you sleep all right? How are your knees this morning?" he asks, his voice deep and full of concern.

After he'd cleaned them up, he walked me to my room last night, tucking me into my bed like I'm some sort of child. I'd been half tempted to ask him to crawl into bed with me and spend the night, but I held back. I didn't want to look too needy.

It's bad enough, how needy I already am. Breaking bad habits, right? I need to remember that.

"I slept okay." I'd lain in bed, wide awake for at least an hour, running over again and again in my head what happened to me out in the parking lot. Wondering how I could have prevented it. I'd kept my head down most of the walk, too focused on getting to Colin's car, thinking of Colin. Of going straight home so I could get him naked. So preoccupied with my wicked thoughts, I never once checked out my surroundings. I'd been easy pickings for that guy; no wonder he came for me.

And I could blame no one but myself for that.

"Are you in any sort of pain?" The soft concern lacing his deep voice almost makes me want to cry, which is so stupid. I'm thinking like such a girl right now I want to smack myself.

"My body aches, yeah. I hit the ground pretty hard when I fell. But my knees are better. They don't hurt as bad." It was sort of true. They still sting, but not as much as last night.

The murderous glow in his eyes says it all. If the guy who did this to me were in the same room with us right now, Colin would be tearing him apart, limb by limb.

"I should call the police and see if they caught the little motherfucker," he mutters, reaching for his cell phone.

"Don't bother. I'm sure they'll never find him." I take another sip, my brain slowly coming awake, along with all of my bitter sarcasm. "I'm low priority in their eyes. I just want to forget last night ever happened."

"A serial armed robber is not low priority, especially in a

college town. Trust me, they're looking for the asshole. And if they're not, I'll call and make sure they are." He lets his cell phone drop onto the table with a loud clang, making me jump in my seat. He notices, remorse filling his gaze, and I hate seeing it. I don't want his sympathy. "Are you all right?"

"Of course I'm all right." I feel defensive, as though his eyes can see right through me. See all my faults and resentment and irritation over this entire mess. I didn't ask for this to happen. Getting robbed and playing the helpless female is so not a role I'm comfortable with. I'd had a nightmare about it. How he knocked me to the ground, yanking my purse out of my grip, calling me a bitch.

This guy didn't just steal my purse and everything in it. I'm afraid he's stolen my strength and courage, too.

"I know you're trying to deal with this in your own way and it's hard. But you've been acting almost like you're . . . mad at me." His mouth sets into a hard line, though his eyes are full of worry. "Are you? Mad at me?"

No way can I be honest. He'll think I'm crazy if I tell him I'm totally mad, though I wouldn't describe it so much as that. Of course, I feel like I'm crazy, because I have no valid reason to be angry with him. What did he do that was so wrong? Help me out? Clean my wounds? Put me to bed and reassure me everything's going to be all right?

Yeah. I'm being ridiculous. I can't help it.

"What happened to me last night just proves once and for all I need to get out of here. I hate this place." I drain my coffee cup, feeling his intense gaze on me. *Uh-oh.*

"Gimme a break. Like it couldn't happen to you somewhere else? Sacramento has a higher crime rate than here," he points out.

"Yeah, and it's a much bigger city, too. We live in Podunkville." I shrug, getting up and going to the coffeemaker so I can pour myself another cup. I keep my back to him, not wanting to have this conversation any longer. Afraid of what I might say if he pushes too much more.

"Does this have anything to do with me? Are you upset with me for some reason? Because you're acting like it." He pushes his chair out and I hear him approach, feel his body heat when he draws near. "Are you blaming me for what happened?"

I whirl around, startled when I find him standing much closer than I'd originally thought. Being faced with acres of naked masculine flesh leaves my mouth dry and I eat him up greedily with my gaze, marveling at all of that gorgeous muscly goodness. Jerking my eyes away from his chest, I look at him, finding him watching me with a look on his face that indicates he can read my every thought.

How freaking embarrassing. I'm supposed to be angry and indifferent, right?

I am so not indifferent. And he knows it.

"Of course I don't blame you," I say. "I'm the idiot who wasn't watching where she was going."

"I should've picked you up at the door," he throws back at me.

"I should've texted asking you to pick me up at the door," I throw right back.

Briefly closing his eyes, he breathes deep, as if he needs to search for the right words to say. "I'm the one who should've watched out for you. I'm your employer. Your friend. Your . . ." His voice trails off.

Stepping toward him, I place my fingers over his mouth, silencing him. Not that he was necessarily going to say anything else. He looks like he's at as much of a loss for words as I am. "Stop talking. We're nothing beyond the word *friend*, right?"

He nods, his eyes shooting daggers at me. But he doesn't say a word.

"Friends are there for each other. And you were there for me last night." I trace his lips with my index finger, the plump lower lip, the finely curved upper one. He has such a beautiful mouth. One I thoroughly enjoy watching when he talks, when he smiles, when he kisses me. I'm tempted to kiss him right now. Just so I can forget for at least a little while that I'm leaving and that I was robbed and that he feels this stupid obligation to me.

I'm not his burden. And that's what it's like—I'm an obligation to take care of in place of my brother watching over me. At least, that's how it started out. He became my hero. Rescuing me when I thought I didn't want to be rescued. Saving me from a life of crime, though he didn't realize that part.

Our relationship has certainly gone beyond the brotherly-sisterly type . . .

"Jen." His voice is deep and rumbling. I feel it reverberate through me all the way down to my bones. He touches me, places his hand on my hip, and pulls me closer to him, our chests brushing. Just like that, my skin is on fire, my braless nipples hardening against my tank top. I want him. Inside me, kissing me, pushing me toward that oblivious, blank space where I can forget everything at least for a little while.

I rest my other hand on his chest, right at the center, and I can feel his heartbeat. It's a rapid, rhythmic pace. Reassuring and strong. Unable to resist, I lean in and brush my lips upon his flesh, right above my fingertips, and he closes his eyes, his expression agonized.

"I want you," he whispers. "But you're hurting from that asshole pushing you. And I can't push myself on you. Not right now."

"You won't hurt me. I'll be fine." I kiss him again, my lips lingering on his warm, hard skin. I settle my hands on his hips, slip my fingers just beneath the waistband of his pajama pants, and touch him, my hands meeting nothing but bare, hot skin. I feel the thrust of his erection through the fabric of his pj's, pushing against my belly, and I know he wants me.

Probably even more than I want him.

"I don't want you to go to work today," he says, abruptly changing the subject.

I can't believe he's talking about work at a time like this. "I already told you, I'm fine. Really." Standing on tiptoe, I kiss his neck, licking him, tasting him, savoring the sound of his moan. I want to distract him, distract both of us. Talking tends to lead us into trouble, especially lately.

Having sex leads us straight into pleasure. And that's what I want right now. Mindless, delicious pleasure with Colin.

"No." He pulls away from me, his expression and body language downright tortured. "I'm not going to do this. Not when you're still recovering from what happened to you last night."

Frustration rips through me, making me angry. "I'm not some delicate doll who needs to be handled with care, Colin. I fell and scraped my knees last night. Big deal."

"You were fucking attacked, Jen. You suffered a tremendous shock. I think you might *still* be in shock. There's no other explanation for why you're acting so odd."

Jackass! I am so done with him diagnosing me all the time. "So you're not going to have sex with me because of what happened last night."

"Yeah."

"You're being ridiculous."

"So are you," he throws back.

We stare at each other, all sorts of tension swirling between us. I both want to jump him and smack him.

Jump him . . .

Or smack him?

Colin

I want to both jump her and smack her, which is the craziest thing ever because I have never had violent thoughts toward a woman before in my life. And hell, she was just mugged, for the love of God. The very thing I should be thinking is how much I want to shake some sense into her.

Those few weak moments when she was touching my mouth, touching my chest, kissing my neck, I was more than ready to cave. Just give in to that uncontrollable urge I feel whenever she's with me. Where I'm desperate to tear her clothes off and make her mine. Brand her, mark her, demand that she say my name when I make her come. Then she'll know who she belongs to.

Me. And no one else.

"You're not working tonight and that's final," I finally growl out because holy shit, I have no idea what else to say to break this almost unbearable tension brewing between us.

"Who are you, my dad?" The sarcasm in her voice is unmistakable.

"No, I'm your fucking boss." I pull away from her and exit the kitchen, needing the escape, but she trails after me, muttering under her breath.

"What the hell did you just say?" I whirl on her, anger running through my veins, making my blood boil. She's getting under my skin, and not in a good way.

"I said that's exactly it. You *are* my fucking boss. As in, you're my boss and we're fucking." She smirks—actually fucking smirks—and crosses her arms in front of her chest, as if daring me to deny it.

I have no answer for her. She's driving me out of my ever-lovin' mind and I have no idea why we're acting this way toward each other. As if we're both full of hostile resentment that we're ready to unleash on each other at any given moment.

It reminds me of a pot primed to boil over—and I think we did just that.

"Is that all I am to you?" I ask, my tone just daring her to say yes.

She shrugs one shoulder, all irritated nonchalance. "So we've known each other for a long time. So what? It's not like we owe each other anything."

My head is spinning. Doesn't she realize I owe her everything? I care about her, more than I want to admit. The closer we get to her leaving, the more I don't want her to go. I need to tell her. I need to let her know what she means to me, but . . .

It's fucking hard. I'm not one to blurt out my feelings. My parents aren't touchy-feeling and rarely talk about their emotions. I hide behind a mask most of the time. Whatever people want to see, I give it to them. With the exception of Jen.

She's the only one who sees the real me.

"Besides, I'm nothing but a burden, right? Don't you get tired of taking care of me all the time? Making sure I'm safe and protected and nothing bad ever happens to me?"

"I let something bad happen to you last night," I say, my voice low, my anger barely contained. The renewed guilt I feel over what happened to her is almost too much for me to handle.

"That wasn't your fault. You can't feel responsible for everything that happens to me. Don't you ever get sick of it?"

"No, I don't. I want to take care of you. Danny would've wanted me to take care of you, too." It's the least I can do. I've already failed her numerous times. I can think of at least three.

"Do you really believe Danny would have wanted us together? Fucking around on the side?" she asks.

I flinch. "Don't call it that."

"Don't call what we're doing what it is? Come on, we don't need to tiptoe around the truth. We're just *fucking* each other until I leave. It doesn't mean anything. We already agreed. You can't back out of it now."

"Why are you trying to pick a fight with me?"

"Doesn't feel so good when someone challenges you, huh? I know that doesn't happen very often," she tosses at me like a giant bomb.

I open my mouth to retort something extra sarcastic right back at her but the doorbell rings, interrupting me. We stare at each other, her eyes narrowing, mine narrowing in return, and we're like two gunslingers ready for a shootout at the O.K. Corral.

Fuck, I think I've been watching too many reality shows on the History channel. I'm starting to sound like them.

"Are you going to get that?" she asks. "I'm sure whoever's on the other side of that door is far more important than I am."

What. The. Hell. I don't get her. She's defiant, angry, and smug. It's like she's completely changed in the last twenty-four hours.

"This conversation is not over," I tell her as I head toward

the door. Thinking it might be the police, I don't bother checking. I unlock the door and throw it open.

"Hello, son."

Well, holy fuck. It's my father. Talk about an unexpected
visit.

I haven't seen him in almost three years.

CHAPTER 17

Colin

"Are you going to let me in?" The man standing on my doorstep could be my future self. I look so much like my father it's frightening. Same height, same build, same features, same hair, though his is liberally streaked with gray now.

He smiles at me, looking like a shark baring all of his teeth, and I barely hold back my grimace. No wonder my mom didn't like me much. I remind her of the man who knocked her up, married her, and then abandoned her, all in a matter of about eighteen months. They pull each other in a constant tug-of-war over me to this day and I'm a grown-ass man. They have nothing to fight over. Their behavior makes absolutely no sense to me.

"Yeah, come in." I open the door wider and Conrad Wilder strides inside, stopping short when he sees Jen standing in the middle of my living room, looking unsure and kind of adorable with it.

My earlier anger melts away, just like that. Dark circles are under her wide brown eyes and she looks from me to my dad, then back at me. She's met my dad before, but it's been a while. It's pretty obvious who he is, though.

"Who's this?" My dad turns to look at me, both eyebrows raised. He's a player, always has been. Women flock to him and he loves it. As he gets older, he likes his women young.

The younger, the better. I bet he's giving me a mental high-five at this very moment.

"Dad, this is Jennifer Cade." I pause as he approaches her with a too-friendly smile and an outstretched hand. "She's Danny's sister."

"Ahhh." He draws the word out, giving me a quick look over his shoulder before he turns on the charm for Jen. "I'm positive we've met before, though it was a long time ago. Conrad Wilder, but you can call me Con."

So fitting that he wants people to call him Con. He's definitely one of the biggest con artists I know. He can talk just about anyone into anything, and that's why the man is richer than God.

"Nice to meet you," Jen says, briefly shaking his hand. She shoots me a look, one that says she needs to get out of here, and I can't blame her. "I'm going to take a shower."

I watch her exit the room, my gaze zeroing in on her swishing hips, her cute ass barely covered by a pair of tiny cotton shorts. Her legs drive me fucking insane.

"She's a cute thing, but skinny. Not your usual type," my dad says the moment he hears Jen shut her bedroom door.

"I don't have a type."

Dad laughs. "You do, too. Blond, petite, with a tiny waist and huge tits—that's your type. Always has been. So what gives with this one? She something serious?"

"We're old friends. That's it," I admit grudgingly.

"Ah, well that's worse. You don't fuck a friend, son. Didn't I teach you anything?" He slaps my back with a laugh, acting like we're nothing but two old buddies hanging out and bagging on women.

That's the biggest problem I've had with him almost my entire life. He treats me like a friend, not like his son. Other than when it's necessary for him to give me advice and be all fake-fatherly, for the most part he wants to talk tits and ass, get drunk, and brag about his net worth.

When I was younger, I thought it was great. Get the old man drunk, talk about the rack on some hot girl, and the next thing I knew, he was handing me a check for thousands of dollars. Now, though, it sucks. I'm getting too old for this shit. And my father is beyond too old. He's so transparent with his frat-boy ways—and he was never a frat boy—it's downright embarrassing.

"I'm not fucking her," I lie through clenched teeth. I hate how he cheapens my relationship with Jen. More than that, I hate how now Jen cheapens our relationship, too. When did I suddenly become the only believer in this equation?

When have I ever been the believer?

"Then what are you doing, son? Having a little piece like that prancing around your house in shorts that should be illegal, where any man can check out those amazing legs? Not smart."

"God, would you stop talking about her like that? It's not like that between us." What sucks is that I don't know what it's really like between us since I'm a confused, screwed-up mess.

"Considering you're pretty damn sensitive about her, that tells me you're taking this way too seriously. Like you have feelings for her. And that gets you nothing but trouble." He plops onto the couch, his gaze shrewd as he studies me. "Danny Cade's sister, huh? I remember meeting her a few times over the years, what with the way you and Danny were so damn close and always together. Though it's been a while since I last saw her."

"She's been living with me the last few months. I found her working at some strip club on the outskirts of town. She had a falling-out with her parents and they called me. Told me they thought they knew where she was and when they realized I was setting up The District close by, they asked me to find her. I got her out of that shit joint and told her she could work for me," I explain, inwardly wincing when I see the expression on his face at the mention of Jen working at a strip club. *Great.* "The Cades knew I would help. I did it for Danny."

"Isn't Danny dead?" Dad looks completely confused.

"Well, yeah, but he'd want me to look out for his baby sister. So I am."

"Did she strip?" he asks. He's looking at me as if my story is complete bullshit. And I refuse to answer him. "Nice arrangement you got here, son. Sounds like a distraction, though, and I need you on top of your game. I've got a proposition for you."

Dread settles in my gut, making it churn. My earlier hunger for breakfast evaporates in an instant. "What are you talking about?" I ask warily as I settle into the chair across from where he's sitting.

He leans forward, resting his elbows on his thighs and watching me intently. "I just acquired a fantastic piece of property in downtown San Francisco. Not too far from the wharf. It's a corner location, near business offices and where the trendy younger set likes to hang out. The building was recently redone, so the renovation costs wouldn't be too bad, and the location gets plenty of traffic on a day-to-day basis. Specifically a night-to-night basis, which is exactly what we want." He rubs his hands together like a greedy salesman—exactly what he is. "It's time to move on, son. Have someone else manage this location in this shit-hole town. I want you to come to San Francisco with me. We can open the new place together. Turn it into something amazing that we could eventually franchise out across the entire country. What do you say?"

"You want to manage a restaurant together?" Crap, that's my biggest sticking point. Working directly with my father is a nightmare of epic proportions. I'd moved on years ago so I could get away with not working directly for him as much as possible. That's always hard, though, when the money starts talking. Because that's when I usually start listening.

"Well, at the start. You know how I am." He'd always had wanderlust and could never stick in one spot for too long. "I won't get in your hair. This'll be your project, completely. I'll hang around, help supervise, take care of the stuff you don't want to deal with, and then when the business is in full swing, I'm outta there. Ready to sell our franchise in all the big West Coast cities at first. Los Angeles, Portland, Seattle. Then we'll sweep out farther east. Las Vegas, Phoenix . . ."

Sounds too good to be true, so I know one thing: there has to be a catch.

"Just got the loan approved for the location and we've moved quickly into escrow," the old man keeps going. "I'm land rich. Rich as a motherfucker, really, but also cash poor. That means I'll probably need some cash loans to take care of expenses and stuff."

There's the catch. I hadn't even really risen to the bait. *Shit.* "You need a loan?" The idea shocks me. My father has never, ever come to me for money. He never needed to. My long dead grandfather had left him a ton of money and though he's at his very soul a con man, Dad is also a very comfortably wealthy con man. He can afford to take risks. He's always the one flashing the big cash stacks, exaggerating about his success, though most of those exaggerations were always based in truth.

The last thing I want to do is let my dad borrow money from me. But what can I do?

He's my father. He might not have been there for me emotionally and he definitely made me work for it, but he always eventually came through when I needed financial help.

I owe him. He's one of the reasons I'm where I am today.

Jen

I'd forgotten how uncomfortable Colin's dad makes me feel, so what just happened was a fresh reminder of the man's ways. He's too slick, too charming, too . . . everything. I don't trust him. He doesn't feel genuine.

I take a hot shower to wash away the awful thoughts that still linger from last night. And the way Conrad Wilder talked, how he looked at me. How he strode into Colin's house as if he owned it, invading our space. Ruining everything.

Thank God I know Colin is not like his father. Yeah, he has a reputation as a player and when I first came to live with him, he flirted with plenty of girls. Even went out with a few. At The District, he's always the charmer, talking to women, making them laugh and smile and vie for his attention. But he never comes across as a total phony.

And lately he hasn't even gone out with any of them. For the last few months he's flirted a little bit at work with customers, but that's it. I'm the only one he's paid any real attention to.

Closing my eyes, I press my forehead against the cool tile, letting the water cascade over me. He's so confusing. Everything he does, how he acts, I can't figure him out. One minute I think he might really want me, then the next he's treating me like a friend or worse, a temporary fling.

You're the one who asked for the temporary fling.

Yeah. I'm such a fool for saying that. No wonder he readily agreed. A man like Colin is always up for a no-strings affair.

I finally shut off the water and step out of the shower, toweling off quickly, preparing for the day. My body still aches, but the pain is probably nothing that a few ibuprofen can't take care of. Colin may have said I'm not going into work, but I so am. No way will I sit around here and do nothing. I'll be climbing the walls in no time. And after having last night's tips stolen, I need the money.

Besides, if Colin's dad is hanging around here tonight when Colin is at work, there is no way in hell I'm staying here with him alone.

Exiting the bathroom that connects to my bedroom, I go to the dresser and open a drawer, slipping on a bra and panties, then a pair of yoga pants and a pale blue tank top. I attempt to grab for my phone, ready to check my text messages, and realize it's gone.

The jackass who stole my purse also took my phone. He's probably not even doing anything with it. My cheap purse has probably been tossed in a garbage bin, full of everything I consider important. He most likely took my cash and left everything else in the trash. Things that matter to me. Stuff that I need.

I sniff, pressing my lips together to hold back the tears as I collapse on my bed. I'm tired. Irritated. Frustrated. A huge ball of confusing emotion swirls within me, and I glance at the bedside table and the landline telephone that sits there.

Yep, Colin's one of the rare few who actually still has a real phone. I grab it and dial the 800 number of my phone company, which turns into a twenty-minute conversation as I cancel my stolen phone and order a new one.

Colin would be proud of me. I actually feel like an adult, taking care of what I need to do.

The moment I hang up, the phone starts to ring. I answer it quickly, something I rarely do since hardly anyone calls the house phone and if they do, it's usually for Colin.

"Oh my God, I took a chance by calling this number," Fable says right after I say hello. She sounds relieved. "Are you all right? I figured your cell was stolen, yeah?"

"Yeah." I sigh, running a hand over my wet hair as I slump against the headboard. "I'm tired, but I'm okay."

We talk for a few minutes, with me explaining that I'm perfectly fine and letting her know about my frustration with Colin. How he doesn't want me to come into work tonight.

"You should totally take the night off. I would if I were you. I bet he'd pay you," she says.

Leave it to Fable to think about the money aspect of it. I usually do, too. We have similar backgrounds, since both of us grew up relatively poor.

"Ha. With my luck he probably won't. That's why I'm going in," I reply.

There's a brief knock on my door before it's thrown open, startling me. "Hey, I gotta go," I murmur to Fable before I hang up without letting her reply. Colin strides into my room, slamming the door behind him. He stops at the foot of my bed, resting his hands on his hips as he glowers at me. As he's still wearing those damn pajama pants and nothing else, I keep my gaze glued on his face.

That muscular bared chest is not going to distract me. I refuse to let it.

"Just because you own the place doesn't mean you can just barge into my room," I say, feeling defensive. On edge. I scoot up the bed till I'm practically sitting among the pile of pillows, my gaze never leaving his.

He looks angry as he runs a hand through his hair, pushing it into complete, sexy disarray. A sure sign that he's frustrated. "I'm sorry about my dad. I didn't expect him to show up. He usually calls before he comes by."

"How often does that happen?"

"Rarely. That's why it was such a surprise." He rolls his eyes, something I don't think I've seen him do since he was a teen. Funny how being around a parent makes us revert in age.

"It's okay. I don't mind that he's here." I shrug, trying to act like it doesn't bother me even though it totally does.

I like having this safe haven with Colin. Hardly anyone ever comes around, so it's pretty much always just me and him. Fable accused me a while ago of playing house with him.

I think she's right.

"He was an ass to you and I hate that."

"You don't have to apologize for him," I say, secretly thankful that he did. At least this way I know Colin is aware of his father's behavior.

"Yeah, I think I do." He sits on the edge of the bed and turns toward me, those beautiful blue eyes studying me, seeing everything and nothing, all at once. "Do I need to apologize for what happened in the living room before he showed up? The fight and the . . . other stuff?"

Hearing him say that reminds me of exactly what was happening between us in the living room, sending a little shiver down my spine. I'd wanted it. There was absolutely no reason for him to apologize for that. "No," I answer, not wishing to say anything else. Why give him anything else? I'm keeping my lips shut.

"Good." He nods, rubbing the back of his neck and looking decidedly uncomfortable and eager to change the subject. "I called the police when you were in the shower."

"Oh?" I try to sound casual but my voice cracks. "Um . . . what did they say? Any news?"

"They haven't found the guy, no surprise. I spoke to a detective who's supposedly in charge of your case and he didn't know shit." Colin practically spits out the last word, his eyes blazing. Seeing him so angry on my behalf makes me feel good, which is silly but I can't help it.

I love having him champion me.

"I told you they wouldn't care," I remind him.

"Yeah, yeah." He smiles faintly, the sight of it momentarily dazzling me, and I try to focus.

But he makes it so damn difficult when he looks at me like that.

"Have you canceled your bank card yet?" he asks when I don't say anything.

I wince, feeling like an idiot. "I haven't."

"Damn it, Jen." He tunnels those long fingers through his already fucked-up hair again and again, messing it up further, and I lean toward him. My fingers are literally itching to run through all that messy hair so I can tug his head, his lips, closer to mine.

"I'll call right now." I reach for the phone again but he stops me, his fingers circling my wrist, tugging me closer to him instead.

"You make me nervous," he murmurs, drawing me so close our faces are inches apart, our lips perfectly aligned. "You need to take better care of yourself, especially if you're going to do this all on your own."

"I can handle myself," I retort, pissed that he's implying I can't.

"Can you really? I'm . . . worried about you. You've never really lived on your own. And the last time you did, you sort of . . . messed it all up."

Understatement of the year. I can't believe he's talking about when I ran away and lived in my stupid, shitty car. I can't go back to those memories, especially with Colin right in front of me. "There were circumstances beyond my control," I remind him. Remind myself, too. "I hadn't been prepared to handle them."

"See, that's the thing about life. It's always throwing circumstances at you that are out of your control. I don't see how you can possibly be prepared for them now. Look at what happened last night." He sends me a pointed look when I continue to stare at him like an idiot. I can't help that he's so beautiful he completely distracts me. "You're moving out on your own in a matter of days, Jen. How are you going to do this?"

"I know, okay? You don't have to make me feel so dumb. I've been . . . I've had a lot on my mind."

"I'm not trying to make you feel dumb," he says, his voice gentle, his expression full of so much concern he makes me want to cry. "I worry about you. I don't like thinking of you out there on your own."

"I don't need you," I mumble, briefly closing my eyes when I see the pain etched across his face.

I'm such a liar. I need him so much. I just hate that I do.

"I know." His voice lowers to a near whisper. "Sometimes I think I'm the one who needs you more."

Tears threaten and I sniff, trying to fight them off. But it's no use. They start filling my eyes and my lips tremble. God, I'm pitiful. I swear I haven't cried this much since Danny died. I don't want to admit I'm crying over Colin so I play it off and blame it on last night, which is still partly true.

"I keep thinking of him. How easily he knocked me to the ground." I keep my head down so I won't see his eyes, his face. I really don't want to see his reaction. "Hearing his voice when he called me a bitch. It was so intense. So scary."

"Damn it, come here." I glance up to find Colin opening

his arms to me and I go to him, closing my eyes when he draws me in close. I press my face against his throat, breathing in his clean, familiar scent, and I slip my arms around his neck, eager to get closer to him.

"I'm sorry you've had to deal with this," he says against my hair, his voice muffled, his strong arms tightening around my waist and pulling me in as close as he can. "The security company, the lights out in the parking lot—all of it's *my* fault. He assaulted you because I gave him the opportunity to do it."

Shoving at his shoulders with all my might, I leap away from him and stand, resting my hands on my hips. "Stop blaming yourself. What happened, what's happening right now, has nothing to do with what you've done."

He frowns up at me. "What the hell are you talking about?"

"All this . . . fucked-up guilt you hang on to, especially when it comes to me. It's ridiculous. You can't continue to be responsible for everything that happens to me, you know? There's more going on between us—you just don't want to acknowledge it."

Colin ignores what I just said. Typical. "It's not . . . guilt." He can barely choke out the word. "I want to take care of you."

"Like I'm an obligation. Some sort of duty you owe to my brother and my family." I throw my hands up into the air, tired of my own voice. "All we do is talk in circles. I say the same thing, you say the same thing, and then everything's fine. But really, everything isn't fine. We just come back to this. Every. Single. Time."

He stands, towering over me. "I hate this. I hate that you think you're some sort of obligation to me. I hate that we have this same stupid argument over and over again." Reaching out, he grabs me, so hard he makes me gasp as he hauls me toward him. "I don't know what else I can do to prove to you that you're more than an obligation to me. So much more."

Finally. I needed to hear those words. So why won't he ask me to stay? Why won't he say he cares about me and wants me and wishes I would stay with him as his girlfriend or whatever he wants to call me? We don't need to define it. I just want to be with him.

Only him.

CHAPTER 18

Colin

"No more talking," I tell her, my hands at her waist, my fingers slipping beneath her tank so I can touch her bare, warm skin. "All I do is fuck it up when we talk." I remember what Fable told me, how every time Drew opens his mouth when they argue he somehow makes it worse. It appears I'm just like him.

The faintest smile curves her lips and she slowly shakes her head. "You're so right." She pauses, worry mixed with desire filling her gaze. "We seem to do our best together when there's no talking at all, don't you think?"

"Well, you seem to like it when I talk to you a little bit." I settle my mouth on hers, keeping it simple, knowing I won't last like this for long. "Like when I whisper all those dirty words in your ear." I kiss her hungrily, earning a soft moan from her when I delve my tongue deep inside her mouth. She tastes like toothpaste, fresh and minty and with a hint of her own, unique flavor. A flavor I could drown in, live on for the rest of my life.

"We can't solve our problems with sex," she tells me when I break away from her to smother her neck with wet kisses. "They're still going to be waiting for us later. They always will."

"Then we'll deal with them later. I've been dying to lose

myself inside you since last night," I murmur against her throat, nibbling it. I love the feel of her skin against my lips, the scent of her, the slightly tangy taste.

She shivers, her hands at my shoulders, trying to push me. Thinking she's trying to put a stop to what we're doing, I reluctantly back away, only to watch in disbelief as she strips her tank top off, revealing the pretty pink bra she's wearing.

"You want to lose yourself inside me, then let's do it," she says eagerly, her voice trembling as she reaches behind her and unhooks her bra. "I'm leaving soon, Colin. I don't want to waste any more time."

My mouth goes dry when she tosses the bra aside, then pushes her yoga pants and underwear off in one smooth movement. She's naked, my favorite thing in the whole freaking world, and without a thought I push her to the bed, quickly kicking off my flannel pants before I'm pushing myself inside her without any warning. No foreplay, nothing beyond the hungry kisses we shared just now.

I'm that desperate to be inside her.

She must be just as desperate. She's wet and hot, opening completely to me, and I move within her easily, rocking against her. Deep. Deeper. Losing myself in her just like I said I wanted to, closing my eyes and letting pure, delicious sensation take over.

"Fuck, you feel so damn good. Tight and hot," I whisper in her ear, holding her close. A little whispery moan falls from her lips at my words. "I wanna stay right here, deep inside your body and never leave."

"That's going to be—awkward when we eventually have to go to work," she murmurs, her voice hitching with my every thrust. Christ, I love that. Hearing her soft gasps, her sweet moans, those delicious little whimpers I swallow with my mouth. I want to fuck her into oblivion. Hell, I want to be fucked into oblivion, too. No thinking, no talking, no past, no future, nothing but the here and now.

With Jen.

"We'll never work again. We'll never leave this bed," I tell her, my voice earnest, my thoughts earnest, too. I would rather stay here with her forever.

Forever.

"Jenny." I whisper her name against her lips, then kiss her deeply, overwhelmed by my thoughts, by the foreign emotion coursing through my veins, making my chest hurt. I care more for her than any other person in my life, even Danny, even my parents, though that's not difficult.

The realization is frightening. Powerful. Liberating.

Jesus. I can't do this now. I can't feel something for her *now,* when she's dead set on leaving me and nothing seems to stop her. We've been fooling each other this entire time. Pretending to be indifferent, acting like we don't matter to each other beyond friendship. The second she moved in, the chemistry between us started to grow. Until it became too overwhelming and we couldn't ignore it any longer. We've become even closer.

I'm falling for her. Completely.

Pushing all thought from my brain, I let my hands wander all over her body as I start to move fast. Faster. Until we're wrapped tight around each other, both of us crying out as our orgasms take us completely over and we lose ourselves in each other, just like we said we wanted.

But now I realize I want even more.

By the time we escaped my room and started getting ready for work, hours had gone by. My father disappeared, leaving me a vague text that he was out scouting the area, whatever the hell that meant. Jen and I had fallen asleep, the two of us exhausted after everything that happened last night, our fight earlier today, and my dad showing up.

It's been an emotional roller coaster the last twenty-four hours. One we're both still trying to recuperate from.

Nothing is said in regard to our earlier fight and I'm thankful she doesn't bring it up. She finally called the bank and canceled her card, and they'll issue her a new one when she goes into the branch tomorrow. Fortunately, the jackass who stole her purse hadn't used her card.

She's lucky. It could have been so much worse. He could have cleaned out her account. Or taken his rage out on her when he had her lying there on the ground. Just thinking about what could have happened sends me into a quiet, seething rage.

So it's best I don't think about it at all.

I let her work her shift because she argues with me that she's perfectly fine to go in and besides, she doesn't want to be alone with her thoughts. Not quite sure what she means by that, I give in because when it comes to Jen, I always want to give in. I can't help myself.

We're halfway through the night and I'm going over paperwork for the new location when I realize I never did talk to her about the job idea that came to me yesterday. The one that would keep her near me. Now it has even more appeal since I've realized I want more. Despite my lingering guilt, I want her in my life. I want a relationship with her.

And I think she still wants that from me, too, if I can convince her that I mean what I say.

Eager to see her, I go search Jen out in the restaurant, finding her working in the bar, and I call her over. She approaches me with a questioning expression. I let my gaze rake over her as I'm prone to do, taking in her bandaged knees with a smile.

The sight of them reminds me of Jenny the nine-year-old, always falling and scraping up her legs and arms. Always trying to keep up with Danny and me.

"Is everything okay?" she asks, her delicate brows furrowed.

"I want to talk to you," I answer, grabbing her by the crook of her arm and glancing about the room. No one's paying us any mind. "Can you come into my office for a few minutes?"

"Um, it's slow, so sure." She shrugs, letting me lead her out of the bar and down the hall toward my office. "If this is your discreet way of getting me alone again, then that was sort of obvious."

"No one was watching us, I checked." Chuckling, I shake my head. "And I really do want to talk to you. Come on."

Leading her into my office, I wave my hand toward a chair, indicating for her to sit. I leave the door open on purpose, knowing it will both prevent me from jumping her and keep my curious employees from thinking I'm banging Jen on top of my desk.

I would really love to bang her on my desk, but not right now.

"What's up?" she asks the moment I sit. She looks agitated, nervous, her knee bouncing up and down in quick, rhythmic succession.

"I have a proposition for you." I lean my forearms on top of my desk and study her, thinking for about the millionth time how damn beautiful she is. "And I'm hoping you'll say yes."

She lifts her brows. "What sort of proposition are you talking about?"

"Well, you know how I'm opening the Redding location,

right?" It's only about ninety minutes north of here, a city of about one hundred thousand residents who love their chain restaurants. I know The District will do great there.

"Right."

"I need someone to help me run it. And I'd like that person to be you." I pause, letting my words sink in.

Jen stares at me, her mouth dropping open, her eyes going wide. "You're serious."

"Absolutely. This keeps you nearby. Actually brings you closer to your parents, though I'm not sure if you care about that part or not."

She's quiet for a moment, her head bent, as if absorbing what I've asked her. Blowing out a harsh breath, she glances up, her gaze meeting mine. "Colin, I really appreciate the offer, but . . ."

"Don't say no," I interrupt, my heart racing at the realization that she's going to turn me down. I know she is. I can feel it in my bones. "I know you refused my earlier offer of helping out in the office here and I get it. You want to get away from me."

She doesn't confirm or deny my statement, which hurts. And makes me feel like a pussy. Instead of dwelling on my feelings, I forge on.

"You're perfect for the position—you just need a little training, and I can do that. You've worked in the restaurant industry for years and you like to take charge. You're efficient, organized, and everyone looks up to you here as a sort of peacekeeper. You manage the floor without me even asking you to and you do it so naturally."

Her eyes widen with surprise. Did she not realize I notice everything about her? How strong she is, what a tremendous asset she is to my business? I not only care about this woman, I admire the hell out of her.

"I need you, Jen. I need you to help me run that location and it has nothing to do with our personal relationship. I swear it."

She's slowly shaking her head, disbelief written all over her pretty face. "I have zero experience running an entire restaurant. You know this. The idea . . . scares the crap out of me."

I wave my hand. "Whatever you need to know, I can teach you. You learn quickly. You're meticulous and you care. I know you won't screw me over or let the place fail. You're loyal to a fault, and that's hard to find in an employee."

"I—I don't know how to manage people, Colin." She's in denial. It's her best skill in the place. "It would be such a huge responsibility . . . and I feel like you're offering it to me only so you can keep me close." Her gaze goes hard, as if she just figured me all out and doesn't like what she sees. "And Redding is even farther north—and farther away from Sacramento."

"It's close to here," I point out.

"Close to *you*," she corrects. "That's it, right? You're trying to keep me close to you? Why?"

This is my chance. I can tell her how I feel about her. I realized after she was attacked last night how much I care for her. How much I don't want her to leave. This is the moment when I can completely change my life forever.

Nerves jump in my gut like little fish jumping in the middle of an otherwise calm lake and I open my mouth, ready to launch into the speech I've been preparing since late last night. "Jen, I need to tell you—"

A rapid knock sounds on my open office door and I glance up to see my goddamn dad standing in the doorway. "Hey," I say irritably, pissed that he's interrupted us.

"Hey, son, got a minute to talk?" He strides into the room

as if he owns it, flashing a brief smile in Jen's direction. "You understand, don't you, honey?"

"Sure. Of course." She stands, tugging on the hem of her dress self-consciously, her surprised, slightly irritated gaze going to mine briefly before looking away.

"We'll talk about this later," I tell her as she starts toward the door, but she doesn't look back once. Her shoulders are stiff, her back ramrod straight. She looks . . . mad.

I wonder what the hell I could have done to offend her. I make her an amazing offer and she's pissed? I don't get it.

My dad rushes to the door the second Jen exits the room and shuts it, turning the lock with a loud click. He turns to look at me, his hands on his hips. "What the hell are you doing?"

I'm taken aback by the hostile tone of his voice. "What do you mean?"

"Offering that little floozy waitress of yours a *manager* position? Are you crazy? How old is she? Nineteen?"

"She's twenty-two, not that it's any of your business. And you gave me a fucking restaurant when I was only nineteen," I point out. He'd done so out of guilt, and maybe I was doing the same, but damn it, I know Jen is capable. I wish she could see how amazing she is.

"That was different. You're my son." He settles into the very chair Jen just vacated, crossing his leg over his opposite knee. "This is just some little girl you're messing around with. She doesn't know the first thing about running a restaurant."

"Don't call her that," I bite out. "She means something to me. I know you don't understand that sort of thing what with your lack of a heart and all, but I care about her."

"What do you mean, my lack of a heart? Oh, I get it." He chuckles, shaking his head. "I'm sure your mom goes on and on about what a heartless bastard I am, right?"

I ignore what he says. This isn't about my parents. I don't want to talk about my mom. "How the hell do you know anything about Jen anyway? You've never spent any time with her, let alone worked with her."

"I know because I've done a little research." The smirk on his face is aggravating as fuck. Smug and knowing, all at once. "I found out your Jennifer Cade has a little secret."

Dread settles over me, my gut sinking. "What are you talking about?"

"You were wrong, son. She wasn't *just* a stripper at that shitty little club. A real popular one, too, not that I'm surprised." He smiles, looking again like the very shark that he is. "She's also a dirty little whore."

CHAPTER 19

Jen

My head is spinning. Colin wants me to manage his new location? Is he crazy? Is this some sort of handout position? Of course it is. I'm not capable of doing what he wants me to do and he knows it. I have no experience managing a restaurant, running a business, handling all of the office-type day-to-day things. Just thinking about juggling all of that responsibility makes me break out into a sweat.

It's the opportunity of a lifetime, but I'm thinking it's more of an "I must take care of you because you're my responsibility" offer. As usual. Does he really believe in me that much? He claims he does. Or is he making the offer because he wants to keep me around and take care of me?

God, the man makes me feel so confused! As if I can do nothing on my own. It all has to come to me as a handout. And when I do try and do something on my own, I almost always fail.

Almost? Try always, you dumbass.

Or I end up dragging myself through the gutter to make a few bucks just to live.

"You okay?" Fable appears before me, her brows scrunched in concern. "You look a little shell-shocked."

"Colin just offered me a job," I blurt out.

She laughs. "Um, I hate to point this out, but don't you already work for him? Oh wait, let me guess. He asked you to be his personal sex slave. I bet that pays well," she adds with an exaggerated waggle of her brows.

I swat her arm, both irritated and amused at her comment. "Shut up, I'm serious."

"Fine, fine. What sort of job did he offer you?"

"He wants me to manage the new location."

Her smile fades. "You mean the restaurant he's opening in Redding?"

I nod. "The very one."

"Um . . . I thought he already had someone lined up."

"So did I, but maybe not? I don't know. But he just offered me the job, not two minutes ago."

"What did you say?" Fable asks.

"I didn't get a chance to answer. He wouldn't let me, and then his dad walked in just as he was about to say something and interrupted us. The jerk," I spit out.

"His dad is here? Really? Wow." She grimaces. "You don't like him, huh?"

"Not at all." I shudder. The man gives me a bad vibe.

"So what are you going to say to Colin?"

"No, of course. I'm not equipped to handle a job like that. Too much pressure." I shrug, feeling let down and not really knowing why. I wish I were good enough to accept the job. I'd jump all over it. But I'm not confident I could do right by him, running the new location on my own. "Besides, it's just a handout. I'd be his puppet and he'd be pulling all the strings."

"God, Jen, he's making you an amazing job offer and you still look at it as charity. Don't you think he wants you to have the position because he believes in you? It would be a huge risk otherwise." She tilts her head. "You are pretty good at wrangling us around here. Everyone listens to you. You tend to take command when Colin's not around."

She's right, I do. But it's just because I feel comfortable here. Colin's never discouraged me from taking control, either. I appreciate that about him.

But leaving me all on my own, taking care of a restaurant and staff as if I know what I'm doing? The idea alone terrifies me.

"I don't know what to think. We weren't able to talk much before his dad barged in and basically told me to leave," I finally answer.

"He sounds like a great guy," Fable says, her normally sweet voice full of sarcasm.

"He's a winner. Thank God, Colin's not like him." Never, in all the years I've known Colin, has he given me a bad vibe.

His father, on the other hand, had a terrible reputation back in Shingletown. Not that he actually lived there or anything. He'd met Colin's mom on a whim, at some sort of wild concert weekend, or so the story went. I overheard Colin telling Danny the tale once long, long ago and I tried my best to memorize every little detail.

They had a brief affair, Colin's mom became pregnant with him, and she called Conrad Wilder up out of the blue and told him he was gonna be a father. He had a girlfriend at the time who kicked him out of the house they shared, he came to Shingletown, moved in with and married Colin's mom, and they were supposed to live happily ever after.

But they didn't. They lived in a crappy too-small shack, neither of them had a job or the ambition to do anything beyond drink (him) and cause arguments (her), which led to Conrad Wilder bailing on his family right before Colin's first birthday. Even weirder, they're still married.

No wonder Colin has such a messed-up view on relationships. Look at the example his parents gave him.

"Families are strange. I totally get that. When I first met Drew's dad, he creeped me out. Now I realize he was just miserable and in a terrible marriage. He's really not that bad." Fable offers me a reassuring smile. "Maybe Colin's dad is stressed out or overworked. Who knows? I'm gonna say this, though. Ask Colin more questions about this potential job he's offering you. Don't just out-and-out refuse him."

"It doesn't matter. I'm leaving for Sacramento in little over a week, Fable. I lined up a roommate and everything," I protest, wincing when I see the crestfallen expression on Fable's face.

"You found a roommate?" she asks, her voice soft.

"Yeah. We confirmed everything today, as a matter of fact. She seems really nice. I sent her a deposit, so . . ." I hate going on about it. The disappointment is clear in Fable's eyes.

"That's awesome. I'm really happy for you." Fable's jaw goes firm, like she's trying to pretend she's fine. I've seen her give the look before. "But I'm dead serious. Talk to him. See what he's offering."

"Like a handout?" I say, trying to joke but secretly meaning it. All of his handouts have strings. Ones I didn't use to mind, since they always involve Colin watching over me. He rarely likes to let me out of his sight.

But I'm really starting to resent his constant need to take care of me. I want more from him.

"Will you stop saying that? It's like you don't think you're worthy of the praise or something. It's really irritating," Fable says, her gaze going over my shoulder. She stands straighter as her eyes go wide. "Uh-oh, here he comes. And he looks pissed."

"Who?" I start to turn but she hisses at me, making me stop.

"Don't look! It's Colin. Oh my God, he's headed over here. I wonder if his dad made him mad," Fable finishes just as Colin approaches.

"Chatting on *my* time, ladies?" He sends a pointed look at Fable, who for once in her life keeps her lips clamped shut. It's a miracle. "I suggest you get back to work."

Not saying a word, she turns tail and takes off, leaving me alone with a man who is very, *very* pissed off.

And I think it's all directed at me.

"I just spoke to my father," he starts, his voice tight, his eyes narrowed. "He had some interesting information."

"About what?" I ask warily.

"About you." He pauses, waiting for my surprise to settle in. "And what you did when you worked at Gold Diggers."

My knees threaten to buckle, and not in a good way. "Wh—what are you talking about?" I know exactly what he's talking about. I've kept this secret from him for months. Almost a year. I never wanted him to know the truth.

Colin steps closer, glancing around as if to ensure we're alone. "You know exactly what I'm talking about."

Panic flares and my brain scrambles. I didn't want him to find out, especially like this. I want to deny it. I want to pretend this isn't happening, but I can't. So I decide to be completely honest.

Even if the truth might cost me everything.

"You already know I was a stripper there," I admit, my voice small. "I danced, but only for a little while. A few months." Regret crashes through me, but I push it aside. I can't say anything more.

"You're lying to me, Jen. Why would you lie to me? I thought I was your friend." He's starting to yell and I shush him, not wanting to draw any attention.

"We shouldn't talk about it out here." I grab hold of his

arm to try and drag him back to his office but he jerks out of my grip, his expression full of disgust and horror.

All of it aimed directly at me.

"You've had plenty of opportunity to tell me the truth. I need to hear you say it." He spits out the last word. "I could've helped you. You know this. God, Jenny, why did you let them *touch* you?"

Dread consumes me and my head spins. How does he know? He's not saying what he knows but I can tell. He looks positively horrified, and I hate it. Hate that this is a part of my past and he's learned about it from someone else. I should have told him. I should have been honest with him from the start. "I refuse to have this conversation out here where anyone could be listening." I reach for him but he steps back, clearly not wanting to be touched. By me. That hurts. "Let's go to your office. Please."

"No," he says vehemently. "Say it, Jen. Tell me what you let them do to you."

Sighing, I throw my head back, staring at the ceiling for a long minute before I finally look at him. "It was only for a couple of months. I was desperate. I started working there as a cocktail waitress like I told you, but the girls who danced would rake in so much money, I became jealous over what they made. Every single one of them encouraged me to dance and after a while, I finally decided why the hell not? So one night I drank a few shots for liquid courage, got up onstage, and proceeded to make an ass of myself the very first time I danced."

I remember the embarrassing moment like it was yesterday. The men that catcalled me and the others who openly laughed. My dancing skills had been subpar at best and I'd been a little drunk and sloppy on my feet. But after a while, I'd gotten into it and danced with wild abandon.

Glancing at Colin, I see he's glaring at me, expecting me to say more. I don't want to say more.

But I do.

"The money that the men threw at me when I danced felt empowering. I—I became addicted to the tips. I needed that money. I was all alone. Soon I was dancing six nights a week, working as much as I could. Making as much money as I could. After I'd built up some confidence, I started to offer lap dances." I look away from Colin, unable to stand to see his reaction. He must hate me so much. "My tips exploded. I saved and saved, ready to put a deposit down on an apartment of my own so I could get away from my awful roommate when one of her creepy boyfriends snuck into my room when I was at work. He searched through my stuff and found the secret stash of cash I kept in a crappy old shoe box under the bed."

"He stole your money." Colin's voice is flat and I refuse to look at him.

"He took it all. My roommate was pissed when I accused her boyfriend of stealing from me. She kicked me out. I was devastated."

Desperate. Scared.

"Why didn't you call your parents? They would've taken you back in."

"They hardly noticed I was gone!" I look at him now, see that he flinched when I yelled my answer. "I left because I didn't seem to matter to them anymore. No one cared. Going home would've been a step backward."

"So you lived in your car instead." The sarcasm in his voice is thick.

"What was I going to do? I felt like I had nowhere else to go. I was embarrassed, Colin. At the very end of my rope. I did things that I'm not proud of. Not proud of at all." Things

I never even told Fable and she's my closest friend. She's the only one who would probably get it.

Colin rescued me within two weeks of the theft, something I'd never told him about either. I don't like talking about my Gold Digger days.

Clearly, neither does Colin.

"Why didn't you tell me all this? I mean, I knew what you were . . . doing, but I sure as hell didn't know everything." He steps away from me and rubs the back of his neck, looking confused. Hurt. Disappointed.

Completely devastated by my confession.

God. He thinks I'm disgusting for what I've done. And he doesn't even know the half of it. "Why is it any of your business, what I've done with my life?" I know why it's his business—I want him to know. He's one of my closest friends.

And now I'm pretty sure I'm in love with him.

"I'm your friend, Jen. If friends can't be honest with each other . . ." His voice trails off, the implication clear.

I'm nothing but a liar and a slut. How dare he jump to conclusions? How dare he judge me? Yeah, I'm not proud of the things I did, but I had no choice. I was alone. I couldn't go back home; my parents were too wrapped up in their own problems to want to deal with mine. They'd ignored me for years and once they lost my brother, it was as if I didn't exist.

My brother. The only one in my family who really noticed me. The only one who seemed to care as we got older. Now he was dead. I had no one.

Just myself.

"Friends don't treat each other like they're trash. At least, not the ones I know," I say, turning away from him and walking out of the room. I don't stop as I head toward the employee room and go to the short row of lockers. I open mine up, grab the old purse I'd started using again after the robbery, and slam the metal door, heading back out into the restaurant. I storm past Colin, my head held high, my gaze anywhere but on him.

"Where the hell do you think you're going?" he barks after me.

I turn to him, my nose tilted into the air. "I'm leaving."

"You leave right now and you're fired," he threatens.

Oh my God. He means it—I can see the grim determination written all over his face. "So fire me, then." I drop my gaze, refusing to look at him. If I do, I might break down and cry.

"Jenny." He whispers my name and I chance a glance at him. "Talk to me." I see the vulnerability in his eyes, the confusion and the sadness. Maybe some of it is tinged with disgust; I don't know. I can't really tell. All I know is that he's judging me and making me feel even worse about my mistakes than I already do. It's better for me to cut my losses and run. Just like I originally planned.

"Don't make me do this," he continues, his deep voice rumbling with agony. "Don't make me fire you."

"Are you serious right now? Go ahead." I flick my chin at him. "Fire me. It'll give me the excuse to get the hell out of this place even sooner."

CHAPTER 20

Colin

I take Jen's hand and drag her back to my office, not giving a shit if anyone sees us arguing. I'm not letting her leave like this. Not until I hear everything she has to say.

"Tell me *everything*," I say to her when we enter my empty office. Thank God, Dad is gone. My entire body is shaking I'm still so damn angry and agitated over my confrontation with Jen.

"There's nothing else to tell," she says, her voice so low I can barely hear her.

She's lying. There's more. What my dad told me . . . I want it all to be a lie.

But I'm scared it's the truth. I remember finding her in that damn car. Hell, I have nightmares about finding her in that guy's car.

The words Dad said still cloud my brain. I'll have nightmares about them, too. I fucking know it.

"You're holding back," I tell her, desperate for her to be honest with me. I need her trust. I feel like I've broken it and I can't stand it.

She lifts her chin, defiance written all over her pretty features. "You know all that you need to know. You always have. I can't believe you're making a big deal about it now."

The words threaten to burst out of me. I can't ask her if

the story my dad told me is the truth. How he went to Gold Diggers and saw a picture of Jen on the wall. That the bartender told him she was one of their best dancers and rumor had it she took money for sex out in the parking lot when she wasn't dancing.

Jesus.

I need to hear her say it. I want her to trust me enough to confess all.

But she won't. I don't understand why. I won't judge her. Will I? Shit, I don't know.

"All I'm asking is for you to be honest with me," I say, my tone pleading. I sound downright desperate.

And that's because I *am* desperate.

"I already said. There's nothing else you need to know." She crosses her arms in front of her chest. "Is that all?"

"You're not going anywhere," I threaten.

"The hell I'm not."

Damn! I can't believe she's pushing me to this. "You walk out, I'm firing you."

"I'm walking out." Her eyes flicker. I see the worry. The fear. It doesn't stop her from telling me she's leaving.

I harden my jaw, glaring at her. "Fine, you're fired, effectively immediately. I'll have your final check for you later this evening."

"Keep it. I don't want your money," she flings at me as she turns on her heel to leave. "It's full of conditions anyway."

All I've ever done is take care of her. Watch over her. "If making sure you're protected and safe are so-called conditions, then you've never protested before," I call after her as she leaves.

She doesn't turn around. Doesn't say another word. I don't understand her. I'm pretty sure she doesn't understand me, either.

No one does.

Dad enters my office minutes later, slowly shaking his head, his expression somber. No doubt he notices the devastated look on my face, because I'm barely keeping my shit together.

"She tell you?" he asks.

"I don't want to talk about it." I start looking through drawers, looking for . . . what? I don't know. If I look at my dad too long, I might break down and cry like a baby.

He sighs. "She's nothing but a whore, son. You really want a girl like that in your life?"

I leap out of my chair and lunge at him, ramming his big body against the wall so fast, the back of his head thumps the wall hard. My face in his, I glare into his eyes, see the fear and confusion swirling in them. "You call her a whore again and I will tear you apart. Do you understand me?"

He releases a harsh, stuttering breath. "You really care about her that much? Even after everything I told you?"

"I don't turn my feelings on and off like a goddamn light switch," I tell him. "I'm not like you."

Dad's eyes darken with anger. "You don't know me."

"You're damn right I don't know you. You never stuck around much. Hell, it's been over two years since the last time I saw you," I yell, furious at my dad, at Jen, at myself.

What the fuck is wrong with me? With everyone in my life? Everything's hard. Nothing's easy. I'm tired of it. I want my life to be simple. I want to be happy.

I want to be with Jen. But again, it's not that easy.

"You never seemed to want me around. Your mother deterred me from being a part of your life every chance she got," he throws back at me.

Stunned by his words, I release my hold on him and step away. "What did you say?"

"You think I didn't want to be a part of your life? You

think I stayed away from you because I wanted to?" He brushes his hands down his front, straightening his shirt that I wrinkled, then runs them through his hair, smoothing out the unruly strands. "Your mother did her best to keep me away from you."

"Why?" I don't believe him. I know she hates him, but she wouldn't force him to stay away from me . . . would she?

I hid away and cried a lot when I was a kid, wishing my dad cared enough to want to spend time with me. She knew this after finding me more than once. I'd been jealous of what Danny had with his dad. A solid, loving father/son relationship. They would go out in the yard and toss a baseball or football back and forth to each other. They'd go fishing together. They included me all the time, always making me feel welcome, but deep down inside, I felt like an intruder. A jealous, unloved interloper.

"She was afraid I'd take you away from her, I think. I don't know. Our getting together was nothing but a chance encounter gone completely out of control. When she told me she was pregnant with you, I tried to do the right thing and marry her. I looked forward to being a father." He pauses and takes a deep breath, his shoulders slumping against the wall he's still leaning against. "Within days of moving in with her, I knew we'd made a bad decision. We didn't get along. We fought all the time. She hated me, resented that I'd impregnated her and took away her freedom."

There's that damn word again. *Freedom*. Jen constantly struggles for it and I constantly try to hold her down. Maybe I'm more like my father than I know.

"I always thought it was you who wanted to stay away," I say, my voice surprisingly calm. Though my head is spinning with everything I've discovered. "Mom said you hated Shingletown and that you were desperate to get away."

He laughs, but there's not much humor in the sound. "Your mom is right. I hated that stupid little mountain town. There was nothing to do, no good jobs. I was struggling. My father had cut me off, was dying and I had no idea. Twenty-eight years old and I should've had my head on straight, you know? I should've had it all figured out by then. But I was nothing but a big kid who wanted to party. I had no real responsibilities. Until you came along."

I had no freaking idea he felt this way. That he suffered with all of this. Of course, he's never really explained himself to me, while my mother would bad-mouth him every chance she got. Still does. I could call her at this very minute and she would call Conrad Wilder the scum of the earth and whatever other horrible name she could come up with.

"So why didn't you two divorce?" That's the one thing that's tripped me up my entire life. If they hated each other so much and couldn't live together, why not get a divorce and be done with it?

"It sounds stupid, but I don't want her out of my life. Crazy, right? Maybe we're just lazy. I don't know." He sounds like he's trying to convince himself. "We've always stayed in contact, your mom and I."

I'm stunned. "Are you serious?"

"Yeah." His chuckle deepens. "We fight most of the time when we talk, so . . ."

Okay, now I'm completely freaked out. "But . . . I thought you hated each other."

"We do. We don't. I don't know. Don't question it, son. Even I don't get it." Pushing away from the wall with a heavy sigh, he goes to a chair and plops down in it. "We may drive each other crazy, but we've always had a connection."

I don't even want to know about this connection. "Have you two seen each other since you . . . first left?"

217

He smiles ruefully. "We have. Never for long, though—we can't be in the same room for more than a day or two before we start arguing."

Sounds familiar. Though Jen and I argue more because we fight our feelings for each other.

I want more with her, but I need to hear the whole truth from her lips. Maybe what the bartender at Gold Diggers told my dad is a lie. I hope it is.

But if it's not . . . then I can deal. I have to deal. She's the only woman I want in my life.

I love her.

Jen

I find a taxi parked a few blocks down from The District and hop in the backseat, rattling off Colin's address and demanding the driver take me there.

"I'm off duty, girlie," he grumbles, starting up the car anyway and shifting into park. "I'm taking a break."

"Please," I say, not about to make a promise of a big tip. He'll probably think I mean something sexual, and that's the last thing I want to deal with.

"Fine." He pulls out onto the street, turning up the radio, and I'm thankful for the sound of the mindless popular song filling the interior of the cab.

The song doesn't chase away my depressing thoughts, though. I should be relieved Colin confronted me, not that I really told him anything. I need to get out of here quick.

And I need to make sure he never, ever finds out everything. I don't like to think about it. It's scary to face what you might do when you're desperate enough. I hate that I let myself become so weak. But I'd been trying my best to earn back all the money I lost. Dancing every night, working for hours in the exclusive lap dance room, touching those men in the most intimate of places in the hopes they would give me extra-big tips, which they did . . .

When the first one propositioned me, I turned him down. I turned plenty of them down. But after everything was stolen and I needed money quick, I finally, reluctantly, agreed one night. At least that guy was handsome. Probably in his early thirties and lonely after a bitter divorce, he told me all about his problems when we met after I got off work. He was nice and kind and gentle, and so very, very nervous. He'd asked for sex at first, but I told him I would only give him oral, so . . . I did.

And felt like the lowest of the low when he pressed the hundred-dollar bill in my palm after I finished. What had I done? What had I become?

A prostitute. A common whore.

I couldn't go back home. Couldn't face my parents after everything I'd done. I was ashamed. Disgusted with myself because I didn't stop after that first time. I did it again. And again.

"Here we are, girlie," the taxi driver says. Interrupting my depressing thoughts, thank God. I didn't want to go there and ended up doing it anyway. "That'll be twenty-two dollars."

I dig through my purse and hand him a twenty and a five as I exit the car, slamming the door behind me. He takes off with a roar, leaving me alone on the sidewalk, the night seeming to close in on me. It's cool, the sky is dark and moonless, and the street is quiet. Past ten o'clock, and pretty much everyone has gone to bed since it's mostly families who live on this street.

Colin and I are the exception. We're definitely not family. Not even close.

Starting up the front walk, I pull out my key and unlock

the door. As soon as I enter the house, car lights from outside illuminate the still dark interior and I hear the garage door start to open. My stomach drops into my toes and my mouth goes dry.

Colin's home.

Swallowing hard, I try to fight off the wave of nausea that threatens and head to the kitchen, where I pour myself a glass of water. I chug it down, wipe my mouth with the back of my hand, and brace myself against the kitchen counter as I wait for him to enter the house.

Better to face him head on than run off and hide in my room. Not that I'm staying long anyway. He'll no doubt kick me out and I'll end up going to Sacramento early. I bet Jason would help me out if I asked him. Maybe I could break down and spend the money to rent a moving truck. I'll call my new roommate first thing tomorrow and see if I can move in a few days sooner. I have a feeling she won't mind. This way I can get settled and find a job right away.

Hopefully.

Finally, Colin enters the house, stopping short when he sees me leaning against the kitchen counter. "How did you get here?"

No *hi, I was worried,* just a *how did you get here,* like he doesn't want me in his house any longer. Oh, how quickly our attitudes change! "I took a taxi."

"A taxi?" he asks incredulously. "How did you find a taxi downtown?" They're usually pretty scarce, so I understand his questioning.

"I don't know." I shrug. Why are we even having this inane conversation? "He was a few blocks down from the restaurant and off duty. I climbed into his car anyway and asked him to drive me here, so he did."

"Jesus." He runs a hand through his hair, clearly frustrated. "I swear to God, your risky behavior is going to get you into serious trouble someday. He could've hurt you."

"I'm a big girl. Besides, didn't I get my quota in this week already when it comes to being attacked by creepy strangers?" I sound like a smug little bitch but I can't help myself. When I feel cornered, I get defensive.

He stares at me as if I've grown two heads. "We need to talk," he says slowly.

"What about?" I lift my chin, going for defiance, but my entire body begins to tremble. I'm this close to falling completely apart.

"About what you did when you worked at Gold Diggers." He flicks his head toward the direction of the living room. "Let's go sit down."

I brace my hands against the edge of the countertop, icy dread slithering down my spine. How did he find out? I know he knows, and I can hardly stand it. "I don't want to. Let's talk here."

"Fine. Whatever." Resting his hands on his hips, he glances around the darkened kitchen. The only light on is the one over the sink. He's frustrated, I can tell. I know him almost as well as I know myself, though I would never have figured he'd react to my secret like this.

Maybe I was foolish to believe he would be more understanding. Maybe it has something to do with the way he found out and not the actual information itself. I should have been the one who told him and I didn't. Someone else beat me to the punch.

I'm at a loss, though, unsure how to explain myself.

"I don't know what you want me to say. I'm sure you don't want to hear all the dirty details." A shudder moves through me, and his eyes narrow. "Not that there are many dirty details . . ." My voice trails off. I'm trying to defuse the situation and not doing a very good job of it.

"Did you sleep with men for money?" He asks the question so quietly, so suddenly, I need to grip the counter tighter for fear I'll slither to the floor. My knees are reduced to jelly by his words, by the look on his face. I wish I could just disappear and forget all of this ever happened.

"What are you talking about?" I whisper, trying to stall. Desperate to stall. I can't lie to him. I have to tell him the truth or I'd never forgive myself. He wouldn't believe me if I denied it anyway. He's already made his assumptions and I'm living up to them.

"Answer me." He raises his voice, the sound sending goose bumps scattering over my arms, and I part my lips. No sound comes out.

I can't deny it because it's true.

"Did you?" he asks again, his voice rough, his eyes full of agony as he storms toward me. He grabs me by my upper arms, his hold firm as he gives me a little shake. "Tell me, God damn it! Did you, Jen?"

I jump when he yells at me, wincing at the fury behind his words. Tears fill my eyes, momentarily blinding me, and then they're flowing down my cheeks, dropping from my face onto the floor. "Yes," I sob, my chest threatening to burst. "I did, okay? Is that what you want to hear? That I fucked around with other men and they paid me?"

His eyes go wide and I swear they shimmer with tears. Actual freaking tears, and I've never seen this man cry beyond the dry sobs in his dreams.

But are those tears for me? Or for the fact that he failed me and broke his promise to my brother? To my family?

"God Jen, I can't believe . . . *why?* Why the hell would you do that? What would your parents think? Or Danny?"

Tearing myself out of his hold, I back away from him, shaking my head. "Don't put all that guilt on me. I do that well enough on my own, trust me."

"You know you could've called them. They would've helped you. You're their daughter." He stresses the last word, and that only pisses me off further.

"Give me a break! They forgot all about me once Danny died. So wrapped up in their grief, he was all they could talk about. You're the same way, with your nightmares about him. He's always hovering in everyone's mind, and I get it. He's in mine, too. But he's gone. We have to keep on living," I cry, wondering how my speech changed track.

"So by living, does that mean you go out doing whatever the hell you want and getting paid for it?"

His words are like a slap in the face. I rear back, my cheeks stinging with embarrassment. He immediately realizes his mistake and starts toward me, but I shake my head, my body vibrating with anger.

"Jen, I'm sorry," he starts to say, but I hold up my hand, silencing him.

"Save it. You'll never understand. No one would. I shouldn't have to defend myself. I was all alone and no one could've saved me. I had nothing." I start to leave the kitchen, ready to make my escape into my bedroom where I can have a good cry. And after I cry, I'll start to pack.

No way can I stay here beyond one more night. This arrangement is over.

"You always had me. Always. I saved you," he reminds me as I exit the room. Pausing, I keep my back to him, waiting for him to say more, which he does. "And I would've come in and saved you sooner if you'd called me. I'd do anything for you, Jen. Remember?"

"Can you forget what I've done?" I slowly turn to face him, scared of what I might find. But I'm facing a blank, expressionless mask.

He blinks once. Twice. The only physical reaction I can see. "I don't know," he says truthfully.

Whoever said the truth hurts was dead on. But it's beyond hurting. It's like a million knives carving into my chest, tearing my heart completely apart.

I don't know if I'll ever be able to put it back together.

CHAPTER 21

Colin

It feels like I'm being taken to the gallows, ready to meet my maker. I'm facing him now, my head bent, my body shaking. He towers over me on a pedestal, his face in shadows.

"You disappointed me," he says, his voice eerily familiar.

I can only offer a small nod, too frightened to speak. I've never been more scared in all my life. It's one thing to know you won't live forever. It's quite another to face your mortality and know it's over.

"You haven't lived your life like I expected you to." He pauses, his breathing heavy, the mood, the darkness that surrounds us, foreboding. "You failed so many people."

"I know." My voice cracks and I clear my throat. I feel like I'm seven years old again. Facing the facts that my dad doesn't care about me and that my mom is bitter and angry all the time. That I have no one in my life who is pure and good, with the exception of Danny and Jenny.

I love them like they're my own family. And I failed them both. I know who this mystery demon is referring to. I don't need the reminder.

"Look at me," the voice commands and I glance up, surprise rendering me completely still when he sheds his hood and reveals that it's Danny who's standing before me. "You let me down. Then you let my sister down."

I was so scared, and all along it's just been Danny standing there. Trying to intimidate me and make me feel bad. For the first time since I can remember, I'm angry. Furious that he's trying to blame me for everything.

Is it really all my fault? Have I been wrong all this time, carrying the guilt around like a shackle around my neck, constantly weighing me down?

"You weren't supposed to sign up for the Marines without me," I point out to him indignantly. We were supposed to do it together. We'd planned it all out, set up a meeting time and everything.

Then my dad showed up, offering me the opportunity I knew would change my life. I'd been so excited to tell Danny, to include him in my good news. We could run the restaurant in Southern California together. Finally we would be able to leave that crap town, have all the women we could ever want, and find success.

Instead, I discovered that he went ahead and signed up without me. No way was I going now. He was furious with me. Disappointed that I wouldn't go with him.

And then he went away and ended up dead.

"I did what I had to do," he says solemnly, his expression hard. Completely unreadable. Though his features are the same, he looks nothing like my best friend. The friend I still miss terribly.

"So stop blaming me for your death," I say, my voice rising.

"Stop blaming yourself," he returns. Sighing heavily, his gaze narrows as he studies me, his eyes so dark they almost appear black. "It's not your fault, what Jenny did."

He called her Jenny. I feel like we're teenagers again, taunting her with the nickname she one day out of the blue deemed childish and silly. We kept calling her Jenny for a solid year just to aggravate her, until their mother finally stepped in and asked us to stop.

So respecting her wishes, we did. I always missed calling her Jenny, though. It's a sweet name, for a sweet girl. Who'd eventually grown up into a sweet and sexy woman.

A woman who sold her body and performed sexual acts for money.

Fuck. I can't get over it.

"You need to get over it," Danny says, as if he can reach inside my thoughts. "Sometimes, we're put into situations we don't know how to get out of. She didn't know how to ask for help. She thought she was doing what was necessary to survive."

"I don't know if I can let it go," I confess, hanging my head in shame. Who am I to judge? I've done many things I'm ashamed of. And Jen has never judged me for any of them.

"Do you love her?" Danny's voice is fierce, and I glance up to see his expression is thunderous. He looks as if he wants to reach out and choke me.

I take a step back, stunned by his reaction, by his words. "I . . . yes. I do." Fuck. The admission staggers me so much my knees threaten to buckle. Reaching out, I brace my hand on the wall, breathing deep, trying to calm my racing heart.

"Then fight for her. Tell her how you feel."

"I can't." The words fall from my lips, broken and sad. I fall to my knees, unable to hold myself up any longer. "I want to but I can't. I said things that hurt her. I might not be able to get past what she did." Despair consumes me, blinds me. "I've ruined it between us."

Danny kicks at my chest, forcing me to look up at him. I

feel small. Powerless. While he's so tall and commanding, standing over me, radiating power and strength.

But he's dead, I remind myself. How can he be stronger than me when he's been dead for nearly two years?

"You keep acting like this and you'll ruin it," he says, his voice like a hiss. "If you can't let go of the past, let go of everything you've done and everything she's done and focus on the here and now, then I can't save you. She can't save you either. You need to live for the present. You and her together."

"I'm afraid she hates me."

"She doesn't hate you. She could never hate you." Danny smiles and shakes his head. "She loves you. She's loved you for years. You've been blind to it all this time."

The realization hits me square in the chest. Jen loves me. I've ignored her, treated her like crap, smothered her with too much attention, fucked her, yelled at her and called her a whore, and she loves me.

I don't deserve her.

"I don't deserve her," I cry, repeating my thoughts. "I don't deserve any of the love she feels for me."

Danny kicks me again, his smile growing. "You really believe that? Then fine. You're right. You don't deserve her. You don't deserve anything good in your life. You're a worthless piece of shit who won't amount to anything."

I open my mouth, ready to protest, but no sound comes out.

"That's right. Don't bother arguing with me because you know it's true." He bends down, his face in mine, his dark eyes staring at me as though he can see that I'm nothing. "Worthless. Just like your father. Just like your mother always said."

"No!"

"Worthless." He's starting to chant, his voice grating on

my nerves, and I clamp my hands over my ears, trying to tune him out. But it's as if his voice has insinuated itself into my brain and it's all I can hear. "A no-good, stupid loser. Didn't your mother use to say that about your father?"

"I'm nothing like him," I protest.

"You're everything like him. You even look like him. You're doomed, Colin. You are turning into your father." Danny kicks me yet again, straight in the gut this time, and I keel over, clutching my ribs. "And there's nothing you can do about it."

I wake up with a jolt, my eyes flashing open, seeing nothing but darkness. My lungs ache with my labored breathing and my entire body is shaking.

Fuck. What a dream. Like nothing I've ever had before.

"Sshh." A soft, sweetly familiar voice breaks the silence and then I feel her. Her hands slide soothingly over my body, down my chest, pressing against my heart. "You're okay. It was just a dream."

It's Jen. After everything I said and did to her, that she would still come to my bed and try to comfort me is . . . overwhelming.

I'm nothing but a selfish asshole, while she constantly gives and gives and gives. And all I do is take.

You give to her, too, jackass. You might not let her know exactly how you feel about her but you're always there. You always want to take care of her.

Yeah, I need to work on that—if she'll still let me.

I slip my arms around her waist before she can make her escape. I've never been more grateful to find her in my bed. She feels damn good, her long, bare legs tangling with mine, her hair brushing against my chin. I breathe deep her scent, holding it, wishing I could keep it with me at all times.

"Was it a bad one?" she asks as she wraps her arms around me and hauls me in close. "You called out my name."

"I did?" I don't remember doing that in the dream, but hell. It was all happening so fast, Danny's words coming at me, carving me up and destroying me like lethal weapons.

"Yeah." She sighs against my bare chest, I feel the gust of warm breath, and like a bastard, my body tightens in response. "You sounded angry. And sad."

I definitely experienced both emotions in my dream. But I want to forget them, push them aside and focus on the woman I have in my arms at this very moment.

The woman I love.

"Jen, I need to say something to you." I take a deep breath, ready to launch into an apology, a plea, to offer her whatever words I can to convince her to stay and never leave me again.

"Don't. Please." She shifts up, her fingers pressing against my mouth to silence me. "There's no need to say anything. I know how you feel."

The hell she does. I part my lips, fully intending to forge on, but before I can get a word out she replaces her fingers with her mouth and kisses me.

Just like that, I'm lost. In the taste of her soft, hungry mouth, in the feel of her warm, slender body. I roll over onto my back and she follows, lying on top of me, our mouths searching, our tongues seeking.

"Make love to me," she whispers against my lips. "One last time, Colin. Please."

One last time? If I have anything to say about it, this is just the beginning. I want to tell her that. I need to tell her how I feel but she's kissing me again, long, hot, drugging kisses that push all rational thought out of my brain, and I'm done for.

Jen

I know I shouldn't do this, but I want just one more chance with him before I go. That's all I'm asking for. I know that together, we're not going to work. He can't deal with my past and what I've done. I can barely deal with it, so how can I expect acceptance from him?

I'd lain awake forever, unable to sleep, my body too restless, my brain too busy with my thoughts, my worries. I heard him yell, though I couldn't understand what he'd said. He sounded so angry, though. Until I heard him call my name.

And then he just sounded sad. Pitiful.

Unable to resist, I'd gone to him just like all the other nights I snuck into his room. He lay in bed clad in just his underwear, the sheets twisted around his legs, baring him to my gaze. His golden hair an absolute mess, the strain and worry his dream was causing him written all over his gorgeous face.

Without thought I slipped into bed with him, untangling the sheet and pulling it over the both of us. He turned to me in his sleep, as if he knew I was there and sought me out. My heart flipped over in my chest and I snuggled close to him, desperate to offer him the comfort he needs one last time.

"I love you," I whispered against his chest, feeling safe knowing he wasn't awake. "I wish you could see that and accept it."

When he finally wakes up, he looks so pleased to find me in his bed that I know we're going to have sex. I want it, literally crave feeling him move within me.

His kisses set me on fire. His hands are all over my body, touching me reverently, as if I am special. I believe that in his eyes, his mind, I *am* special, and the thought fills me with so much warmth, so much love, I almost want to cry.

I focus instead on him. On his beautiful body, the way he looks at me when I put my mouth on his in a hard, hot kiss. I kiss him everywhere, memorizing his every line and muscle with my lips, branding him as mine.

Because he is mine. We will belong to each other forever, even if we can't be together.

I strip his underwear off with trembling fingers, touching him everywhere I can. His stomach, his legs, his erection. His hands shake when he reaches for me and helps me shed my clothes. Within minutes we are a tangled mess of arms and legs, our mouths fused, our bodies connected, as he pushes inside me. So deep, I cry out in pure, exquisite pleasure.

I asked him to make love to me, and God, he does, so perfectly. This isn't a fast, hard coming together for us. He takes his time with me, as do I with him. His touch, his mouth and hands and fingers, are gentle, reverent, searching as they skim over my body, paying particular attention to all the right places. The spots he knows arouse me, give me so much pleasure I'm afraid I might fall completely apart far too soon. I feel worshiped, beautiful, loved.

Loved.

Maybe I'm reading too much into it. Maybe I'm projecting my own feelings onto him, but I feel so completely connected to him in this very moment. As if he understands me and I understand him. That we're able to toss aside all past hurts and mistakes and are both finally ready to focus on the here and now.

Wishful thinking, I suppose, since I know it's not true. But I can't help it.

And when he moves inside me so deep, deeper, until he's a complete and total part of me, my orgasm slowly takes over, washing over my skin, through my veins, pulsing through my bones. It feels like an awakening. A realization. My breath lodges in my throat, my belly flutters, and my heart threatens to leap out of my chest.

I've never felt so lost, so found, so utterly . . . confused.

So fitting. I've been confused when it comes to Colin since the day I met him.

"I hate that I'm taking part in this," Fable whispers to me when I meet her at the curb in front of Colin's house. She'd driven Drew's truck over to pick me up. I'd texted her hours ago, basically begging her to do it. She agreed, no questions asked, but now she's balking. Can I blame her? It's five in the morning, the sun isn't even up yet, and I'm leaving like a thief in the night.

For good.

"Well, I really appreciate you taking part in this because I don't know how I'd get out of here otherwise." I throw my one suitcase into the backseat of Drew's extended-cab truck and climb into the passenger seat, looking at Fable expectantly. "You ready to go?"

She's sitting in the driver's seat, looking exceptionally tiny in such a huge vehicle, her small hands gripping the steering wheel. Her long blond hair is piled on top of her head in a sloppy bun and her sleepy-looking face is devoid of makeup, but she's still beautiful. She wears Old Navy sweats and a T-shirt, fake Uggs covering her feet. I'm wearing almost the same damn thing in different colors, though I don't bother pointing out that we're practically twinsies.

Now is not the time for cutesy-type stuff. I need to make my escape. And Fable is uncomfortable enough already with the situation.

"You should tell him you're leaving," she blurts out, her imploring eyes meeting mine. "It's the least you can do."

"I left him a note." I tear my gaze away from hers, staring

at the dark, quiet house. That was the hardest thing I've ever done, walking away from him. Leaving his bed while he lay there sleeping peacefully . . . I'd wanted to slip right back beneath the covers and hold him close. Never let him go.

But I didn't. I had to go. It was best for both of us.

At least, that's what I tell myself.

"A note is a really chicken-shit thing to do," Fable says softly. "Trust me, I hate notes. It's much better to pour out your feelings to someone in person."

"You love Drew's poems," I point out. "And he's always pouring his heart out in those." A big, buff football player with a romantic heart, the guy is downright swoon-worthy.

My overprotective, sort-of-demanding Colin is swoon-worthy, too. I just refuse to think about him like that any longer. It's too hard. My heart hurts, I miss him so much.

And I haven't even left him yet.

"Yeah, I love his poems now. But when he first left me, he left behind a note that both broke my very soul and filled me with so much hope that I knew he'd come back to me." She smiles, but it's sad. "He didn't."

"What?" I'm incredulous. "What are you talking about?" I thought they were perfect for each other. That they had the perfect relationship. Yeah, I knew they had some trouble and things were rocky at first, but I had no idea he'd bailed on her and didn't come back.

"Remember that night when the frat boys were having the party and Drew was there? And he almost got into a fight with that one asshole?" Fable shudders at the memory.

"Yeah, of course I remember." That had been quite the drama-filled evening. It had also brought Fable and me closer together. I realized then that she could become my friend.

And she did. She's now my very best friend and I'm leaving her, too.

"That was the first night I saw him after over two months," Fable admits.

Here I thought their relationship was the ideal we should all aspire to. "Fable, I had no idea . . ."

She waves a hand, dismissing my words, clearly uncomfortable with my sympathy. "Yeah, yeah. It was a mess, but eventually we figured everything out and made it work, so look at us now. We're getting married."

Jealousy clutches at my heart, makes me wish I could have that easy acceptance from Colin, but I know it's never going to happen. He will forever hold what I did in the past against me. I can't blame him.

I hold it against me, too.

"Whatever he did," she says softly, breaking through my thoughts, "whatever you've done, none of it matters if you love each other enough."

I really hate when she pulls the mind-reader stuff. "I wish I could believe that," I mutter resentfully. "You make it sound so easy."

"It *is* easy when you face all your problems together. Easier, I should say. Fighting your battles separately won't work. Trust me. The battles just grow larger and longer."

"Please don't lecture me and try to keep me here," I whisper, my voice nothing but a ragged rasp. "We need to go, Fable. Now. He might wake up and realize I'm gone."

Her lips disappearing into a thin line, she shifts the truck into drive and pulls away from the sidewalk, driving slowly through the neighborhood I've lived in for little over a year. Tears threaten as I stare at the houses that we pass by and I don't hold them back, letting them flow freely down my cheeks.

"Why, Jen?" Fable's sad voice makes me turn and look at her. "Why are you leaving when you so clearly don't want to?

What's so bad about this place, huh? You have me, you have Drew, you have everyone who works at The District, and you have Colin. We all support you and care about you. So why won't you stay?"

I rub the back of my neck, my fingers tracing over the stupid, beautiful tattoo. Colin cares for me. Perhaps he even loves me. Can he accept what happened? What I did? I don't know. We may have had sex and shared a beautiful moment together, but we didn't talk about anything.

Before I give myself—and my heart—to Colin completely, I need to make sure he's ready. And I don't think he's there yet.

So it's best to get it over with now, right? Leave him before he can really break my heart . . .

"There's more going on than you know," I admit to Fable, my voice shaky, my stomach roiling. I feel sick; I've hardly eaten anything since lunch yesterday and I think I might puke. Closing my eyes briefly, I try to stop the tears, searching for some sort of inner strength. "I've done things in my past I'm not proud of."

"I thought he knew you were a stripper?" she asks gently.

Nodding, I brush at the tears still streaming down my cheeks. "There's other stuff, too. Bad stuff I couldn't tell you." I take a deep, shuddering breath. "Really bad stuff, Fable. You might hate me for it. I know he does."

Fable pulls over the truck and puts it into park, then turns to look at me. "Whatever you've done, I don't care. It will never, ever bother me because you're my friend and I will never judge you. You can choose to tell me all about it or keep it your secret—I totally understand and respect your decision." She pauses, her gaze gentling, so full of genuine concern it makes me want to cry harder. Just collapse in her arms and absorb some of her strength for a while. "But if you want to talk about it, I'm here for you. I want you to know that."

I nod, hardly able to speak, too overcome by her kind and easy acceptance. "I—I let men pay me money for sex," I blurt out, needing to tell her, needing to get everything off my chest.

She doesn't blink, doesn't react whatsoever, though I see sympathy fill her gaze. "Oh Jen . . ."

"I know, right? I'm nothing but a whore. Not that I got paid for having intercourse with anyone, but I handed out blow jobs for cash." I shake my head, disgusted at the words, at the realization of what I've done. I cheapened myself. Sold my body like a common slut. I'm so ashamed, I wish I could crawl inside a hole and never, ever come out.

"You did what you had to do, I'm sure." Fable reaches for me over the center console and I go to her, letting her envelop me in a hug. She holds me close, patting my back, making soothing noises as I start to cry in earnest on her shoulder. I can't believe I'm falling apart like this. Talk about embarrassing.

But it also feels good. Liberating. This secret has boiled within me for so long, I thought I might burst. I believed I could forget all about it. Just push the dirty memories from my mind and pretend it never happened.

It did happen, though. I can't forget it. Everyone thinks I'm good, sweet, and kind Jen, but I'm not. I'm a fraud.

"I don't know how Colin found out, but he knew everything. *Everything.*" My voice chokes up and I shake my head. "God, I hated the way he looked at me. Like I was the most disgusting thing on this planet."

"I doubt that. I've seen the way he looks at you and it's more like you're the sexiest, most beautiful woman on this planet in his eyes," Fable says. "He loves you, Jen. He has to. I'm sure he can look past your mistakes and forgive you."

"Yeah, well, I doubt that," I mutter, wishing what Fable said were true.

But wishes are for fools. So I guess I'm one of them.

CHAPTER 22

Colin

"She's gone, and I think you know where she went," I growl into my cell phone, not giving a shit who might hear me. "So you'd better fuckin' tell me."

I'm at work, the place is bustling, and I'm hiding out in my office, seeking privacy though I keep the door wide open. Maybe one of my employees will overhear me and offer up some information about Jen. I have my suspicions. I'm guessing she fled to Sacramento early, but I want confirmation.

And then I want to go to Sac and find her so I can bring her back here. To her home, where she belongs.

With me.

"Don't you dare curse at me, Colin. I know you're my boss, but that gives you no right to talk to me like that." Fable sighs, sounding completely put out that I'm calling her, but I really don't give a shit. "Listen, it's my day off and I don't have time to deal with you right now. I'm exhausted. Maybe we can talk about this tomorrow."

She's being just as rude as I am. I can tell when she's trying to avoid something and she is most definitely trying to avoid me. The little sneak. She knows everything—I can feel it in my bones. "Did you help her leave this morning?"

Finding Jen gone, her stuff packed up and her bedroom empty, made me lose my shit. As in, I threw a framed picture of Danny and me against the wall, the glass shattering all over the floor. I'd felt only a hint of satisfaction at destroying something before the remorse kicked in.

And the sadness. Then the anger.

Jesus, I really know how to fuck things up.

Fable is silent for so long I'm afraid she hung up, until she finally says one, simple word.

"Yes."

Okay. Now we're getting somewhere. "Tell me where you took her, Fable. I need to know. I need to find her."

"Why, so you can chase her down and force her to come back to work for you after you fired her? Pretend that everything is exactly the same? Because it's so not and you know it." She pauses. "I know what she told you, Colin. What she did. She admitted everything to me. And you're being a complete jackass for not accepting her in spite of it. It shouldn't matter. It's all a part of her past. You need to forget about it and focus on the present."

Damn it, she sounds just like Danny in my dream. I know Fable is right, but I can't help myself. It both breaks my heart and fills me with uncontrollable rage, what Jen's done. How she cheapened herself when she's worth so much more. "I know. You're right," I murmur. "So if I'm going to accept what happened and fight to bring her back here, I need to know where she is. I need you to tell me."

"I took her to the bus station," Fable admits grudgingly, her voice soft. "She was going to Sacramento. She got it all arranged with her new roomie and she's moving in early."

Just as I thought, but I need more. "And where does her new roommate live? What part of the city?"

"That I'm not sure. She mentioned Citrus Heights, I think, but I don't know. One of those suburbs out there that's close to Sacramento. That's as far as it went, though, information-wise."

"And what about her address? Did you get that?" It's a long shot, but I have to ask.

"No." Fable sighs. "I told her to text me when she got there and she said she would, but she hasn't. And she should've been there by now."

Worry claws at my throat. Jen bought a new cell; she'd picked it up yesterday afternoon before work. I already tried to call her. Text her. Multiple times. I left her a few pleading, desperate voice-mail messages. She hasn't responded to any of them. And that stupid, useless note she left on my pillow, for the love of God, had been nothing. Just remembering it pisses me off.

> *Thank you for everything you did for me. You mean more to me than you'll ever know. I'll miss you.*
>
> *Take care,*
> *Jen*

She signed it fucking *Take care*. What the hell? I don't even merit a *Love, Jen*. She didn't even acknowledge me by name.

"Have you talked to her? She hasn't answered any of my calls or texts," I say, running a hand through my hair.

"I've tried. She hasn't answered my calls or texts either." She sounds downright exasperated. *Great*. The feeling's mutual. "I'm worried, too, you know. I didn't want to take her to the bus station. I tried my best to convince her to stay."

I know Fable's telling the truth. She didn't want Jen to leave either. "Let me know if you hear from her, okay? And I'll do the same for you."

241

"Okay. Yeah, that sounds good." She sighs. "I'm sorry I yelled at you, Colin. I'm just worried about her."

"So am I." I hang up before I say something really stupid and pitiful, glancing up at my open doorway to find my dad standing there, looking almost afraid to come inside.

Great. He's the absolute last person I want to see. "Weren't you leaving to go see Mom?" I ask.

Chuckling, he enters the room and settles into one of the chairs that sit across from my desk. "I'm taking off later today. She's working."

I lift my brows. Well. That's news to me. "Where at?"

"The diner in the next town over. You know, the one that your Jennifer Cade used to work at?" How the hell he knows this stuff about Jen is beyond me. It's like the guy keeps up on the small-town gossip even long after he's gone. "That's what your mother told me, at least."

Ah, well that makes more sense. Mom always did like Jen. "I'm still mad at you." I decide to be forthright with him and not beat around the bush. A new thing for me, since I'm usually all about avoiding confrontation.

He blows out a harsh breath. "You needed to know, son. It's best you have all the facts when you're dealing with a woman. You don't want to end up like me and your mother."

That's the damn truth. Funny thing is, though, even after I learned the truth, I'm realizing that I still want Jen. That I'm in love with her and will do whatever it takes to get her back into my life.

"Did she admit to everything?" he asks when I don't speak.

I nod. I really don't want to have this discussion with him, so I don't go into too much detail. "I was mad at first. Freaked out. We got in a big fight and she moved out of my place this morning before I even woke up."

"Huh. Well, that was easy, wasn't it? You got rid of her with no fuss, no muss."

I grit my teeth together, holding back the angry words I want to hurl at him. The man is completely dense. No wonder he drives my mother insane. "I want her back."

"What?" His eyes practically bug out of his head. "You've got to be kidding."

"I'm not," I say flatly, clearing my throat. I'm about to admit something major and I don't want him to pass judgment. "I'm in love with her."

He chuckles. Of course he does, the asshole. "You're crazy. Crazy, just like your mother. Always looking for trouble and finding it real easy."

"Sounds like you, too, you know," I bite out.

"Yeah. Yeah, you're right. I like a little trouble now and again myself." He sits up straighter, his expression going blank. "Speaking of that, I wanted to talk to you about that San Francisco location and the loan you promised . . ."

I didn't promise him shit, but I'm not going to press that point. "Forget San Francisco, Dad. I'm not doing it. I have my hands full and I'm perfectly content staying here." I eye him carefully. "You didn't already sign any papers, did you?" *Please tell me he didn't.*

"No, I was waiting for your okay." He sighs and leans back in his chair. "I knew you were going to refuse me. We could've made a lot of money together."

"Yeah, well, maybe someday, but not now." I want him out of my office. I need to be alone with my thoughts. I need to figure out how I'm going to get to Jen.

"Uh, how about that loan though, son? I need some

money to get me through. I have a few things pending, payments due, and I need a little help." He looks decidedly uncomfortable, which I'm thankful for. If this came too easy for
him, I'm afraid he'd soon be constantly asking me for money.

"Sure. I can do it." He helped me so much early on,
though it always came with conditions. And it definitely
hadn't been easy. We tried to work together but we're like oil
and water. We just don't mix well.

Opening up a desk drawer, I pull out the company check-
book, then grab a pen. "How much do you need?"

"One hundred thousand dollars."

My pen skids across the check I'm about to write at the
staggering amount that just fell from his lips. I glance up at
him. "Are you fucking serious?"

He nods, his expression miserable. "You're going to think
I'm a fucking fool, but I got some thugs breathing down my
neck. Gambling debt I owe from way back. I gotta pay it by
Monday and or I'm in deep shit."

"Sounds like you're already in deep shit," I say, setting the
pen down and leaning back in my chair. I run my fingers
through my hair, clutching it tight for a moment before I release it. How does he always end up in these risky situations?
He grew up spoiled and turned reckless at an early age. The
man likes living on the edge. He always has. I had no idea he
had a gambling problem, though. "Hell, I really don't have
that kind of money to spare."

"Come on, Colin. I'd do it for you," he pleads.

Ouch, thanks for the guilt. Love you, too, Dad. Not that
I'd ever deny him, but hell. That's a lot of money.

"Yeah, things might get a little tight for you for a bit, but
you always bounce back. I know it. You're a Wilder." He
grins, his over-bleached teeth seeming to glow. "We're just
alike. I know you're raking it in here. And you have your new

restaurant opening up soon. That's going to be a huge success—I don't doubt it for one minute."

Shit. I really do have that kind of money to loan him, but what he's asking for is no loan. I'll never get one dime of it back. "How about fifty," I offer.

The unmistakable disappointment etched across his face isn't easy to ignore. "I guess that'll work. I'll take what I can get. Maybe they'll only break one of my legs instead of both."

I write him a check for seventy-five, because I'm a sucker and he's my dad. If he's really involved with guys who'll physically hurt him, I could never live with myself if they really did break his legs.

Tearing the check off, I hand it to him, then see his face go from disappointed to relieved in an instant. "Thanks, son. I'll pay it back as soon as I can," he says.

Sure he will.

"I have to ask a favor from *you*, though," I say as I watch him fold the check and put it in the pocket of his button-down shirt.

"Anything," he says eagerly. "Whatever you need, I'm here for you."

"I need you to help me locate Jen." I ignore his flabbergasted look. "Use your wily ways and track her down. I know you can do it. You can dig up information on anyone and anything."

"But I'm leaving in less than an hour," he whines.

I silence him with a look. "You owe me. I'll give you the other twenty-five if you find her."

Ah, greed always talks when it comes to Con Wilder. It usually talks to me, too, as loath as I am to admit it. "Well, now you're talkin'."

I barely restrain from rolling my eyes. "Find her in the next few hours and that twenty-five thousand is yours." I can't believe I'm essentially paying him to find Jen, but a desperate man falls to desperate measures.

And I am beyond desperate to find Jen.

Jen

The bus ride took a lot longer than I thought it would. It felt like we stopped in every single town along the way, which I really think we did. I was stuck on that gross, stinky, hot bus for so long, my phone battery died. Then I realized I'd forgotten to pack my charger. I bet it's still plugged in at the kitchen counter in Colin's house.

Talk about a bonehead move. Yet again, I don't think things through.

Tired, frustrated, and hungry, I finally arrive at the bus station in Sacramento, thankful my new roommate, Angela, is kind enough to come pick me up. I pull my suitcase behind me, my giant purse filled with everything I couldn't fit in my luggage slung over my arm, when I think I spot her.

Dread fills my gut the moment I see her face. She is the complete opposite of me. Short and curvy, with bright, bleached blond hair and a fake tan, she comes running over to me, a big smile curving her freshly pink-glossed lips.

"You're Jennifer?" she asks, clapping her hands together like a seal.

Shit. She is way too enthusiastic for her own good. "I am. You must be Angela."

"It's so good to finally meet you!" She wraps me in a bear hug, holding me so tight I'm afraid she might suffocate me. I carefully detach myself from her grip, offering her a faint smile in return for her giant grin. "Is that all your stuff? Wow, you pack light."

"It's everything I own," I say, trying to joke but feeling sort of dumb.

"You don't have a bed or any furniture?"

"Um . . ." My voice trails off and I clutch my purse even closer to my side. Colin made good on his promise and had brought home my final check the night before. Though I'd told him I didn't want it, I took it anyway. Thank God. I need every single dollar I can get.

You'll never make it on your own.

I ignore the rude voice in my head.

"Hey, I'll take you to the Goodwill tomorrow, or Target or Walmart. Wherever you want to go—we'll find you something. You can sleep on the couch tonight. I'll make sure and warn Roger you're going to be there." She giggles as we emerge outside into the parking lot of the bus station, the waning late afternoon sun warm on my skin.

"Who's Roger?" I ask.

"My boyfriend, silly. He stays over a lot. I hope you don't mind." She tosses her hair over her shoulder. "He's really nice. I'm sure you two will get along great."

"No, of course I don't mind. I bet he's a great guy," I say, not really meaning it. I mind like crazy. I had no idea I'd have to deal with a near live-in boyfriend. Just great.

"So hey! I worked earlier today and my boss said she's looking to hire someone part-time at the store." Her smile never, ever fades. I wonder if her cheeks hurt. "Would you be interested?"

"Absolutely," I say, a hint of excitement filling me. I'm not as cheerful as Angela, but maybe if I hang out with her for a bit, my mood will brighten.

Maybe.

"We'll stop by there tomorrow, too, and you can fill out

an application." She stops at a candy-apple-red Volkswagen Bug, clapping her hands together again. Reminding me of an overenthusiastic little kid at her birthday party when she sees all her presents. "This is my car! Let's get you loaded up."

Oh. My. God. I don't know if I'll be able to handle this chick. She's obnoxious as hell and I have zero tolerance for any bimbos at the moment. Not that she's a bimbo. I don't know her at all, so I need to chill.

And I need to remember to be grateful. She came and picked me up from the bus station. I know that was a long drive from her apartment. She might have even found me a job. And she wants to help me find some furniture.

I think this has the potential to really work out. Maybe I can move on and truly forget my past once and for all. Start a new future and finally find that freedom I've been so desperately seeking . . .

Hours later, I've come to the conclusion that she never, *ever* stops talking, my new roommate. Angela ordered in Chinese for dinner, enough to feed an overindulging family of eight, and then her boyfriend showed up, all sullen and moody. With the typical boy band, swing-it-constantly-out-of-his-eyes sandy-brown hair and glittery golden eyes. He, on the other hand, doesn't talk much at all, but I don't like the way he looks at me.

It gives me the creeps.

Deciding to ignore him, I instead concentrate on Angela, who prattles on and on, telling me essentially her entire life story. I pretend that I'm listening. That I'm not nodding off in the middle of our conversation, trying my best to stay awake. Considering I've been up since before five A.M., I'm having a heck of a time.

"You're tired," Angela says with a sympathetic look.

"Let's get you a pillow and a blanket and you can crash out on the couch. Sounds good?"

"Yeah." I nod gratefully, offering her a small smile. "Sounds awesome. I can barely keep my eyes open."

"I'm boring you with my endless talking." She flashes the creepy boyfriend a look. "Rodge says I talk too much."

Rodge is one hundred percent correct, but I'm not about to validate anything he says. He gives me such a bad vibe I don't know what to think about him. "I don't mind," I tell her, neither confirming nor denying her statement. "You're so sweet to help me out. You don't know how much this means to me."

"You're helping me out, too, you know. I've had a hard time finding a roommate, and Rodge didn't want to move in. Says I'll try and take away his independence." She sends him a withering stare. There's unmistakable tension between these two and not the good kind. "I think we're going to make a perfect match."

I don't know if I'd go that far, but I'm so damn grateful for her and everything she's already done for me, I can only nod in agreement. "Yeah," I say weakly, glaring at Roger when I catch him staring at me. Again. "We're the perfect match."

CHAPTER 23

Jen

"I need your forgiveness," he whispers in my ear. *"I've hurt you and I'm sorry. I want you back in my life, Jenny. I need you."*

My heart expands, making my chest so tight I'm afraid it might burst. *"I forgive you, Colin,"* I say, throwing my arms around his warm, familiar body and hugging him tight. *"Thank you for coming for me."*

"I can't live without you. I couldn't not come for you." He holds me tight, his mouth pressed against my cheek in the sweetest of kisses. *"I love you, Jen. So much I can hardly stand it."*

I burst out laughing. Only Colin would make love sound painful. But it's a good kind of pain. One I revel in, especially when it comes from him. *"I love you, too."*

He holds me tighter, his arms like bands around me, my face smothered against his chest. At first it's comforting and I relax in his hold. But his arms squeeze me even tighter and I suddenly feel like I can't breathe.

"Colin." I try to push at his chest, but my arms are trapped in between our bodies. *"Stop. Please. Let me go."*

"Just let me hold you," he whispers, his voice sharp. Foreign. *"That's all I want. Just to hold you."*

I'm struggling now, trying to duck under and out of his

arms, but it's no use. I can't break free. Panic fills me, threatens to bubble out of my throat, and I part my lips, ready to scream. He slaps his hand over my mouth, silencing me. He doesn't smell like Colin. The scent of sweat and fear hits my nostrils and I grimace beneath his soft, damp palm.

"Shut up," he hisses, his voice reminding me of the guy who stole my purse. My panic grows and I'm thrashing about in his restrictive arms, anything to get out of his grip.

But I can't.

"Knock that shit off," he continues, his hot, heavy breath in my face. I wrinkle my nose. This . . . isn't Colin. My skin crawls when I feel this strange man's hand skim down my back, cupping my butt and hauling me close to his unmistakable erection.

Oh, God. This stranger, this unknown man, is going to rape me.

"You know you want it. Just let it happen. It can be our little dirty secret."

Dirty secrets. I have enough of those to last a lifetime. I definitely don't need any more.

I open my eyes to discover my nightmare is a reality. And it's not Colin holding me too tight with his strong arms, his hand still clamped against my mouth.

It's Roger.

A muffled scream escapes me, and he thrusts his face in mine, his golden eyes blazing with unmistakable fury. "Shut the fuck up," he mutters. "I know you want it. You were looking at me all night."

He was the one who looked at *me*, not that I'm able to tell him that. I can't speak at all with his hand covering my mouth. My heart's racing and I swear to God I'm going to have a panic attack if he doesn't let me go. I struggle against him again, yelling the word *please* against his hand again and again.

His brows lower as he glares at me hard. "If I drop my hand, you promise not to scream?"

I nod furiously, willing to promise just about anything so I can breathe again. My muscles are tense, my body so rigid I'm afraid I might shatter.

Slowly he removes his hand from my face and I take a long, deep breath, exhaling through pursed lips. I'm shaking, trying my best to act like it's no big deal that Roger is lying on top of me on his girlfriend's couch. His hands are everywhere, his mouth pressed against my neck, and I press my lips together, breathing through my nose.

Oh God, he really is going to rape me. All while his girlfriend is sleeping just a few feet away.

"You yell and I'll tell Angie you asked for it. That you came on to me. She'll believe me over you. She always does," he threatens, his hand gripping my left breast so hard tears spring to my eyes. I'm going to have bruises from the rough way he's touching me.

He's disgusting, and clearly he's done this sort of thing before. Poor Angela! She has a total douchebag for a boyfriend. A douchebag who's going to force himself on me and there's nothing I can do about it.

"Your tits are small." He squeezes me again, then delves his hand beneath my T-shirt to touch my bare breasts. He pinches my nipple and I bite my lip at the intense pain that shoots through me. "I bet you're a decent fuck, though. And those sexy lips would look real nice wrapped around my dick."

I can't take it. I can't. Shutting my eyes against his words, I think of myself not so long ago, on my knees and with a stranger's penis in my mouth. How my brain would shut down every time I did it, how I'd become numb to the men's grunts and groans, to the way they touched me, their hands in my hair, their guttural voices encouraging me to suck harder, take it deeper.

Remembering when I snuck into Colin's office and gave him a blow job. The first one that I actually enjoyed. How powerful I'd felt, how much pleasure it had given me to see the rapturous expression on his beautiful face, the sweet, sexy things he said to me. His fingers delving into my hair, lifting it away so he could watch.

"Let me go," I tell Roger, my voice firm. "Right now, or I'll scream loud enough to wake up the entire building."

"Do it and you're fucked." He laughs, the sound mirthless. "Both figuratively and for real."

I don't care. Maybe this has happened enough times that Angela will believe me over her boyfriend. I have to at least try.

No way can I let this pig touch me any longer.

Parting my lips, I scream, the sound loud and shrill in the otherwise quiet. A door slams open and Roger leaps away from me and off the couch just as an overhead light comes on.

"What the hell is going on?" Angela's standing in the middle of the living room, her eyes wide as they go from me to Roger and back to me.

I sit up, tugging my shirt back into place, wincing when the soft fabric skims over my aching nipple. A shiver moves through me. God, that jerk is rough. "Your boyfriend jumped me."

"Baby, she jumped *me*. I came out here for a glass of water and she attacked me." He goes to Angela, grabbing her upper arms and giving her a little shake. "She's been looking at me all night like she wanted to eat me up. Remember how I told you that before we went to bed?"

She eyes him warily before her gaze goes to mine. "Are you only wearing your underwear?"

I glance down. I'm wearing an oversized T-shirt that once belonged to Danny and it hits me almost at my knees, it's so huge. "Am I asking for him to jump me because of what I'm wearing?"

Her eyes narrow as she continues to contemplate me. "No bra either, huh."

Crossing my arms over my chest, I chance a look at Roger. His expression is smug, confident. *Asshole!* "I was asleep, Angela. I wake up and he's lying on top of me, trying to kiss me!"

"Liar," Roger murmurs. "You were begging for it, your hands all over me. You said you wanted to suck my . . ."

"Shut up! Stop it!" Angela screams, placing her hands over her ears, again reminding me of a little kid. "You need to go, Jen. I can't have you living here."

"Wait . . . *what?*" Did she really just say that?

Her expression is full of remorse as she drops her hands to her sides. "You'll tempt him. Roger . . . he's a recovering sex addict."

Recovering, my ass! Does she really believe that? "Angela, he said he's done this sort of thing before and that you always believe him."

"It *has* happened before. He's in therapy now." She slowly shakes her head. "I'd hoped he was healed, but I guess not. It doesn't help, how you're dressed."

"How am I dressed inappropriately?" I jump to my feet, the blanket falling away from my body and onto the floor. "Look at me!"

"Yes, look at you." She's wearing pajama pants and a matching top, completely covered from head to toe. I can tell she's wearing a bra and her feet are covered in socks.

Weird.

"I can see your legs—and your chest through your shirt. It's totally inappropriate." She actually has the nerve to shudder. "You need to go. I can't have you as a roommate. Roger can't handle it, so neither can I."

Funny, how Roger has clammed up completely. "I'll leave first thing tomorrow," I say firmly, ignoring the panic that fills me yet again.

Where will I go? Where will I stay? I can't keep doing this.

"No." She drags the word out, dropping her head so she's not looking at me. "You need to leave. Right now."

"But . . . where will I go?" My voice is small. I sound pitiful. I feel pitiful.

Kicked out yet again.

"That's not my problem now, is it?" She looks to Roger, who's standing right next to her. "We'll stay in the bedroom so we won't get in your way, but I'm going to have to ask you to pack your stuff and leave."

"What about my deposit?" My head is spinning so fast I'm getting dizzy. I fall heavily onto the couch, trying to breathe through the uncontrollable shivers racking my body. "I need that money."

"Nonrefundable. Didn't you read the fine print?" She sighs, as if she's the one who's being put out on the street. "I'm sorry this didn't work out, Jen. I had high hopes."

I don't say a word. I'm afraid if I open my mouth, the insults will start flying and I won't be able to stop them. I'll end up calling her every horrible name I can come up with and she might kick me out without my stuff. Now *that* would suck.

So I remain quiet, looking up just as I see Roger trail behind her down the hall toward her bedroom. He turns to look at me after Angela has slipped inside her room, his glittering eyes full of hate and lust. He flicks his tongue at me in a dirty gesture and I give him the finger, making him laugh just before he slams the door.

Jumping at the sound, I wrap my arms around me to ward off the chills. I guess Roger was right in what he said earlier.

I'm completely fucked.

Colin

Somehow, some way, my dad got the name and address of Jen's new roommate within a few hours, just like I asked. I didn't question how he did it. Didn't really want to know, truthfully. My dad's always had a bit of a devious, criminal streak running through him. He knows some shady characters. Gangster types the average person wouldn't dare associate with.

But my dad isn't the average person. He doesn't give a shit. He actually believes having "those sorts of people"—his quote, not mine—in his back pocket is a good thing.

Scary.

I gladly handed over that twenty-five-thousand-dollar check to him, relief flooding me when he gave me the name and address on a slip of paper. I stuffed it in my jeans pocket and took off for Sacramento, letting Fable know I knew where Jen was before I left. Not caring that it was late at night or that it would take me hours to get there.

I need to get to Jen. I have to find her. There's no way I'm leaving that place without her. We belong together. And if it takes me hours to convince her of that, then I'll do it. I'm that determined to make her mine.

The drive was easy since it was the middle of the night and traffic was light. I find the street Angela Blackburn's apartment complex is on quickly, thanks to Siri on my phone. I'm cruising it slowly, looking for the address and complex name, when the beams from my headlights land on a tall, slender figure walking along the sidewalk, pulling a giant black suitcase behind her.

My heart lurches in my chest and I pull over fast, rolling down the passenger-side window as I follow along beside her. She picks up her pace, her head averted, like she's afraid to look at me. Probably thinks I'm some sort of creep stalking her in the middle of the night, not that I can blame her.

Fear grips my chest and I hate that she's so frightened. What the hell is she doing out here all alone in the dark with her purse and her suitcase?

"Jen!" I call to her, and she stops short. I hit the brakes just in time to see her bent over and looking through the open car window, her dark gaze going wide when she sees it's me. "Get in the car."

"Wh—what are you doing here?" Her voice shakes and she looks scared out of her mind. It's taking everything within me not to run out of my car, grab her, and sling her over my shoulder like some sort of caveman.

"I've come for you," I say simply, shifting my car into park. I climb out and go to her, stopping right in front of her. She tilts her head back, staring up at me with so much relief and happiness in her gaze, the sight of it makes my heart swell. "You really think I can stay away from you, Jenny? You know I always find you eventually."

Her eyes fill with tears, and seeing them nearly rips me apart. "How did you know I needed you?"

I melt at her words. Grabbing her, I pull her in for a hug, the tension coiled tight in my chest easing when she slips her arms around me and buries her face against my shirt. "Because I needed you, too. I can't live without you," I murmur into her silky hair.

"Oh God." I stop her from saying another word with my

lips, kissing her, swallowing her sobs, tasting her with my tongue. She feels good, so right in my arms. I can't believe I found her so easily, walking down the goddamn street in the middle of the night, for Christ's sake.

"What are you doing out here anyway?" I ask once I break the kiss, brushing the hair away from her forehead. I can't stop looking at her, touching her. I can't believe I have her standing in front of me. She's been gone less than twenty-four hours and it felt like a goddamn lifetime.

I never want her out of my sight again.

"My new roommate kicked me out," she says, her voice shaking.

Blood roars in my ears at her words. "What the fuck! *Why?*"

She starts to cry again and I gently push her away so I can look at her pretty, tearstained face. Reaching out, I brush the tears away from her cheeks with my thumb. "Her b-boyfriend tried to r-rape me," she stutters out on a sob.

"Are you fucking serious?" My blood is boiling as I clench my left hand into a fist. *Hell no, she did not just say that.* "Take me back there. Right now."

I start for the car but she grabs me, halting my progress. "No, Colin. Please. I don't want you to get into any trouble. They're not worth it."

"He tried to fucking *rape* you, Jen. Smashing his face in with my fist and hearing his bones crunch will definitely be worth it." I'm fucking fuming, I'm so worked up. All I can see is an angry red haze across my eyes as I grab her suitcase and open the door, tossing it into the backseat.

"Trust me. He's a douchebag and she's an idiot. If you go there and lay a hand on him, they'll press charges and you'll go to jail." She grabs hold of me and shakes my shoulders, forcing me to focus on her. "I don't want you to get arrested,

Colin. Please. I need you here with me, not locked away in a jail cell."

Her words seep into my enraged brain and I blow out a harsh breath as reality comes crashing back over me. "You're right. I know you're right," I admit, my voice, my heart, beginning to calm. "But I wish I could. I'd tear him apart for you. You know that, right?"

"I know." She smiles, the sight of it knocking the breath out of me, and she leans up on her tiptoes, brushing my mouth with hers. "I love you, Colin. Thank you for rescuing me."

"God, I love you, too." I crush her to me, kissing her again, stealing her lips, her breath, her heart, just like she stole mine. God, she completely owns me; she has for months. Years. And she belongs to me. She's mine.

We're in this together.

It might have taken us a damn long time to figure it out and make it work, but thank Christ we did before it was too late.

"I'm tired of wasting time," she whispers against my lips when we finally break apart. "I want to come back. I want to live with you if you'll have me."

As if she has to ask. "I'll have you as long as you'll have me. I'm . . . sorry for what I said earlier. How I treated you."

"Of course I'll have you." She smiles, her eyes full of happiness mixed with lingering sadness. "I'm sorry I kept the truth from you. I was afraid."

"Never be afraid with me. You're my everything." I can't believe how lucky I am, that this woman is a part of my world. "I can't imagine my life without you."

"You're my everything, too," she admits softly, her head bent, her slender fingers plucking at the front of my shirt. Her innocent touch heats my blood, sets my skin on fire. I never want to be apart from her again.

"Will you come with me?" I ask her, needing to hear her say yes. "Be a part of my life, Jenny. I need you. I love you." I don't know if I'll ever be able to stop saying I love her.

She slowly lifts her head, her gaze meeting mine once more. The sadness is gone. Tears still fill her eyes and stream down her cheeks, but she looks happy. "I love you, too. So much."

Pulling away from her, I grab her hand and lead her over to my car, opening the passenger door for her. "Get in, baby. I need to take you home."

CHAPTER 24

Jen

"Look at you!" Fable whistles low when I stop directly in front of her. "Dressed up, all hot shit and manager-like."

"Stop it." My cheeks heat with embarrassment and I give her shoulder a gentle shove before I smooth my hands over my sleek black pencil skirt. "It's only temporary, remember?"

"Of course." She rolls her eyes, the gigantic smile on her face giving her away that she's not as irritated as she's putting on. "Colin can't live without you and you can't live without him, blah, blah, blah. I still say you should stay here and take over this place completely. You could probably run it better than anyone else."

"Yeah, right." She might be exaggerating, but her words still fill me with warmth and pride. She's so close to the truth about Colin and me it's funny. We just haven't admitted it to anyone yet.

The moment Colin brought me home—well, after we indulged in each other for hours in his bed—he sat me down and told me he was making me the manager of The District's new Redding location.

I protested again and again and we ended up arguing for hours, which was silly, but hey, that's how we work. We finally came to a compromise: I would run the Redding restaurant temporarily while he went in search of a permanent manager.

It's not that I didn't want the position or didn't believe in myself. I preferred working with him. We're a team, Colin and I. So when he asked me to join him instead and run the original location while he looked into expanding The District chain, I agreed readily.

We'll make the announcement soon, when he finds a new manager to replace me. In the meantime, I'll make the ninety-minute trek each way five days a week. We can stand it. It's temporary. Plus, he helped me buy a new car. A used Honda that I love, that isn't filled with bad memories and is reliable.

"I'm serious." Fable grabs my hand and pulls me into a fierce hug. "I'm so proud of you. You're doing an amazing job here. Colin gushes about you to everyone all the time. He's such a sap."

Tears threaten and I blink them away, irritated with myself. I've been an emotional mess lately. I blame the constant driving back and forth, overseeing the new restaurant's opening. The stress and the excitement and the anticipation—it's all combined to make me a complete wreck.

A happy wreck, though. Life is good. I have friends who care about me. I've attempted to contact my parents and though we've talked only briefly, I plan on going back home and seeing them someday soon. It's a step in the right direction. Our relationship isn't ruined forever, but it's definitely not perfect. I need to fix it. They need to fix it, too, and I hope they realize how their neglect affected me.

Colin promised he'll go with me back to Shingletown. He says he's ready to see his mom again, too.

And then there's Colin. He's so supportive, so encouraging. I don't look at his treatment of me as coddling or controlling any longer. It's just his way, a way that I've come to accept. He just wants to take care of those he loves. And he loves me. Passionately. Whole-heartedly.

Completely.

The dreams have mostly stopped. Of course, I'm in bed with him every night and I think that helps. But I also believe he's found peace with Danny's death and let go of all the guilt that weighed him down. He confessed to me what happened between him and Danny the day my brother joined the military. As if it were some sort of deep, dark secret.

I'd suspected some of it but never had any confirmation. Danny had seemed irritated with Colin before he left. I'd tried to ask why, but he always cut me off or worse, told me it was none of my damn business.

So I left it alone.

Colin was so relieved after making his confession, he hugged me close in bed and proceeded to cry against my chest. Shedding his tears, shedding his guilt. Afterward, he admitted he felt cleansed and that he was so thankful for my easy acceptance.

As if he had no idea *his* easy acceptance made it that much more possible for me to deal with what I've done. The choices I've made. He doesn't hold them against me.

He just . . . holds *me*. And tells me he loves me.

Constantly.

"Break it up, break it up." Colin approaches, using his stern boss voice, saying what he always does when he finds Fable and me together. "Don't you two need to get back to work?"

"I'm here as a guest," Fable says smugly. "So no bossing me around tonight."

"And I run this joint," I say teasingly. "Or haven't you heard?"

"Who's the crazy guy who put you in charge?" He slips

his arm around my shoulders and kisses me, his soft, warm lips lingering. I lean into the kiss, then step away, slowly shaking my head. "Hey, I need to maintain a certain image here, you know? No kissing on the job."

"Well, that's a damn shame," he drawls, smiling at me. The sight of his smile sends a bolt of longing through me so strong, I nearly sway toward him.

"Stop, you two. You're making me sick," Fable says, wrinkling her nose.

"Gimme a break," Colin says, rolling his eyes with a smile. "Where's *your* boy toy? I know you two can't keep your hands off each other."

"He's scoping out a table with Owen." Fable stands straighter, her expression going serious. "Thanks for giving me the night off and letting us come for the opening tonight, Colin, and for hiring Owen part-time. He's so excited to start working at the restaurant he can barely stand it."

Colin hired Owen as a busboy. He'll start after the football season ends, right when the busy holiday season starts. He's applied for a work license and everything, taking his first real job very seriously. Fable is so happy she can hardly stand it. She's trying so hard to keep her brother on track, as is Drew.

I love that Colin wants to help them out, too. He's careful, though, never wanting to offend Fable since she can be kinda prickly when it comes to so-called handouts.

No wonder we're such good friends.

He likes Owen a lot and is confident he'll be a great worker, and so am I. All five of us have hung out together more than once. Colin and I have invited all three of them over for dinner. Drew and Colin seem to be getting along well, too, which I think is awesome. Fable, Drew, and Owen—they all feel like they're a part of my family.

So does Colin, but he's always felt like family to me. Now we've taken it that much more seriously . . .

He's become my everything.

"I'm gonna put that brother of yours to work," Colin promises Fable, his arm lowering to slide around my waist. He pulls me in so I'm nestled at his side. We're a perfect fit and I gaze up at him adoringly. "I know he can handle it, though."

Fable nods and smiles, her gaze going from me to Colin. "You two are so damn cute together. Took you long enough."

"I'm pretty sure you've already said that to us," I remind her wryly.

"And it needs to be said a few more times, I think." She steps toward us both and kisses my cheek, then Colin's. "I gotta go find my men. I'll talk to you later, Jen?"

"I'll need you to rescue me, yeah," I say as she waves at us and then walks away.

"She's a good friend," Colin says close to my ear.

I nod, smiling up at him. "The best. But so are you."

He kisses me, like he can't help it. "Right back at ya, baby."

Warmth suffuses me, his love taking hold and giving me the courage I need to keep on top of this night, on the most important day of my career. "I need to go manage the front entry," I tell him, kissing his cheek. "Wish me luck?"

"No." He drops a kiss on the tip of my nose as I glare at him. "You don't need it. You got this and you know it."

I love his confidence in me. I freaking need it, especially right now. I'm a wreck. "I'm nervous," I whisper. "So thank you for that."

"Anytime, babe. You know I've got your back." He hugs me, his mouth at my ear, nibbling on it. "I love you. So much."

"I love you, too." My heart swells, and the nausea that plagued me the last hour or so evaporates completely.

Having this man by my side, I'm the luckiest girl in the world.

Colin

I watch her move about the restaurant, handling everything with calm efficiency, and pride ripples through me. She greets everyone who enters the door with a warm smile and introduces herself to the chamber of commerce members we invited for The District's grand opening.

The parking lot is full, yet the people keep on coming. A local radio station set up outside, broadcasting live and encouraging their listeners to come and check us out. Every table is occupied, the bar is at full capacity, and the front lobby has so many people waiting to be seated they spill outside, waiting on benches, their kids dancing to the top-forty music the radio station is playing.

It's a rousing success, all thanks to Jen. I wanted her to stay here in Redding permanently, more than willing to sacrifice and endure a long-distance relationship so she could take on this management position. She's so damn good at it, I'm afraid the guy I have lined up to replace her won't measure up.

Of course, no one can measure up to my Jen.

She refused, though. Simply told me she couldn't stand to be that far away from me. She loves me too damn much and didn't want us to be apart.

How can I refuse her?

"Hello, son."

My spine stiffens, and I slowly turn around to find my dad standing before me.

"Hey," I greet him weakly, giving him a quick hug. "How are you?"

"I'm good. Look at you, all dressed up. Quite the restaurant you have here. Looks good."

"Thanks." He drives me crazy, but I can't help but be proud at his meager compliment. He took his father's restaurant and turned it into something more. And I've gone and done the same, over and over again. I want him to be proud of me. Despite our tangled past, I'm still the kid who wants his dad's approval.

I'm also pleased he showed up. I'd extended the invitation out of courtesy, never believing he'd actually come.

"Kind of surprised you came," I say, immediately feeling like a jackass for saying it.

"Well, you did invite me," Dad reminds me. "And I'm never one to pass up a free meal."

I laugh. Thank God he relieved the tension.

"I saw your Jenny."

"Yeah?" Warmth fills me at his calling her my Jenny. She *is* mine. Glad he realizes that, too.

"She looks nervous. I told her not to worry. She can handle it." That he even said that shocks the hell out of me. Maybe he's doing it just to make me happy, I don't know. I'm glad for his support of Jen, though. I don't want to fight.

I'm so damn sick of fighting.

"So. How's work going for you?" I ask pointedly. He gives me some vague answer but I accept it. After I gave him the money, we had a long talk about his gambling problem and how he needed to get it under control. My dad's compulsive ways finally got him into major trouble, and luckily enough I was able to bail him out. But I warned him I wouldn't do it again. He needed to seek out help. So he did, in the form of a therapist, whom he sees once a week.

After ensuring my dad has a table to eat at, I take off toward the front of the restaurant in search of Jen. I find her standing by the hostess's desk, leaning against it as if she needs it to hold her up. Her shoulders are slumped and her head is bent, but she has a giant smile on her face.

Tired but happy, that's how I read her.

The moment she spots me headed toward her, her eyes light up and she comes for me until we meet in the middle. "Hi," she greets me breathlessly. "I didn't think I'd ever see you again."

Laughing, I reach out and tuck a stray strand of hair behind her ear. "Why do you say that?"

"Have you seen how busy this place is? It's crazy." Her smile fades the slightest bit though her eyes are still sparkling. "I saw your dad."

"I know. He told me."

"He was nice to me." She smiles.

"I'm glad." I drift my index finger down her soft cheek, getting momentarily lost in her eyes. I could almost forget we're at the restaurant.

Almost.

"He said he's happy that we're together." Jen leans into me, pressing her forehead to my chin, a sweet, trusting gesture. "So am I, I told him."

Fuck yes, I'll second that. "Baby, as soon as we can, let's get out of here. I want to take you home."

"Colin." She rolls her eyes, pulling away from me. "This is my restaurant and we're having our opening night. I can't just bail."

"Oh yes, you can. Especially when the owner of said restaurant tells you to." I cross my arms in front of my chest, going all mean boss on her. "Your work is done here tonight. Let's go home."

"But . . ."

"No buts," I tell her. "We're leaving. Now."

She smiles, her eyes full of promise. "I really like it when you use that stern voice on me."

"I know. Why do you think I use it?" Chuckling, I place my hand at the small of her back and steer her through the crowd, making our way to the short hallway that leads to the manager's office. The moment I get her in there, I shut and lock the door, pressing her against the wall with my body, effectively trapping her there.

She places her hands on my shoulders, not to push me away but to pull me closer to her. Our lips meet and cling. I slide my tongue against hers, taking the kiss deeper, and she moans into my mouth before breaking her lips from mine. "We so shouldn't do this here."

"Why? We christened *my* office. Let's do the same for yours."

She rolls her eyes but she's smiling, her hands running down the front of my chest slowly, feeling every inch of me. I harden, ready to take her right here against the wall, but I don't want to push if she's not into it.

This is something else we've discussed extensively. Her past, and how certain things still trigger the bad memories. I've come to grips with what she's done, trying my best not to let it bother me. Though I'd be a damn liar if I said it didn't . . .

But what she did has nothing to do with who we are now. I know that, and so does she.

"What would you say if I wanted to take on the managerial position here after all?" she asks, her voice casual though I see the apprehension in her eyes.

My heart tightens and my first response is an automatic *hell, no.* But that's not fair. "Is that what you really want?"

She slowly shakes her head. "No. I just wanted to hear you say I could do whatever I wanted. I shouldn't test you." Sighing, she pulls me in closer, so close a piece of paper couldn't fit between our two bodies. "I can't wait to work with you, as your partner."

"I can't wait either," I answer. "Maybe someday you can be my partner in every sense of the word."

Her eyes go huge. "Are you serious?"

"Absolutely." I nod, not surprised to realize I am. "Now that you're truly mine, I want to make it real."

"It's already real," she murmurs.

"I know, but I'm making it permanent. You'll be mine." Leaning in, I kiss her. Once, twice, our lips clinging, our bodies heating until I pull away first. "I'll be yours. We can work together. Get engaged. Get married."

"Oh my God," she breathes, those dark brown eyes of hers still wide and full of hope and excitement.

"Does that work for you?" I ask, and she nods.

"You really want to marry me?"

"I'd do anything for you," I vow solemnly. "Haven't you realized that yet?"

"I have." Smiling, she kisses me, wrapping her arms around my neck and squeezing me close. "I love you so much, Colin Wilder."

"I love you, too, Jennifer Lynn Cade." I slip my hand up, curving my fingers around her neck, lightly tracing the butterfly tattoo that I've touched hundreds of times before. A shiver moves through her and I smile.

Her smile grows. "Remember that time you woke me up and called me sweet cheeks?"

"Hell yeah." My voice goes soft and my body goes hard as I nuzzle the side of her face. "You do have a pretty sweet pair of cheeks, you know."

"So do you," she whispers. "Maybe you should go settle those sweet cheeks of yours on the desk so we can fool around on top of it."

I raise my brows. "Fool around, you say?" That sounds promising.

Of course, anytime I can be with her, naked and alone, is promising. The more we're together, the better it gets. Something I believed wasn't possible.

Slowly she nods. "Yeah. Though, hmm." Pulling out of my embrace, she turns and studies the desk, tapping her pursed lips with her index finger. I let my greedy gaze roam the length of her, taking in the crisp white shirt, the sexy-as-hell black skirt that fits her body like a glove. Just looking at her makes me break out in a sweat.

"Are you thinking what I'm thinking, sweet cheeks?" I ask her, my voice gruff, my body tight.

She glances over her shoulder at me, her eyes sultry and full of want. "If you're thinking of bending me over the desk and testing its strength, then yes. I'm most definitely thinking what you're thinking."

Damn, she's a mind reader. "Then let's go test it out, baby." Cupping her ass with both of my hands, I press against her and guide her toward the desk, where I proceed to strip her and spread her out like my own personal feast.

Making her mine.

Forever.

Acknowledgments

What a year. I'm so incredibly excited to have the One Week Girlfriend series with Bantam/Random House. I know it's in good hands. A big thank-you to my editor, Shauna Summers, who helped me so much with this book and made it ten times better with her suggestions. Thanks to my agent, Kimberly Whalen, for helping me find Shauna and Bantam. I think we're all a good match.

To my critique partner, Katy Evans, who read a very rough version of this book and gave me that light-bulb moment/idea I so desperately needed. Thank you, my friend, I don't know what I would do without you.

Gotta mention Kati Rodriguez and KP Simmon for keeping me on task and helping me out when I send those last minute emails that start with, "Can you . . ." Thank you, ladies. Your help is invaluable.

To my husband, who is my rock. A big thank-you and I'm sorry to my kids for all the extra time I spent planted at my desk, especially these last few months. I hope the epic summer trip to Seattle and Disney World made up for that.

I must always, always thank the readers. And the reviewers and the bloggers and everyone out there who's offered me so much support for my books. Thank you, thank you from the bottom of my heart. Words cannot convey how much I appreciate each and every one of you. This has been such a wild ride and it's made that much more wildly awesome by talking with all of you via email, Facebook, Twitter, and in person. I've met so many wonderful people this year! Y'all rock.

Jen and Colin's story is different from Drew + Fable's because it had to be. And it's sexier—because it had to be. These two are older, they have a past, a shared history that in my eyes made their getting together inevitable. They aren't Drew + Fable and I'm going to be honest—that scared me as I wrote their book. So I hope you all love their story and that your wariness in regard to Colin's intentions is gone. I love Colin. And I love Jen. I especially love these two together.

The Maguire family never takes the easy road when it comes to love, and Fable's younger brother, Owen, is no exception.

Monica Murphy continues her bestselling New Adult One Week Girlfriend series with *FOUR YEARS LATER*

The sexy story of two college kids with nothing in common but a bunch of baggage and a burning attraction.

Read on for an exclusive sneak peek

Coming soon from Bantam Books

CHAPTER 1

It doesn't matter what people think about you. It's what you think about yourself that counts.

—Unknown

Owen

I wait outside in the hallway, slumped in a chair with my head bent down, staring at my grungy black Chucks. The closed door to my immediate left is composed mostly of glass, hazy and distorting, but I know who's inside. I can hear the low murmur of their voices but I don't really hear the words.

That's okay. I know what they're saying about me.

My counselor. My coach. My sister. My brother-in-law. They're all inside, talking about my future. Or lack thereof.

Tilting my head back, I stare at the ceiling, wondering yet again how the hell I got here. A few years ago, life was good. Hell, last summer life was really good. I was on the team. Running on that field like my feet were fire and I couldn't ever be stopped. Coach approved, a big grin on his face when he'd tell me, *You're just like Drew.*

Yeah. That made me proud as shit. I idolize my brother-in-law. He makes me feel safe. He understands me when Fable never, ever could. Not that she doesn't try the best she can, but she's a girl. She doesn't get it.

Thinking of girls makes my heart feel like it's made out of lead. Solid and thick and impenetrable. I haven't been with a girl since . . . I don't know. A few weeks? I miss'em. Their smiles and their laughter and the way they gasp when I dive in all smooth-like and kiss them. Their soft skin and how easy it all was. Clothes falling off and legs and arms tangled up.

Being on the football team meant I could get all the tail that I could ever want. But if I don't have the grades, I can't stay on the team. If I can't stop smoking weed, then I'm kicked off the team. If I get caught one more time drinking at one of the bars while I'm underage, I'm definitely off the fucking team forever. Zero tolerance, baby.

None of us practice what the team rules preach.

The glass door swings open and my college counselor peeks her head out, her expression grim, her gaze distant when she stares at me. "You can come in now, Owen."

Without a word I stand and shuffle inside the room, unable to look at anyone for fear I'll see all that disappointment flashing in their eyes. The only one I chance a glance at is Drew, and his expression is full of so much sympathy I almost want to grab him in a tackle hug and beg him to make it all better.

But I can't do that. I'm a grown-ass man—or so Mom tells me.

Fuck. There's my biggest secret. I can hardly stand to think of her, let alone when Fable is sitting right next to me. She would flip. Out. If she knew the truth.

She doesn't know. No one knows Mom is back in town and begging me to help her. She asks me to get her weed and I do. She gives me beer as payment and I drink it. Handing over all the spare money that I make.

I'm working at The District, where I'm a waiter when I'm not in class or at practice or supposed to be studying or whatever the hell. I'm making decent money, I'm on a football scholarship, and Drew plays for the NFL, for the love of God, so Fable and Drew have no problems. They live in the Bay Area, he plays for the 49ers, and he's one loaded mother-fucker.

But I refuse to take a handout from them beyond their helping me pay for school expenses and my apartment, which I share, thank you very much, to ease the burden. Mom blew back into town last spring, when my freshman year was winding down. Knowing I have a soft spot for her, that I'm easily manipulated by her words.

Your sister's rich, she tells me. *That little bitch won't give me a dime, but I know you will, sweetie. You're my precious baby boy, remember? The one who always watched out for me. You want to protect me right? I need you, Owen. Please.*

She says "please," and like a sucker I hand over all the available cash I have to her.

"We've been discussing your future here at length, Owen," my counselor says. Her voice is raspy, like she's smoked about fifty thousand packs of smokes too many, and I focus all my attention on her, not wanting to see the disappointment written all over Fable's face. "There are some things we're willing to look past. You're young. You've made some mistakes. There are many on your team who've made the same mistakes."

Hell yeah, there are. Those guys are my friends. We made those mistakes together.

"Your grades are suffering. Your sister is afraid you work too much and she called your boss." Holy. Shit. I can't believe she did that. But hell, the owner is her friend and former boss, Colin. He'll rat me out fast, I guess, even though he doesn't really work there any longer. He and Jen moved on right after I graduated high school. They're in Southern California now, opening one restaurant after another, all over the place.

"What did my boss say?" I bite out, furious. My job is

mine and no one else's. It's the only thing that gives me free-dom, a little bit of pocket money that I earned all on my own. Not a handout from Drew. Not an allowance to keep a roof over my head and my cell phone bill paid.

It's money that's mine because I earned it.

"That you're working in excess of thirty hours a week." Dolores—that's my counselor's name. She sounds like a man and she's ancient. She's probably worked at this college as long as it's been around and considering that was around the turn of the twentieth century, this bitch is old as dirt. "That's too much, Owen. When do you have time to study?"

Never, I want to say, but I keep my mouth shut.

"All your grades have slipped tremendously, but you're failing English Comp. That's the class we need you to focus on at the moment," Dolores the man-lady says.

"Which I can't believe," Fable says, causing me to look at her. Ah hell, she's pissed. Her green eyes—which look just like mine—are full of angry fire and her mouth is screwed up so tight, I'm afraid she's going to spit nails. "You've always done so well in English. Once upon a time, you actually liked to write."

Once upon a time, I had all the hours in the world to write. Well, not really, but I could carve out enough time to get the words down. It was therapeutic. I copied Drew at first with it. The guy used to always scribble a bunch of non-sense that made my sister look like she wanted to faint, and I wanted to do the same. Not faint or make my sister faint, but touch people with words.

So I became a carbon copy of Drew Callahan. I played football, I wrote, I studied, I tried my best to do the right thing. I'm a little more outgoing than Drew, though. Girls are my thing. So are my friends. And beer. Oh, and weed.

All of that equals not doing the right thing, despite my intentions.

I tried to kick the drug habit, as they call it. And I did. But then Mom came back around, and now I have a smoking buddy.

That is all sorts of fucked up.

"I don't have any time," I say with a shrug.

"Right. Working a job you don't even need, you little shit." Fable hisses the last word at me, and it stings like she's lashed at my skin with a whip. Drew settles his hand on her arm, sending her a look that says chill the hell out.

So she does. He has that sort of effect on her. The two of them together are so perfect for each other it's kind of disgusting. I miss them. I'm alone, adrift in this town I grew up in, going to school here because this is what I wanted. Independence from them.

Now I wish I would've moved with them. Gone to Stanford like they originally wanted me to. Well, like Fable wanted me to. Drew told her not to push. The more she pushes, the more I pull away.

And I did. With the Stanford thing, with the move-in-with-my-sister-and-her-husband-in-the-big-ass-mansion thing. All of it, I said no to.

I'm one stupid asshole aren't I?

"We've found you a tutor," the counselor says, pretending as if my sister's outburst hadn't happened. "You're going to meet with her in an hour."

"I have to be at work in an hour," I start, but Fable butts in.

"No, you don't. You're on probation."

"Probation from work?" I turn to her, incredulous. What the hell is she talking about?

"Until you get your shi—act together, you're not working.

You need to focus. On school more than anything," Fable says. When I open my mouth to protest, she narrows her eyes. I shut the hell up. "They're benching you on the team, too. You need to move fast before you lose everything. I mean it."

Shit.

Chelsea

The classroom is quiet and smells like old books and chalk dust, even though I bet there hasn't been a chalkboard in here for years. We're meeting in one of the original buildings on campus, where the air is thick with generations of students past and everything is drafty and old, broken down and historic looking.

I feel very shiny and brand new, and that's a feeling I haven't had in a while. I'd almost forgotten what it was like. I got my hair cut yesterday—splurged for the blow-dry treatment, too, so it falls in perfect waves just past my shoulders. Waves I don't normally bother to make happen since my hair is boringly straight. I'm wearing a new pair of jeans and a cardigan sweater I picked up at Old Navy yesterday with the 30-percent-off coupon they sent me via email. Mom would be proud of my newly found thrifty ways.

I don't have a choice. Being frugal has become a way of life.

Now I'm waiting for the new student I'm going to tutor for the rest of the semester. It's already October, so we don't have much time to turn his grades around; not that I'm worried. I'm good at my job. So good, I get the tough cases, and supposedly this one is extra tough.

I've been a tutor since I was a freshman in college, and considering I graduated high school over a year early and I'm now a junior, I'm going on three years. I have a lot of experience. I'm not bragging when I say I'm smart. I'm what some people might call a prodigy.

More like I'm too smart for my own good.

All I know about the guy I'm going to tutor is that he's a football player and he's failing English. Considering I don't pay attention to any of the sports teams at my college, I have no idea who he is beyond his name. My first instinct is that he's a punk ass with a chip on his shoulder who hates the idea of being tutored by little old me.

Whatever. I don't let it bother me. I'll simply collect my check every two weeks and send what I can to Mom. I've dealt with plenty of punk athletes in the past who are resentful that they have to do schoolwork in the first place. More than one whined at me in the past, "Who cares about my grades? I just wanna play ball."

They think they can get by on playing ball and that's it. Doesn't matter what ball it is, either. Football, baseball, basketball . . . if they're good at it, they think they're invincible. They believe it'll take them so far they'll never need anything else.

Relying on one thing and one thing only for your happiness, your expenses, your entire life, doesn't work. Mom is living proof of that.

So am I.

Glancing at my phone, I see my new student is almost ten minutes late. I'm only giving him fifty minutes, then. I have to go to my other job after this and don't have time to wait for him. I work some nights and weekends at a crappy little diner downtown and I don't really like it there. The boss is an arrogant jerk and the customers are grouchy. But the tips are decent, and I need whatever dollars I can get.

We're two broke girls, Mom and I. Dad left us with nothing.

I hate him. I sorta hate guys in general. Once, when I was almost fourteen and suffering in high school as the young kid no one liked with hardly any friends, I went through a stage where I believed I was a lesbian. I told the few friends I had, I told my parents, I told everyone who would listen to me that I liked girls. I never told them the reason why I'd decided I was a lesbian.

Sixteen-year-old Cody Curtis had stuck his tongue down my throat, his rough, inexperienced hands roaming all over me one Saturday night at a birthday party gone wild, and I almost gagged. I decided right then and there if that's what boys do to girls, I would have no part of it. I'd rather become an ostracized lesbian than deal with guys who wanted to grab my butt and lick the roof of my mouth.

Funny thing was, no one believed me. Not my parents or my friends. They all thought it was a stage. Especially my best friend, Kari, who *knew* Cody stuck his tongue down my throat and how much I hated it.

They were right. It was a total stage that wasn't really a stage at all. More like a front. But I've never been really comfortable around guys. They give me even a hint of attention and I think they have ulterior motives. They want something from me I don't want to give.

My body. My mind. My soul.

They'll take everything, then destroy me. Walk away without a backward glance. Look at Dad. He's done it time and again. He leaves. My mom cries. He comes back. She gives in. He decimates her, piece by piece, until she's a broken crumble of human spirit on the ground, and then he's gone. This time for good.

I'm the one left who has to pick up the pieces. Glue her

back together and tell her she's strong. She's tough. She doesn't need him. We both don't need him.

But I'm lying. I think she does need him. And I need him too, only to keep her together more than anything else. I don't love him, not anymore. He's stomped all over that love until he's made me resentful.

Seeing what he does to Mom makes me really wish I would have stuck to that lesbian deal. Or maybe I should just become asexual. That would work too. I like it here in my little world that makes sense, with school and tutoring and plans to go on to get my master's degree. I can be whatever I want. I don't need a man to define me. Kari's afraid I'll never want to graduate college because I like school too much. She thinks something's wrong with that.

It's hard to confess to her how scared I am of the real world.

A creak sounds, startling me out of my thoughts, and the classroom door swings open. A boy struts in—there's no other way to describe his walk. It's all effortless grace and smooth movement He's tall and broad, and with a menacing glower on his face. A face that is . . . holy wow, it's beautiful!

All thoughts of returning to my so-called lesbian ways are thrown right out the window. If I'm as smart as I claim to be, I'll go chasing after them and snatch them back up. Pretend this gorgeous boy doesn't exist.

"You my tutor?" He stops just in front of the table that I'm sitting behind and I leap to my feet, pushing the chair back with so much force it falls to the side with a loud clatter.

My cheeks are hot, but I ignore the fallen chair as though I didn't knock it over. I am the biggest dork on the planet. "Yeah. You're Owen?" I wince. *Yeah*. I'm supposed to bring up his English grade and I can't even utter a proper yes.

"Yeah." He flicks his chin at me. It's a firm chin and jaw that's covered in golden stubble that doesn't match the color of the hair on his head. That's brown. A rich, golden brown, though, that hints he could almost be a blond if he sat in the sun long enough. "I don't have time for this shit, though. I gotta go to work."

Oh. Not even a minute in and he's blowing me off and cursing at me. Jerk. "You're late."

"I know. Told you I don't have time."

"I don't think you have a choice." Turning, I bend over and grab my chair, righting it. When I turn back to face him, his gaze quickly lifts to my face, as if he'd been checking out my butt, and I swear my cheeks are on fire.

More over the fact that I actually liked catching him most likely checking out my butt.

What is wrong with me?

"I really don't need your help," he says, his gaze locking with mine. "I'm usually pretty good at English."

I'm at a loss for words just looking at him, which is pitiful. His eyes are green. A deep, intense green that is so beautiful, they're almost painful to stare into. A girl could get lost in eyes like those. I bet a thousand girls before me already have. "Really?" I ask, my voice full of contempt. "Because according to your teacher, you're failing."

His generous mouth sets into a hard line, the lush fullness that could be considered almost feminine if he didn't have all those harsh angles in his face to offset it disappearing in an instant. "This is such bullshit," he mutters, running a hand through his hair, messing it up completely.

It's a good look for him. That I'm even thinking this makes me want to punch myself. Where did my lesbian plans go? My asexual plans? Shoved aside because of a good-looking guy sauntering into a room full of attitude and doing his best to get away from me?

I'm not one of those girls. I'm smart. Boys don't interest me and I'm okay with that. I have a protective shell that's surrounded me for years, but I had no idea it was so thin.

He's shattered through it with one look of his too-green eyes and he doesn't even know it. I refuse to hand over the power.

"Why don't we sit down and go over everything," I suggest, settling in my chair and scooting it close to the table.

He doesn't follow my lead. Still standing above me, he's so tall, his shoulders so broad, he's all I can see. I tilt my head back, hating how it feels like he has the upper hand. Hating more how he looks down at me like I'm nothing. Like he could walk away right now and forget I even exist.

Which he probably could.

"Can't we just say I come and see you every week and you get paid and we pretend everything's fine? You turn in your little reports and I turn in my assignments, take my barely passing grade and call it good?" he asks as he reaches out and grips the back of the chair he's standing in front of. His fingers are long; they curl around the edge of the chair so tightly his knuckles turn white. He's tense.

Great. So am I. "Um, that would be lying. And cheating," I say slowly, letting my words sink in.

"So? I can make this happen. I just need to catch up on my assignments, right?" He makes it sound so easy.

"You failed three tests already," I point out, not even bothering to look at the sheet that breaks down his epic failure of English Advanced Comp. I studied it before he arrived. Memorized it, really. "You're also taking a creative writing class and you're close to failing that one as well."

"I thought . . ." His voice trails off and he exhales, his nostrils flaring slightly. "I thought it would be easy."

"Apparently not." I raise a brow, proud of my calm, cool demeanor. Inside my nerves are starting a riot in my belly.

"I'll pay you extra," he blurts. "I can't . . . I gotta work."

His offer shocks me, and all I can do is blink.

"Maybe . . ." I take a deep breath. "Maybe we could meet at another time? Is that the problem? Does this time not work for you?"

"It doesn't. Not at all." He shakes his head. "I don't want to do this. No offense, but I don't have time for this shit."

And with that final statement, he turns on his heel and leaves.

PHOTO: COLBY RAIMER

New York Times and *USA Today* bestselling author MONICA MURPHY is a native Californian who lives in the foothills of Yosemite. A wife and mother of three, she writes new adult contemporary romance and is the author of *One Week Girlfriend, Second Chance Boyfriend, Three Broken Promises,* and *Four Years Later.*

monicamurphyauthor.com
missmonicamurphy@gmail.com
www.facebook.com/MonicaMurphyauthor
www.facebook.com/DrewAndFableOfficial
www.twitter.com/MsMonicaMurphy

Read all of **MONICA MURPHY'S** Addictive New Novels

One Week Girlfriend: Available Now

An utterly addictive and sexy story about a fierce, determined young woman who's just trying to make ends meet, and the hot college football quarterback who makes her an offer she can't refuse.

Second Chance Boyfriend: Available Now

The exhilarating conclusion to Drew and Fable's story as Drew fights to show Fable why they're destined to share a love that lasts forever.

Three Broken Promises: On Sale December 2013

Colin feels responsible for his best friend's death in the Iraq War, and vows to make it up to the one person who was devastated the most: his friend's sister. Colin takes Jennifer under his wing, but Jennifer isn't interested in Colin's charity or his guilt. Instead, she wants his love . . .

Four Years Later: On Sale Spring 2014

About to start college, Owen Maguire is stunned when his mother waltzes back into his life four years after having abandoned their family. Owen's afraid that he'll revert to his bad habits under the burden of his mother, until he meets a girl who's ready to show him how to love.

Visit Monica's website: **MonicaMurphyAuthor.com**
Join Monica on Facebook: **Facebook/MonicaMurphyAuthor**
Follow Monica on Twitter: **@MsMonicaMurphy**

BANTAM TRADE PAPERBACKS AND EBOOKS